RIVER
RULES

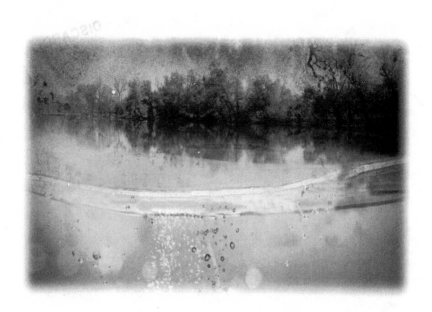

RIVER RULES

STEVIE Z. FISCHER

GREEN WRITERS PRESS   *Brattleboro, Vermont*

Printed in the United States

10 9 8 7 6 5 4 3 2 1

Green Writers Press is a Vermont-based publisher whose mission is to spread a message of hope and renewal through the words and images we publish. Throughout we will adhere to our commitment to preserving and protecting the natural resources of the earth. To that end, a percentage of our proceeds will be donated to environmental activist groups and The Southern Poverty Law Foundation. Green Writers Press gratefully acknowledges support from individual donors, friends, and readers to help support the environment and our publishing initiative. Green Place Books curates books that tell literary and compelling stories with a focus on writing about place—these books are more personal stories, memoir, and biographies.

Giving Voice to Writers & Artists Who Will Make the World a Better Place
Green Writers Press | Brattleboro, Vermont
www.greenwriterspress.com

ISBN: 978-1-7327434-7-2

COVER DESIGN: Asha Hossain Design, LLC
INTERIOR DESIGN: Rachael Peretic

PRINTED ON PAPER WITH PULP THAT COMES FROM FSC (FOREST STEWARDSHIP COUNCIL)-CERTIFIED, MANAGED FORESTS THAT GUARANTEE RESPONSIBLE ENVIRONMENTAL, SOCIAL, AND ECONOMIC PRACTICES. ALL WOOD-PRODUCT COMPONENTS USED IN BLACK & WHITE OR STANDARD COLOR PAPERBACK BOOKS, UTILIZING EITHER CREAM OR WHITE BOOKBLOCK PAPER, THAT ARE ARE SUSTAINABLE FORESTRY INITIATIVE® (SFI®) CERTIFIED SOURCING.

To Edith

"Who hears the fishes when they cry?"

—HENRY THOREAU, *1839 Observation of Lowell*

"Well, we'll know better next time."

—TOM STOPPARD, *Rosencrantz and Guildenstern Are Dead*

PART 1

TWO YEARS AGO

CHAPTER 1

WHEN PETER RUSSO DISCOVERED THAT SAUNDERS Construction got hired as the general contractor for the Zenergy fuel cell site in his beloved hometown of Bridgeville, Connecticut, his chest practically exploded. Not only had Brock Saunders sold his older brother, Jeff, a worthless investment in the biggest Ponzi scheme outside of Bernie Madoff, almost causing the Russo family to lose their farm in the late 1980's, but Brock had date-raped one of Peter's best friends two years before the scheme went bust.

The light from a brilliant peach and purple early-May sunset illuminated the fuel cell construction site as Peter grimly took stock of the land's devastation. Astonishingly located in a pleasant residential neighborhood that hadn't guessed an electricity-generating behemoth was being built in the treed expanse abutting the road, Peter found Saunders Construction signs plastered all over the chain link fence surrounding the property. How Saunders got hired to do the site work for Zenergy's fuel cell facility, adjacent to a natural gas pipeline that most people welcomed because it freed them from the tyranny of oil, didn't rank as public knowledge. Neither did how Zenergy somehow obtained the wooded tract in the leafy riverfront town. Yet the facility was just about up and running.

"Satan with a backhoe loader," Peter, hale and hearty at fifty four, explained to Brutus, his rescue pit bull and stalwart companion. "Zenergy steals the land. Saunders guts it and builds a butt-ugly industrial eyesore that belongs on the Jersey Turnpike. No way it should be in a residential neighborhood. And Saunders should be in jail, not fucking Bridgeville up the ass again."

Reluctant to tell Nancy Yates about Saunders's involvement, Peter didn't mention it or anything else about his newly hatched plan to give Zenergy and Saunders a raised middle finger. He also knew to stay away from Saunders in person; the last time Peter saw him had been after Nancy broke down and told him everything.

"Yeah, I shoved him. So what?" Peter said to the police officer Brock flagged down at the ferry landing, where Peter found him standing alongside his precious Porsche. Peter's best buddy, John Tomassi, had just joined the force, and told him privately in no uncertain terms to stay away from Saunders.

"He's a piece of shit, but he'll bring charges the next time. For once in your life, think about consequences." Tomassi grabbed him by the shoulder and squeezed hard with his meaty paw.

"Jesus, alright. Lay off. But what he did should have consequences, too."

"Nancy didn't report it. End of story as far as you and Brock are concerned."

But, it wasn't, not by a long shot. Peter knew the last thing Nancy's poor health, depression and anxiety needed was a reminder of Brock's violations let alone his reappearance in Bridgeville after being run out by burned investors who wanted him tarred and feathered or, better yet, roasted alive on a spit.

Peter poked around the Zenergy fuel cell facility site for much longer than anyone suspected. On every evening excursion, he spat on Brock's photoshopped face adorning the Saunders signs.

"Rot in hell, Brockie."

The perpetual smirk on Brock Saunders's face had been a fixture since toddlerhood. An only child, his mother coddled him while his father beat the shit out of him, favoring a jab-cross- hook punch combination. Whenever possible, Brock could be found outside, where he loved to catch frogs and kill them. Taller and meaner than most kids his age, he bullied almost everyone except the farm boys like Jeff Russo, his school classmate who brawled with ferocity. Brock focused his rifle scope elsewhere, spreading suffering and fear among the more defenseless. No mercy kills; just prolonged agony that the adults in charge either didn't know about, care about or view as more than boys will be boys. The rewards of hyper-masculinity as practiced in American schoolboy Darwinism were good to Brock. A quick study, he branched out into sexual predation in his teens, twisting the bodies and souls of young women, preferably defenseless ones, like screw tops.

In his twenties, Brock's father called in a few favors after Brock fucked up too many times at the family construction firm and got him a marketing gig for Pioneer Premium Properties, a high-flying real estate developer. Brock sold $50,000 units of can't-miss real estate investments to almost everyone he knew. In those heady go-go times, New England commercial real estate ran hotter than the sun. All Brock had to do was reserve a meeting space, offer a full bar with passed hors d'oeuvres, dim the lights for a short dog-and-pony slide carousel, and voila. Eager investors, now including average folks like teachers, farmers, small business owners, and retirees pressed checks into his hands. No one wanted to miss the boat to riches and tax write-offs, although the small-potatoes investors didn't even belong in the same universe with the real estate scheme. Somehow, big-time accountants, auditors and bankers blessed it all; their names, synonymous with fiduciary standards, impressing everyone.

How Jeff and the family patriarch, Artie Russo, got sucked in, given what Jeff, twenty-five at the time, knew about Brock infuriated Peter.

"You gave that scumbag $50,000? What the fuck is wrong with you?" Peter shouted at Jeff and his father. Artie and Peter never had a good relationship, even before Artie ruled from on high that Jeff would get the farm, freezing out his independent-minded younger son who left home after dropping out of community college. Peter kept his distance, finding steady work on the booming aerospace assembly lines that prospered in the area.

"You're a good for nothing ingrate," Artie yelled in response. "You don't know shit. What did you ever do for me?"

"Oh, right. Everything's all about you. For once in your life, admit it. You fucked up. I know this wasn't only Jeff's idea."

Jeff muttered something inaudible. Peter leaned towards him. "What?"

"Didn't want to miss out. Sure thing—everyone said."

"Yeah," Artie said, jutting out the chin that both his sons had inherited. His wife, Peter and Jeff's mother, died earlier that year after driving drunk into a tree, saddling Jeff with Artie's constant presence on the farm that desperately needed modernizing.

"Oh, so you'd jump off a building if everyone said to?" Peter barked a laugh and poked Jeff in the ribs to see if he got the richness of being able to throw Artie's mantra from their youth right back in his face. But Jeff, slumped in a chair, his head in his hands, didn't stir. To this day, only Peter knew how close he came to taking his own life.

CHAPTER 2

PETER SNEERED AT THE BIG ZENERGY SIGNS THREATENING doom and damnation for anyone who dared trespass.

"Oh yeah? Just try." The promise of arrest, fines and prosecution egged him on. Creative revenge could indeed be a dish eaten cold. "I answer to a higher power. Count on it."

The gap he'd jimmied in the chain-link fence surrounding the fuel cell went undetected. Peter searched online for information about how the chemical reaction in the huge fuel cell converted natural gas into electricity. He learned that Zenergy had big contracts for selling the electricity it would generate in Bridgeville. But when it came out that contractually, only 15 percent of the electricity would go to town residents who already paid through the nose, Peter took it as a personal challenge.

"Game on."

There were a lot of if's involved in his decision that beauty would be his weapon of choice. Brock Saunders sullied everything and everyone he touched. Saunders Construction's involvement leaked an even more putrid stench that just added to his zeal. If Zenergy had just located the brutally industrial facility on the business side of town, if Zenergy had just acted in good faith by actually asking permission to build in Bridgeville, if Zenergy had just wanted to be a good neighbor and share some electricity, if Zenergy hadn't hired Saunders to kill every living tree in sight. Brutus agreed with him—the desecration of a modest neighborhood of small ranch houses and modest capes smacked of complete disrespect, a Saunders specialty.

"Disrespect can't go unpunished, right, buddy?" As the only living creature with knowledge of Peter's secret mission, Brutus's opinion counted for a lot. "Gotta swing for the fences here, B."

Peter wore a miner's helmet to explore when the sun went down. He created a schematic of the site and labelled the pathetic plants Saunders' sub-contractors slapped into the ground.

"Ten dead, four beyond hope and three on life support. Atrocious, Brutus. And there's not an ounce of topsoil."

The invasion of cement trucks and earthmoving equipment left an alien landscape in stark contrast to Bridgeville's towering oaks, maples, and pine trees. A world of hurt, decorated with cigarette butts, cans, bottles, fast-food wrappers, styrofoam, ketchup packets, and used condoms.

"Not on my watch," Peter said, double-gloving and shoving it all into big plastic bags. The condoms were the worst. It was probably just kids looking for a place to hump, but still. "Not cool."

Peter ripped out the raggedy dwarf Arborvitae quickly; the holes hadn't been dug deep enough for petunias. Round-the-clock nurturing in the ICU wouldn't have helped these babies.

Armed with spades, shovels and a pitchfork, Peter coasted his pickup truck with his headlights off into a small clearing near some evergreens. A security firm patrolled the site after eleven, so he made sure he was always out by 10:30. Expertly, he mixed manure and topsoil in a barrel, all from the Russo farm's stockpiles. He added time-honored growth boosters: coffee grounds, rotting banana peels, pulverized sea shells, and fresh water from the brook near his house.

"Brutus, we were meant to do this, dude. Look at this.

Just pitiful, fucking pitiful." Brutus lifted a leg and pissed. "My feelings exactly, buddy."

Peter worked methodically for a week straight. Jeff, who Peter left completely in the dark, including about Brock Saunders's resurrection after his prolonged exile from Bridgeville, quizzed him about his evening activities and seemed to think Peter had finally gotten over the heartbreak of Carmen Fiori, who had cut him off at the knees two years ago.

"At least tell me your new lady's name, Romeo. She's gotta be a saint or blind to put up with you. C'mon, Pete, dish."

"Hey, don't jinx me." Peter wiggled his hips.

Jeff shook his head. "I feel sorry for her. You look like you're having a seizure." The two brothers laughed, and in that moment, they looked almost like twins, although Jeff, two years older at fifty-six and more weathered by the sun, outweighed Peter by about twenty pounds. Jeff and Peter had the same thick dark hair shot with gray, the same deep brown eyes and the same strong chins. They both would have scoffed at being called handsome, but age had been kind to them.

Nancy called him a few times during his nocturnal excursions and left messages about her latest travails with online dating.

"Another dagger to my heart," she said. "He might've been the one."

Since this happened with amazing frequency, Peter barely had to glance at the guy's bio and headshot to know that Nancy had leaped again before she looked.

"He lives on a boat, Nance. You get seasick on an escalator." Peter held his hands up in disbelief. "Plus, he looks like a gerbil."

"Only in profile."

"The one from last week collected shrunken heads."

"Bullshit. He collected Russian fur hats, the kind with earflaps."

"Same difference."

Peter tried not to whistle or hum—nothing to draw attention to himself. He counted on Brutus to keep quiet, too, so he packed Brutus a little care package every night: a juicy bone, an old tennis ball, and a ripped dish towel. Brutus had more joy in destroying a dish towel than most people experience at Christmas.

A few times Peter felt like he wasn't alone up there in the woods. It couldn't be the security people; they stuck to the paved front of the fuel cell and never came early. It had to be nocturnal animals foraging for food. So, he tethered Brutus to a tree; there was no point of him chasing after some raccoon or fox. Fisher cats were mean as hell, too.

When the soil finally smelled fecund and ripe, Peter rechecked his selections. "Let's see. Mountain laurel, pink azalea, holly, and Stella De Oro day lilies in purple and yellow. OK, time to cook with gas."

The first night went well. He dug deep into the newly fertile soil, gently lowering the bushes and plants. But then it rained like hell for two days straight. Thunder, lightning and high winds shut everything down. Once he got back up there, tire-spinning mud and quicksand kept him from parking close.

"Shit. I can't do this all in one trip." He lugged his tools and the remaining plants in two trips. On the second one, he stumbled over Brutus and landed on a shovel blade with his right hand.

"Fuck." He sucked on his butchered hand and soldiered on.

Throbbing pain and swelling made it difficult to grip the bloody shovel. Perspiration stung his eyes and big ropes of snot hung from his nose. At 10:50, he looked at his trusty Timex and knew it was way past time to get out of there.

Pain and fatigue made him woozy. Steadying his legs against Brutus who braced himself to provide a sturdy base, Peter surveyed the fruit of his labor as he gathered up his tools.

"Fucking A+, my man." It looked so good, phenomenal actually, until blaring sirens and flashing lights cut through the dark. Cop cars, ambulances, and fire trucks seemed to burst out of nowhere.

CHAPTER 3

"WHAT THE HELL?" PETER'S BODY REFUSED TO MOVE. Sitting down heavily on a nearby boulder, he pulled Brutus close and hugged him tight with his good arm.

"I love you, buddy." Peter whispered as Brutus's powerful chest expanded and contracted in perfect rhythm. Brutus licked Peter's cheek and looked at him expectantly.

"I don't know what's happening. Just sit tight, B. Sit like you've never sat before."

The cops swarmed closer and closer. They had to be locked and loaded, ready to counter any threat. Peter knew their adrenaline rush was off the charts. He prayed with all his might the cops wouldn't shoot Brutus. He heard the clicking of weapons and looked down in horror as the red laser dot landed on his chest.

"This is Bridgeville Police: drop your weapon and come out with your hands high in the air. Walk slowly," a loud male voice commanded.

Peter staggered to his feet, hands above his head. "Fellas, I'm coming out. I'm unarmed—it's Peter Russo. But my dog is here; don't shoot him."

Brutus started barking like a madman. Peter inched forward slowly just as instructed. He got on his knees and begged them not to hurt Brutus. Guns trained, they patted him down and cuffed his hands behind his back.

"Jesus, he's covered in blood."

"My dog, guys, my dog."

"Shut your mouth!"

"Wait, Russo? Peter Russo is that you?" One of the younger cops, who Peter recognized as Kenny Johnson, a skilled baseball player who almost played in college, nodded at him and said something inaudible to the others. All but two of them lowered their weapons and asked him what the hell he was doing at the facility in the dead of night.

An ambulance sped past them and Peter asked, "What's going on? What's this all about?"

The loudest, biggest cop, who Peter didn't recognize, yelled at him. "Maybe *you* should tell us."

"I don't believe this. Everybody's up here to arrest me for what, trespassing? Jesus, I only planted some bushes and flowers."

"This is no time for bullshit, Russo. You know damn well what's going down here. Where's your truck?"

"What . . ."

"Shut it." Herding him into the backseat of a squad car, someone squashed his head down hard.

"My dog, what are you going to do with him?"

When they got down to Peter's truck, the caravan of cops stopped. Weapons drawn, they fanned out in a circle. The bright lights illuminated the truck, and the command to exit the vehicle with hands in the air crackled through the loudspeaker.

"There's nobody in there," Peter said.

"Shut up."

The responders closing in on the truck were armed to the teeth. They captured it and tore open the front doors.

"Clear," came the response. "Got his wallet and ID. It's Peter Russo."

One of the other cops who knew Peter from fishing down by the ferry, Billy O'Leary, came up to the back window of the patrol car. "Man, you are in deep kimchee," he said. "Is that Brutus back there?" Peter nodded.

"Hey," O'Leary yelled out. "I'm handling the dog. Calling Animal Control right now."

"That fucking dog is low priority."

"OK—listen," O'Leary said into his cellphone. "We've got a clusterfuck up here at the fuel cell. We need you to handle an agitated pit bull tied up to a tree. It belongs to the suspect."

"Get over here," the officer in charge yelled.

"What?" O'Leary talked quickly on his phone as he looked at Peter. "Judgment call. Don't shoot the dog unless it's absolutely necessary."

CHAPTER 4

AT THE STATION, PETER WAS FINGERPRINTED, photographed, swabbed, and booked. They left him in his bloody and mud-sodden clothes. His injured hand pulsated and swelled gruesomely while the cops conferred. Peter decided against playing the card of asking to see his buddy, Sergeant John Tomassi. If he was in the station, Tomassi would make his way over soon enough.

Finally, the senior arresting officer took him to the interrogation room, read him his rights again and sat him down.

"I want my lawyer," Peter said. An EMT tried to clean his wound but wasn't happy about the bleeding.

"You should've taken him to the ER for stitches," she said. "I don't know if these butterfly bandages will hold the edges together." Nobody appeared too concerned.

"Make your call, Russo." Trying to hold the phone in his left hand and dial with his right, he kept dropping the phone and messing up the numbers. His right hand was as useful as a brick. Finally, he got through to Lori Welles, his good friend who happened to be a very successful local attorney.

"Lori," Peter said. "Wake up, this is urgent."

Lori mumbled something incoherent, so Peter spoke louder. "It's me, Peter Russo."

"Hello? Peter," she said, in a voice muffled with sleep. "Why are you calling me this late?"

"Lori, get over to the Bridgeville police station as fast as you can. I've been arrested and there's a wall of shit coming at me. They're going to shoot Brutus—you've got to save him."

"Don't say another word to anyone, Peter." Lori cleared her throat and pushed her sleeping lover in the back. "I'm on my way. Who's going to shoot Brutus?" Her groggy partner rolled over to the far edge of the king-sized bed, out of Lori 's reach.

"Brutus is tied to a tree up at the fuel cell on Maple Street, and he's going bananas. Animal Control could kill him. You gotta call Jeff and get Marti in on this. Brutus needs all the help he can get."

Lori hung up and reached for Martina Dunn, shaking her by the shoulder until she roused. Marti, a tall and athletic wine merchant in West Hadley, did not wake easily.

Lori pulled the covers off and showed no mercy as she maneuvered a naked Marti out of bed.

"Goddammit," Marti yelled, rolling onto her back and rubbing her eyes.

"For fuck's sake, Marti. Wake up! I need you." Lori's tension rose as she got Marti up to speed. "Peter's in trouble, and Brutus is about to be shot by Animal Control. I'll go handle Peter, but I really need you to pull the stops out for Brutus."

"Lor, breathe. Teamwork, babe." Marti hugged her hard. "I'll call my ex."

They each threw on sweats, grabbed their cell phones and jumped into their respective cars. Lori roared down the road while Marti, driving wildly through the dark as she tried to focus, regretted her generous nightcap of French brandy when she barely missed a galloping deer.

Nobody worked a phone like Marti. She could chew out vendors and purr to customers simultaneously. She jumped into action, calling her old girlfriend, the one woman on the planet who could keep Brutus alive. Her ex not only wrote for the Hatfield Gazette, the biggest paper in the area, but she loved animals passionately—actually more than people. Plus, her brother ran the West Hadley Public Works Department.

"You want me to do what?"

"Two things, really." Marti tamped down her rapid-fire speech, courtesy of her New Jersey upbringing, to a slower pace. "First, threaten Bridgeville's mayor you'll publish all the dirt you have on him unless he makes Brutus priority number one."

"Peter's Brutus?"

"Yes—haven't you been listening to anything I said?"

"Yeah, but it's two in the morning and I was having a great dream about an orgy. Everyone wanted a piece of me."

Marti heard loud yawning that sounded halfway to snoring. "Wake up, come on."

"OK, ok. What's the second thing? Wait, don't tell me. Call my brother and get one of his Animal Control people over there, right?"

"Exactly. Please, please."

"You owe me, bitch."

No sooner had Marti hung up than Bridgeville's mayor learned that allegations of campaign irregularities would be made public unless he called Animal Control and instructed them to let West Hadley take the lead in dealing with Brutus.

Marti waited anxiously, driving through the humid night and clutching her phone. When the call came through, Marti answered it in a nanosecond.

"Talk to me."

"Ok, listen. My brother got Animal Control to send an officer who's trained in something called non-lethal animal subjugation. Now, there's a mouthful. And Bridgeville's gonna let West Hadley do their non-lethal thing."

"You're the best—I really owe you, babe. How about a bottle of primo wine?"

"Sure, a bottle of 2015 Chateau Lafite Rothschild and we're close to even. Maybe throw in your fine self for old time's sake."

"What?" Marti relaxed her death grip on the phone. "You'll like the 2015 Mouton Rothschild better. It's just like me—finesse and power."

"Tramp."

"Ha. Trust me, put it away for twenty years and drink it for a great occasion. Then you'll thank me."

Marti and her ex made kissing sounds before they hung up. Lori texted that Jeff was on his way and would meet her in the parking lot.

When Marti eased into the space next to Jeff's pickup, he ran over in a panic. "Nobody's telling me what's what with Pete or why Brutus is a dead man walking!"

Marti calmed him down as they waited for Animal Control from Bridgeville and West Hadley. Explaining the situation as best she could somehow upset Jeff even more.

"I'm gonna kill Pete. And, they're gonna try non-lethal subjugation? The fuck does that mean?" Jeff seethed as he handed her his spare flashlight.

"Look, I don't know, either. I think there's a dart gun. I mean, how hard could it be to shoot a dart into Brutus? He's huge."

The West Hadley and Bridgeville Animal Control trucks arrived back to back. It became immediately obvious that neither town's personnel wanted to see the other there.

"I got the OK from the chief to let this shitshow happen for exactly five minutes," the Bridgeville Animal Control officer said. "And you do know it's the middle of the night, and I'm not getting overtime."

"Back off. It's our technology," the West Hadley guy said, brandishing the gun. "I've got three tranquilizer darts. One should be plenty."

Two Bridgeville cops hiked through the woods with the tense group to the approximate area where Brutus remained tied to a tree.

"Call out to him, Jeff," Marti urged. "He knows your voice."

"Brutus, buddy. Where are you?" Jeff searched unsuccessfully in his pockets for a dog treat. Luckily, one of the cops had some Snausages in his car, meant for his own pup. He ran back to get them while the group waited.

Brutus barked savagely, making him easy to locate with the powerful flashlights they all clutched.

"Healthy set of lungs on that dog."

The cop with the Snausages returned breathlessly and nudged Jeff to holler for Brutus.

"This baby," the West Hadley officer said, "is a shoo-in at ten yards."

"So, you've done this before?" Marti, Jeff and Snausage cop voiced this concern simultaneously.

"Uh, no, not really."

"What does that mean?" Marti ventured.

"We just got it, but I watched the training video a couple times. No worries." The West Hadley officer caressed his new toy.

Marti, Jeff and Snausage cop exchanged worried looks. The other cop yawned and scratched his balls. The Bridgeville Animal guy spat and kicked the ground in disgust.

"OK, this is how it's gonna go," West Hadley said. "You," nodding towards Snausage cop, "throw the treat close to him. When he bends down to get it, I'll shoot the dart. Piece of cake."

The first attempt was wide of the mark. Brutus retrieved the Snausage too quickly.

The second attempt hit the tree. The Bridgeville Animal guy threw his hands up in anger and stomped away.

"Hey, can I see that gun?" Officer Snausage examined it carefully. "How about that dart?"

"Look folks, this is fucked up." Jeff's voice bristled with frustration and anger. "We've got exactly one dart and one Snausage left. This is it—one and done, right, Officer Piece of Cake?"

"Bite me."

"You first. You better watch your tone, son."

Officer Snausage whirled into action. He threw the Snausage and fired the dart into Brutus's flank. After a few seconds of yelping confusion, Brutus crashed to the ground.

"Hey, man. Not cool," West Hadley protested.

"Thank God," Marti shouted.

"Great shot." The other Bridgeville cop high-fived Snausage cop.

Jeff pumped his arms in the air. "You're my man."

"You're not my type, Russo," Officer Snausage said, puffed up with pride. Then he grinned and accepted a hearty fist bump.

CHAPTER 5

SERGEANT JOHN TOMASSI PEERED OVER HIS BIFOCALS at Peter, his boyhood chum since they were fat boys playing side by side on the offensive line in Mighty Mites football forty-five years ago. Peter stood before him, disheveled, muddy, bloody, and arrested.

"What the fuck, Russo?" Tomassi's fearsome unibrow amplified his frown. His permanent five o'clock shadow seemed to darken as if to reflect his extreme irritation at Peter's arrest at the Zenergy fuel cell facility. "I got one hour left in my shift, and now I gotta deal with you getting arrested on a goddamn boatload of charges."

"So, tell you what, John, just let me go." Peter's stocky build and graying dark hair matched Tomassi's. He shrugged as Tomassi took his glasses off with one hand and dramatically massaged the bridge of his nose with the other. "Just sayin' since of all the paperwork, it might be easier." He stared straight into Tomassi's bloodshot eyes, hoping to see some softening, a flicker of their long friendship.

"No can do. Zenergy's got weight; they even got departments in the area to put out an alert and a BOLO about suspicious activity near their facility. Asshole," he snorted at Peter.

"Really? Since when do they get to dictate what cops should be on the lookout for? Unbelievable." Peter shifted uneasily on the ugly linoleum floor, finally sitting down in an uncomfortable plastic chair.

"You're going to enjoy a nice long Memorial Day weekend here on account of all the courts being closed until Tuesday." Tomassi popped a breath mint and leafed through his notepad. "Your brother called. Not to alarm you or anything, but evidently pit bulls like Brutus can't tolerate the drug in the tranquilizer dart they shot him with."

"Shit." Peter picked at the blood-soaked bandage on his hand before wiping away a tear that trickled down his cheek. "Why did your guys have to go in so heavy? Locked and loaded 'cause of me and Brutus? They could've killed us."

"What don't you get? You just had to be a wise-ass, with your flowers and bushes. I'm not even gonna talk about the attack on Lou Stulow, the security guard." Seeing Peter shake his head no, Tomassi held up his calloused hand. "Save it for your lawyer. Now, back to someone I actually care about—Brutus. Yeah, he's gonna stay another day in the animal hospital. Jeff also said he wouldn't be coming to visit you until he could feel enough brotherly love not to freaking strangle you." Tomassi checked his watch. "I'm outta here in five. Lemme give you a piece of advice: zip it and make like a boy scout from here on in." He patted Peter gruffly on the back and then swatted him hard in the head with his notepad.

"Thanks."

"De nada. Lori handling it?"

"What?"

"You're deaf *and* stupid? I might stop by on Memorial Day with one of Donna's amazing chili hot dogs if you play your cards right." Tomassi left the room with all the grace of a wounded hippo, slamming the door behind him.

Lori Welles, forty-five and proudly out for basically her entire life, entered the room with her dark hair pulled up in a top-knot like a Japanese samurai. Beautiful, even at that hour and without make-up, she looked royally peeved.

"I want to slap you. And I want to cut open your head to see if you have an actual brain in there. But, then I might get arrested, and that would be about as useful here as a cat at a dog show."

"I can't pay you, Lor. I've got like a negative balance. Maybe just get me through the weekend and I'll wing it from there. Or we can barter, right?"

Peter's bank account, never flush, had shriveled to an all-time low. None of his friends had any spare change, either. That is, none except for Carmen Fiori, who ran her family's apple orchard like Warren Buffet. But when Carmen dumped him, she made it very clear that he was never to darken her doorstep.

"Don't worry about that now," Lori said. "Let's sort through everything and get the assault charge thrown out. Obviously, it's circumstantial bullshit. But I'm swamped with work, literally up to my neck. We gotta get you out of here. I need someone to help out."

"OK, good. But just not Vic Baldini, I'm begging you. I know you use him sometimes, but anyone else. The shitty late-night commercials, the bad comb-over . . .

"Peter could have listed a million reasons, but Lori honed in on his major reservation.

"And he's Carmen's ex brother-in-law, yadda, yadda. Beggars can't be choosers. If I can get him to help, he's on the case."

"Oy."

"He's a good tactician with a nose for the kill. Just close your eyes when you talk to him if you're such a priss. Maybe he'll figure out how to get you off for being mentally deficient."

"I thought you were on my side. What's this, tough love?"

"You shouldn't have posted so much trash-talking about Zenergy on Facebook. Combine it with Saunders Construction, and you know I mean the history Brock has with your family. By the way, does Jeff know that Saunders is back in the game in Bridgeville? I hope to God I won't have to defend him, too, once he finds out." She rubbed her eyes, and Peter saw how sleepy she looked.

"You're working too hard. Sorry to add more to your plate."

"You're like family. I'd be insulted if you called anyone else. But, everything I just said plus the guard getting assaulted while you were up there recreating the Garden of Eden makes you look bad. Really bad."

Peter swatted away the comment. "Oh, so it's OK for Zenergy to poison our air and water? That assault on the guard wasn't me, and they're morons if they think I did it. He's gonna be OK, right?'

Lori shrugged. "Hope so. It's a messy head wound, and they can be tricky."

"They better hurry with the blood tests from my clothes and everything. It's my own blood for Chrissake. I wanna get home to Brutus, the poor guy. And my hand hurts like hell." He held it up to show her.

"Boo-hoo. Suck it up cupcake. Here's a smooch to make it better.' Lori smiled and blew him a kiss.

CHAPTER 6

AFTER LORI TOOK OFF, A GUARD ESCORTED PETER BACK to his cell. He looked around to see if he had company at chez Bridgeville PD. "Anyone else here?"

"Yo, Pops," a young man called out. "What you here for?"

Peter saw a tattooed set of arms sticking through the bars of the cell near him. "Same as you—nothing."

The young man laughed and called out to the cell next to him, "Hey, el Viejo—aight!"

"Hey, Pops," another young male voice said. "Over here. You ever coach a Little League team in Hatfield?"

Peter tried to get a closer look at the young men, especially the one who asked about baseball. Short, muscular and just as tatted out, he had sleek dark hair cut in an elaborate buzz but Peter didn't recognize him.

"I coached Little League with the Big Brothers program in Hatfield about ten or so years ago," he said, trying to retrieve this buried memory. "Help me here; did you play on that team?"

"Man, I knew I remembered you!" The young man crouched into a baseball hitting stance. "You always told me to be 'baseball ready' and I never forget a voice. You got old, Coach."

Peter chuckled. "You could say that again. What else do you remember? What's your name?"

"Marco. What the hell you doing here, Coach?

"This is all a misunderstanding. It'll be settled soon."

"Ain't no misunderstanding if you in here with us,

Pops, on this fine Memorial Day weekend," the first guy said, stroking his black knife-edged goatee. "Hey, I'm Paco."

"Pleased to meet you. I kind of like being Pops, but my real name is Peter."

"What your kids call you?" Paco asked.

"Divorced, no kids. At least none that I know of."

"Coach, 'member that sweet time I hit the winning inside-the-park homerun against West Hadley?"

"Marco—wow. That's a blast from the past. Of course, I remember, but do you remember that I bought the team Dairy Queen after every game?" Peter asked, recalling just how excited the boys got when they piled into coaches' cars, win or lose, and they got to order ice cream at the walk-up window.

"Man—you went broke on us! Blizzards were the bomb."

"You asked for every kind of candy in the world to be mixed into yours. You still have teeth?" Peter pretended to count as Marco laughed, flashing a smile that a beaver would love.

"So, like serious now, Coach. What you get arrested for?"

"Long story, guys."

"You see us goin' anywhere?" Paco said, his voice filled with frustration. Peter knew better than to ask what they had been arrested for. It would probably depress the hell out of him and they would tell him if they felt like it. "We got nothin' but time, Pops."

Peter sighed. "They arrested me for trespassing, vandalism and aggravated assault."

"What the what?" Marco yelled. "No way."

"Aggravated assault ain't you, Pops," Paco said solemnly.

"Thank you. At least somebody aside from my family and lawyer gets that. But I definitely was trespassing." Peter thought for a minute. "Vandalism could go either way."

"Hey, Coach," Marco said after a pause, employing the regretful tone a surgeon might use for a terminally ill patient who has weeks to live. "That aggro assault charge could be some real shit. You gotta get a good attorney."

"Chow time," Officer Kenny Johnson came in and announced. "Peter, I see you've made friends."

"I'm a friendly guy, Officer."

"He coached me in Little League," Marco said proudly.

"No shit," Kenny raised an eyebrow. "Me, too."

"Wait a minute, Kenny," Peter said. "When you go home, can you get ahold of a team picture from about ten years ago? You played at least one season on the mixed team for Bridgeville and Hatfield, right?"

"Yeah, I did." Kenny, twenty-four, looked exactly the same as he did at thirteen, with curious eyes and plain features. He still wore his brown hair high and tight, and his tall muscular build made his babyface even more noticeable.

"Damn," Marco said. "Are you that KJ kid who could hit like anything?"

"You gotta be kidding me," Paco said loudly. "What is this a fucking reunion? I never got no Little League. I was in the Dominican trying to play street ball with a stick and some raggedy ass kids."

Kenny walked over to Marco and they slapped hands. "Marco, I'm not gonna talk about what you're doing here. But, you were Derek Jeter at shortstop. Man, you had his hands and wheels."

"Yeah, back in the day. Get that picture, Officer KJ. Aight?"

Peter shook his head in wonder. Cosmic coincidences like this one didn't just happen. Once he got out of jail, he'd have to ask Ian Edwards, his karma-obsessed friend and occasional personal trainer, how to explain the force that pulled off this phenomenon. It wasn't random, that's for sure. Suddenly, Peter wanted nothing more than to go for a pre-dawn walk down by the river, dogs off-leash, birds singing, water flowing, cool wind in his face, and not a soul in sight.

CHAPTER 7

PETER GOT TO SEE IAN MUCH SOONER THAN HE EXPECTED.

Ian Edwards and his business partner, Andre Jackson, were very serious about trying to salvage their fitness clients from the scrap heap. Ian's clients tended to be spiritual and broken somehow or else highly entertained by his idiosyncrasies, while Andre's wanted to get ripped and lose weight. Yet, Be It Gym aka BIG worked. In fact, they were turning away clients. They created their business partnership after their mutual employer, Ladies in Fitness Together (LiFT), went bankrupt during the Great Recession. Never particularly close, they still felt a kinship and the urgent need for both a paycheck and a gym facility. So, they looked at each other and shrugged, why not?

At first, business was so slow that Andre auctioned off personal training sessions at fundraisers for PeeWee football and Little League, which is how Peter entered the BIG orbit. Ian ended up offering cheap Pilates classes through the Adult Education program in two towns. They grew the business and kept the hype to a minimum, personalizing the experience for each client.

"Don't sit on furniture, don't lift weights, don't eat meat, and avoid sex," Ian counseled. The white ex-cop from the UK preached the virtues of vegetarianism, tee-totaling, discomfort, and celibacy. He claimed to have bedded more women than he cared to remember, including the one he trailed to the States like a lovesick puppy in his earlier unenlightened days.

"There's always a gutting betrayal in love," he said to an incredulous Andre. "That's why country music grabs people's hearts. You know, somebody done someone wrong. It's the human condition." Now, enlightened and evolved, Ian's dedication to asceticism simmered steadily but never too explosively; Lao Tzu's warning that the brightest flame burns half as long adorned an elaborate tattoo down the inside of Ian's left arm.

"That's bullshit," Andre said, whenever one of his clients seemed swayed by Ian's list of don'ts. "You gotta lift weights, eat more protein and boogie on. But really, don't sit so much."

Andre, a handsome African American in his mid-thirties, was a devoted dad with three kids and deep roots in the community. No longer together with the kids' mother, he lived for the time he got to spend with them. Andre's high school sports feats were still legend, but he had moved on to a few careers since those days. Many people remembered him as the best phlebotomist who ever took their blood or inserted an IV when he worked at the local hospital.

Ian's yoga devotions and British accent made him unusual in Bridgeville, but aside from that he blended in easily. A frequent patron of the Alewife Java Hut, Bridgeville's most popular coffee shop, he looked like every other hipster wannabe late-thirties dad, with his shaved head, tattoos and lean build. Except he wasn't a dad or a hipster.

"Children are to be pitied," he said. "Look at the condition of the world that they've been born into! They're fucked."

"You need to get a life, dude, you know—take your mind off all the negative shit," Andre said. "I'm not even talking about a new woman. Maybe some kind of plant to begin with; you'd probably forget to feed a pet, so start with a cactus."

"I include you in my prayers for mankind, Andre. I have a special one for you," Ian said, extending his middle finger with a flourish.

"Right back at you."

But Ian could be surprising, with an abiding love for technology and a nest-egg. Although this at times conflicted with attaining nirvana, it ensured that he kept up his private investigator license, hard-earned when he toiled for Discreet Review, a marital infidelity powerhouse.

Lori had enjoyed some weird yet deep chats with Ian, including the revelation about his PI license. She filed that nugget in the back of her steel-trap mind in case she ever needed some outside-the-box work done. Now was that time.

CHAPTER 8

AROUND 5:45 A.M. ON THE FRIDAY OF PETER'S ARREST, Andre propped open the gym's front door to enjoy the sunrise and the sweet-smelling fresh air.

Ian, on his way over, greeted the day, too. "Here comes

the sun," he sang happily, unwilling to shield his eyes from the mesmerizing yellow light.

Andre bopped to the beat of the radio, vacuuming every inch of the gym, his usual routine. Ian wandered in after parking his car, grabbed an oil can to adjust an annoying squeaky spring on the Pilates Reformer, and suddenly started screaming once he saw the unholy mess.

"Andre! Oh, no—What the fuck?"

Andre couldn't hear him over the vacuum, so Ian ran over and yanked the plug out of the wall.

"What have you done?" Ian yelled in a very un-Zen manner.

"What is your damn problem this time, man?" Andre followed Ian over to the Pilates corner and there, stuck in a previously gleaming Reformer machine, lay a big mangled bird.

Ian and Andre glared at each other as they beheld the Canada goose lying bloody and quite dead in the Pilates Reformer.

"Fuck me, this is really bad," Ian sputtered, pacing between foam rollers, yoga mats and clean fluffy white towels.

"Fuck you is right." Andre owned up to being a total neat-freak and germaphobe. In fact, this had led to a serious conflict in his phlebotomy career. He was not about to let this colossal dead goose, which looked like it could feed twenty-five hearty eaters at Thanksgiving, besmirch his gym. Blood needed to be where it belonged: in veins, arteries and test tubes.

"Don't touch anything," Ian commanded, keeping his distance and ignoring the latex gloves Andre threw in his direction.

"C'mon, already. Let's just throw it in the trash and be done with it." Andre stuffed feathers and assorted body parts into the bag.

"Why you think this was an accident is beyond me. This could be a message." The ex-cop couldn't stop spinning investigatory habits drilled into his head. "Who had access? Motive? Opportunity? Is anything missing?" Ian recoiled as one of the goose's bloody legs fell on the floor near him.

"This never happened," Andre snapped and threw a big towel at Ian, motioning him to start cleaning. "We got to be careful about people poking their nose into our business. You tell just anybody and they tell somebody and pretty soon we're gonna get closed down. Probably blamed, too, for animal cruelty or some shit. Unbelievable."

"Shut up, Andre. This is seriously unlucky back where I come from."

"Seems to me finding a dead bird in your gym isn't lucky anywhere."

"No, you don't get it. There's serious religious omens and superstitions at play here. All is not well." Ian kept wringing the towel and taking deep breaths.

"Man, you need to get a grip. It's just a damn stupid dead bird." Andre headed off to the dumpster with a disgusted look.

Ian was still looking up dead bird omens on his smartphone when Andre came back in. "Hey, enough of this crap," Andre said. "I'm going to the Alewife for coffee. You want anything?'

"What? Did you know in Scotland finding a dead bird is a bad omen for supper? You might be served the corpse if you don't spit on it immediately. Do you still have the bag?"

"Get a hold of yourself, man. Get the big-boy underpants on." Andre tried unsuccessfully not to laugh. He knew from experience Ian could be very touchy and might sulk for days, confusing clients into thinking they had angered him somehow. That was bad for business, and Andre prided himself on providing a quality product.

Ian stalked off outside and soon returned, wiping his mouth on the back of his hand.

"Oh, no—you didn't," Andre said. "This is no way for a dude in touch with his third eye to behave."

"Go on, ignore the obvious, Andre. You don't have an enlightened bone in your body."

"I'm ignoring your crazy, asshole."

"This goose omen is too much; it's a warning from the universe." Ian grabbed his water bottle and baseball cap. "I'll be back for my eight o'clock."

"Later, man." Andre left soon after to go the Alewife for his beloved morning java.

When he got back twenty minutes later, the dead goose and the overwhelming smell of disinfectant annoyed him so much that he felt his blood pressure rising.

Andre found some pine-scented candles and lit them near the Reformer. Checking his phone for new messages, he found three urgent texts from Lori starting at seven A.M.

Lori picked up right away. "Peter Russo's in jail on a crazy-ass assault charge. Can you talk Ian into getting over to Vic Baldini's office for a quick meet-and-greet and doing some PI stuff? I had to get Vic in on this because I'm up to my eyeballs in work. I swear to God, Peter needs Ian. And tell him to act like a human being—not like some space cadet."

He's on it," Andre said. "I'll get him back here and then over to this Vic guy's office ASAP."

"Don't you have to ask him?"

"Hell, no. He'll do it. Call you back soon."

Andre drummed his fingers impatiently as he waited for Ian to answer his phone. "C'mon, pick up, man."

"What, Andre. I'm up a tree so this better be important."

"Dude, get the fuck down. Peter Russo's in trouble, and Lori says he needs your help."

"Is this some kind of joke? Don't mess with my tree time."

"No, this is real. Get back here," Andre yelled.

"OK." Ian started to chant loudly, and Andre's blood pressure climbed even higher. "Ian, you OK?"

"No. None of us are. It's the goose, don't you get it? The goose is only the beginning."

CHAPTER 9

"YEAH," LORI SAID AS VIC SHOT DOWN THE IDEA ON the phone. "I know you think he's a village idiot, but first of all, you don't really know him. Second of all, he's got a unique way of cutting to the chase. Peter's got a huge problem, and the sooner we uncover what the hell went down, the sooner he's home. You know what Memorial Day weekend is like around here; nothing gets done. I want Ian on the case."

"Lori, he's too psycho. Once I was behind him in line for coffee at the Alewife, and I'm talking on my phone, he turns around and stares at me without blinking with those spooky blue eyes for like five minutes. If I hadn't wanted a latte so bad, I would've split."

Lori smiled. Ian did that to people when he thought they had just uttered something spectacularly stupid. "Vic, you don't talk on the phone; you yell. Look, just because you're opposites doesn't mean that he's not the guy to break this bullshit down."

Vic exhaled loudly. "I got my own PI, and I don't like flakes."

"Listen, someone had to have a beef with the guard that got violent the same night Peter was gardening up there like a moron. Ian's on his way—make nice."

About an hour later at Vic's wood-paneled office decorated in haute Ralph Lauren, replete with antlered deer heads on the walls, Ian and Vic sized each other up unblinkingly.

"I can't believe you're a PI," Vic said. He glanced up and down, curling his lip in palpable dismay. "Hey, Bob Marley," he nodded at Ian's T-shirt, "you carry a gun?"

"Absolutely not. Guns kill, and I'm not a killer. But I do have this," Ian said, taking the high road by not pulling the deer heads off the wall and beating Vic with them. "You can find out more about someone with the ultimate tool." He held out his iPhone.

"Hey, that's actually true." Vic, chubby and sporting a shiny golf shirt at least a size too small, stroked his comb-over like it was a beloved pet.

"Social media tells all. And, I have these," Ian pointed to his eyes, ears, skull, and heart.

"Yeah, me too. And a ten-foot shlong. My regular guy is on a cruise, and this is a rush job. Add Lori on my ass, and you're hired. I gotta know your rates."

"$125 an hour and twenty-six cents per mile."

"What? Those are for top-notch PI's."

"Of whom I am one," Ian said primly. "Besides, Vic—I have to eat and pay rent."

"Alright, fine—it's not my dime, anyway. On the down-low, an anonymous someone's paying the bills, and she wants her identity to remain secret. So, shhh." Vic put his finger to his lips.

"Oh, I bet it's Carmen Fiori. That wasn't very hard to figure out. But I won't tell." Ian chuckled before saying, "I'll need an advance."

"You're not as dumb as you look. Now we're gonna do this my way. Find out who the guard is shtupping. Who, what, when, where, how. Why, I don't give a shit—oldest story in the book. Stay away from him. You don't want to get hit with a tampering charge."

"Anything else?" Ian asked, already thinking of ten million modifications, his mouth puckered like he just ate a lemon.

"You got a problem? Tough shit. I started out with a slip-and-fall law firm. You know, personal injury. People who take a tumble at Home Depot and get money. I already forgot what you never knew about greed and the itsy-bitsy line between opportunity and extortion."

"Vic, I'm not critiquing." Ian held up his hands in supplication. "Don't forget that I was a beat cop back in the day."

"England," Vic snorted derisively.

"What, you think everybody spends all day bowing and curtseying? Like I said, I'm not judging."

"Bullshit. Everybody judges. But you know what? Out on my own, I play both sides of the ball, and every client gets a thousand percent of me. Defendant, plaintiff, whatever. I return every phone call; every lonely little old lady hears back from me. I climb into the foxhole with my clients. Give me conflict any day. I eat it for breakfast on a spoon. You want tactics? I got tactics. I could get you a settlement for a hangnail. I go to war for my clients, and you want me on your side. Just ask Lori and Carm." Vic panted after his long monologue and reached into his pocket for his ever-present Chapstick. "Cherry's the best."

"You're actually foaming at the mouth," Ian marveled. "Calm down. I'll do it your way."

"I'm only getting warmed up; this is first gear. You don't want to see third gear."

"Definitely not. But you need a meditation intervention to detach from your anger. Negative energy is a killer."

"Yeah, yeah." Vic rested his sockless loafer-clad foot on a leather stool. "I'll take it under advisement."

Ian quickly gulped some room-temperature water from his ever-present thermos. "Tell me what you need for Peter's defense."

"It's fricking Memorial Day weekend. The cops got the parade, beer-soaked picnics; they're not ultra-motivated to investigate until Tuesday, I'm betting. So you do the legwork. Get all the dirt, everything, because that leads us to who wants him dead. Then find a loose link and exploit the hell out of it. Get it done like yesterday."

"I'll circle back to you soon."

"Buddy, if you're too busy helping housewives lose cellulite, let me know. I'll find someone else before the door hits you in the ass on your way out."

Ian gritted his teeth into a smile. "No worries, mate. I include you in my special prayers."

"Thanks. A little extra in the God department couldn't hurt."

CHAPTER 10

THE FRIDAY MORNING OF PETER'S ARREST, CARMEN Fiori, forty-nine and unaware of this momentous event, stood naked in front of the full-length mirror in her huge bedroom closet and critically assessed her petite silhouette. The light from the antique wall sconces and the soft earth tones that graced her inner sanctuary, built out of her cheating ex-husband's closet, were designed to flatter.

"The legs are the last thing to go." Carmen still approved of her shapely legs and the black shoulder-length bob framing her brown eyes, Roman nose and rose-bud lips, a look she'd tinkered with for years. Just like Cleopatra, her studious young grandson, Jimmy, suggested, delightedly showing her a picture from his favorite book on ancient Egypt. But Carmen frowned at her drooping breasts.

"Damn gravity."

Carmen strapped the girls into a sag-defying padded bra and stepped into her basic spring uniform of tan capris, a black V-necked sweater and sneakers. As she did her makeup, adroitly applying concealer to her under-eye bags, she decided Botox could wait another month.

Amped after a big cup of high-test espresso, Carmen walked the hilly expanse of Fiori Orchards, armed with her iPad and phone. She saw some rot on the Honeycrisps in Section A and photographed it carefully. Back in the house, she sent the pictures to the specialists at the state Apple Council. Absentmindedly, sipping at her second cup of coffee, she scrolled through her new text messages and almost fell over when she read Lori Welles's brief text about Peter's arrest.

WTF, she texted back.

Peter had muscled into her sex fantasies for almost a whole year. Carmen's sixteen-speed vibrator worked impeccably, but she never came with such shuddering fulfilment as when Peter crowded into the picture. She recognized the irony; the man she couldn't kick out fast enough needed to be in her head for the earth to move. Just thinking about him in this unguarded moment made her pulsate, an electric charge that juiced her pants and splashed her coffee.

"Oh my God, Carmen. Get a grip."

Carmen had shut Peter out abruptly from her life two years ago, right after her daughter, Becky, died at twenty-three, high and drunk after yet another night of partying at the quarry. Although Peter supported her lovingly when her mother finally passed away from Alzheimer's, a gut-wrenching shadow of her former self, Carmen couldn't handle him after Becky died. She knew he cared about Becky and Jimmy, but the double whammy of losing her mother and her only child in three years destroyed her world.

After the overwhelming awfulness of Becky's funeral, which Carmen remembered in precise detail, she forced him to leave. She felt her edges sharp as glass and didn't hesitate to skewer even the well-wishers. When a woman came up to her at the gas station and said she was so brave, Carmen stared at her with disgust.

"Here's a word of advice, die before your children so you don't have to be brave."

Carmen boiled it down to simple calculations, all of them zero-sum decisions: cling to Peter and depend utterly on him or crawl out of the wreckage and depend on herself, somehow rising like a phoenix from the ashes of her life. And it had to be her, not only for Jimmy's sake but for her own. So, she built an impregnable iron fortress, reinforced with barbed wire and snarling wolves, to chase Peter away and keep him out for good.

"You destroyed your own happiness," her grief counselor said when Carmen could finally do more than cry during their sessions.

"I hate happy. It's bullshit, and what you're really talking about is love, isn't it?" Carmen jumped up from the armchair she usually curled up in. "Romantic love or whatever ridiculous fucking name you want—it makes you blind and stupid. Look at what my being in love with Peter did. It doesn't have a place in my life anymore."

"Is that fair to him? To yourself?"

"I don't want to talk about it. We're done here." She never went back.

Carmen was raising Becky's son, the introspective Jimmy, now eight years old. He devoured books and delighted in impressing his grandma with his unusual interests, currently pyramids and pharaohs. Whoever Jimmy's father had been, Becky, then seventeen, couldn't remember or wouldn't say when she told her mother she was pregnant.

"I'll get an abortion, Ma. It's just a stupid mistake; I'm sorry."

"That's my grandchild, not just a stupid mistake," Carmen yelled, shocking them both. They locked eyes as they stood wordlessly frozen in place.

Finally, through tears, Carmen spoke first. "I'm sorry, but I'm not sorry I said it. Of course, it's your choice. I absolutely believe that." She wiped her face and blew her nose noisily. Becky did the same, only louder, and they cried in each other's arms.

Becky loved Jimmy and made sure to give him the Fiori last name, but being a teen mom sucked, in her own words.

"Jimmy Fiori is gonna know where he's from. I can't give him much, but I can give him our history," she said to her grandfather, who slowly embraced the whole situation. Becky worked at the orchard after Jimmy's birth and earned her GED. Carmen paid her a generous salary and helped with Jimmy, but Becky didn't step up the way Carmen thought she should.

"I need a life," she complained to Carmen. "I'm missing

all the fun. I want to go out with my friends. Why can't you watch him more?"

"Becky, you can't go out every night and party. I'm happy to do three nights a week. And you better be using birth control."

"Butt out, Mom."

"You just asked me for more help, so I'll butt in every now and then, thank you very much. I've got a life, too." Carmen bit back the pointed observation that Becky was acting like a spoiled brat. She didn't want to go there again.

Peter used to come over once Jimmy, who slept like a log, went to bed. And Carmen spent a lot of time at Peter's cottage. She huddled with Annie, Jeff's wife, to scout through the attic for old black-and-white pictures of the Russo clan and farm. After checking with Peter, who gave her carte blanche to do whatever she wanted, she got them framed and hung them artfully on the walls. She also moved his collection of rubber chickens to a shelf in the garage.

Lori panicked when Carmen spiraled into an absolute recluse after Becky died, only able to surface from the depths of her personal hell for Jimmy and the orchard. Anything and anyone else, including Peter had to go, not that Lori understood what happened there. But Lori knew Carmen would do anything to help Peter out of jam.

Lori and Carmen went way back to elementary school. Feisty and always ready to fight for a cause, Carmen took no prisoners, even as a kid. When Lori, younger by a few years, needed protection from schoolyard bullies who taunted her for being different, shouts of "dyke" ringing through the air, Carmen made them pay. She also taught Lori a few key moves, like the best way to kick someone in the groin.

Carmen's fingers danced madly as she and Lori exchanged texts. When Vic called her to complain about ruining his Memorial Day plans, Carmen set him straight.

"You're doing it or I'll make your life a living hell. Obviously, I'm footing the bill. It's Pete, for Christ's sake. And don't tell him it's me or I'll hunt you down, so help me God."

"OK, I got it. Try a little decaf, would ya? But hey, you're the boss."

"Damn straight and don't forget it." Carmen's ex-husband Anthony Baldini, better known as Ant, had hit the road long ago. A hard partier who never met a vice he couldn't master, he didn't have Vic's ambition, loyalty, or smarts. The Baldini's hailed from West Hadley where their used-car dealer lots were celebrated for their trashiness. Carmen had never taken the Baldini name, and Becky couldn't wait to legally change her last name to Fiori when she turned sixteen.

A few hours later, Carmen spoke to Lori on the phone. "How bad is it, Lor? Pete didn't assault anyone, I know it like I know my name. But Saunders being involved must've made him crazy. I get that. But, if I was talking to him, I'd kill him for being such a pig-headed ass."

Lori sighed. "I know. I've asked Ian Edwards, you know, the personal trainer who's partners with Andre at BIG? He's a trip and a half, but he's also a licensed PI and sharp as a tack. You're going to pay his bill, too, Ms. Moneybags."

"Only under two conditions—I want to meet Ian face to face, and Pete never finds out I'm doing this."

"Don't you think Peter will suspect something? I mean he knows Vic is your ex brother-in-law."

"Yeah, but he also knows Vic is an ambulance chaser who wins cases. And you work with him sometimes. It's just a small-town connection. You know, the usual incest."

Carmen busied herself with prowling the orchard for more rot, disease and insects. The orchard laborers stayed far away, sensing her mood. But whenever she saw a potential problem, she summoned Miguel, the foreman who was her first hire when she took over the business and who she trusted with her life. She knew his boyfriend, backstory and immigration woes. He called her La Luchadora, the strong fighting woman who never quits.

"Don't forget who doesn't take shit," Carmen reminded him.

"Don't I know it."

Carmen's humble Mediterranean heritage—her parents joked that her baby bottles were a mixture of olive oil, red wine and milk—informed her life. No processed food, no crap from anyone except the loser she ended up married to for twelve years, no surrender. Even as a girl, she'd cultivated her own vegetable patch, eagerly asking her beloved grandmother, Nonna, for recipes from the old country.

"It's peasant food," her mother said disdainfully. "Don't listen to her. Such nonsense. Since when is American cooking not good enough for you?"

Nonna taught her how to pluck zucchini blossoms at daybreak and to stuff them with meat, rice, and cheese. Carmen learned how to get rid of evil spirits, how to put a curse on someone, how to use every part of a chicken, and how to save the blood for Nonna's secret sauce.

When her father, Aldo Fiori, finally washed his hands of his two slacker sons and loser son-in-law, he put Carmen in charge of Fiori Orchards. Painstakingly, she dragged it out of the Stone Age.

"We're gonna stop being like every other dinosaur orchard around here. I want sustainable horticulture," she said to Peter.

"Whore-what?"

"Ha-ha." She slapped away his wandering hands.

Her brothers were furious at Aldo for passing them over. Carmen knew they were dunces, indulged by their mother until they thought the sun rose and set on their command.

"Better you than them," Aldo said to Carmen, waving off the whining protests. "I didn't work my ass off to have them run it into the ground."

Nick, Carmen's older brother and a womanizing layabout, still irritated Aldo immensely whenever they crossed paths. Frank, her younger brother, owed money to just about everyone. Frank's gambling addiction, made much worse by Bridgeville's proximity to three enticing casinos, kept him in and out of rehab, hospital emergency rooms and permanently in Aldo's shithouse. But little Jimmy, his only great-grandchild, made Aldo smile.

CHAPTER 11

EARLY SATURDAY MORNING, JEFF, STILL APOPLECTIC, came by with warm freshly-baked crumb cakes from Rudy's for the cops and a bombastic expletive-laden diatribe for his brother. He showed Peter a take-out cup of steaming coffee from the Alewife Java Hut, Peter's favorite morning haunt, and refused to give it to him.

"Oh, come on, Jeff. The coffee here is pure rotgut."

"You don't deserve it."

After finally handing Peter the coffee and ranting for at least five minutes, Jeff calmed down sufficiently to inform him that Ian was on the case as a private investigator.

"Lori's busy, Vic's busy—no one imagined you would be such an asshole. They need someone to get all the goods double-time on who might've attacked the guard. Lori tapped Ian to do the leg-work, and Vic's in, too. BPD's not gonna give you special treatment. There's a line." Jeff said, tilting his chair onto the back two legs. "That yoga freak has a current PI license, can you believe it?"

"You gotta be shitting me," Peter said. "Maybe I forgot that minor detail about Ian, but I thought I knew as much about him as any earthling could, outside of Andre."

"Hey, Nancy's coming to see you today. Get ready—she's fit to be tied."

Nancy Yates had a work ethic that would shame the most industrious honey bee. She got ahead by busting her ass off. After the ugly divorce that left her financially strapped with two furious young sons, who still hated her as grown-ups, a steady paycheck and good benefits, including full psych coverage thanks to Brock Saunders, became her reason for being. When recessions and constant mergers generated layoffs in the financial services sector, Nancy hung on, sometimes by her fingertips. Nancy's cosmic clusterfuck as an aging single woman with major health problems and a handful of nothing fed the flames of her stress. It made her crazy. But what Peter had done made her practically certifiable.

Nancy burst into the interview room ready for blood.

"You jackass. If I could go back in time, I'd give you four flat tires every night just in case you hot-wired the ignition." Nancy, currently a blonde, pounded the table with the heel of her well-manicured hand, barely able to fit her bulk into the molded plastic chair. Morbidly obese now, she sat with difficulty. Her blue eyes blazed angrily.

Peter acknowledged Nancy's fury with a vigorous head nod. "Mea culpa, but something had to be done, so I did it. I am not going to let those corporate bastards and government lackeys scorch the earth."

Officer Billy O'Leary listened to the conversation with disapproval.

"Russo, come on. Just keep quiet like Tomassi told you."

"None of this would've happened if those Zenergy ratfucks showed some respect for nature. Wait, that's an insult to rodents. And I'm not even mentioning how no one living near the fuel cell has a prayer of selling their houses or—"

"Enough!" Nancy said. "We get it. But you're on a big shit list now. The cops, the town, the state, and probably even the FBI. They'll be watching everything you do and say."

Peter waved at imaginary cameras and gave a spirited thumbs-up.

"So why did Lori bring Vic in? I mean aside from the obvious. I saw his latest profile on OKCupid. Tell me he's a better lawyer than a liar. According to him, he looks like George Clooney and has a net worth like Bill Gates."

"Ha—he's a dead ringer for a warthog," Peter said. "And by obvious, you mean I need a sketchy operator to help my case? Or do you mean because Lori's so in demand and had to scrape under a rock for a quick side-kick? Or do you mean Vic's old connection to Carmen, the woman who doesn't give a flying shit about me? Whatever. Lori's lead on this, not that I know how the hell I'll pay. I want my freedom back. But I'm not done."

"Shut up, Peter." Nancy held up a finger in warning.

Jeff wandered in and nodded to O'Leary. "Hey, Nance."

"Your idiot brother."

"Yup." Jeff pulled over a chair. "Look, sorry to butt

in on your time with Mr. Jerkoff, but I just had a good thought on the food truck."

"Did it hurt?" Peter asked. "Steam is coming out your ears."

"Listen to me. Now that Rachel's officially celiac, on top of everything else, I want to do something positive for her. Plus I can swing a barter deal for a truck. And you obviously need more of a hobby than being a pain in everybody's ass. So, the timing could work."

Jeff and Peter had kicked the food truck idea around for the past year or so, but everything got derailed when Jeff's twenty-two-year-old daughter, Rachel, got busted for heroin possession six months earlier.

"Wait, are you saying that you wanna do gluten-free?"

"Yeah. I mean, we still do breakfast and lunch for downtown Hatfield during the week and farmers' markets on Saturdays. Just everything's gluten-free."

"That's not a money-maker. Any gluten-free baked stuff I've tasted absolutely sucked."

"Actually," Nancy interjected. "Gluten-free is hot, so Rachel's problem kind of gives you an opportunity. You bake your own." She paused and stared at Peter. "Jeff, has he always been this slow?"

"Would it kill you to come to the point?" Peter asked, suddenly irritable as his lack of sleep, throbbing hand and pent-up anger at his predicament kicked in.

"Einstein," Jeff said. "Rachel's almost done with cooking school—specializing in baking. Does any of this ring a bell?"

"Oh, yeah."

"We could hire a full-time baker and let Rach learn the ropes."

"Easy peasy. Are we actually gonna shit or get off the pot?" Peter raised his eyes towards the ceiling tiles and lightly pumped his hands in a modified praise-Jesus.

"Try some recipes, buy some potholders and a couple of baking sheets. If it tastes halfway decent and doesn't poison our friends, we fire on all cylinders."

"Time's up," O'Leary announced. He motioned for Jeff and Nancy to leave. "Jesus, Russo—potholders? It's all about silicone oven mitts, man."

"But you're going to need a dedicated baking facility if you actually go into production." Nancy struggled to rise from the chair. Waving off Jeff's help, she turned to O'Leary and pointed at Peter. "I'd shackle that one if I were you."

"Ditto." Jeff pointed his fingers at his eyes and then at Peter's. "I'm watching you."

"Look before you go, I gotta tell you something, and you're not gonna like it."

"What now?" Nancy looked at Jeff and rolled her eyes.

"Don't kill the messenger, but, I don't know—maybe it helps you understand. So, Saunders Construction did the Zenergy site." Peter waited anxiously to gauge their reaction.

"What? Saunders? If that motherfucker's back in town, so help me God," Jeff said angrily.

Nancy clutched at Peter's arm, raking it with her nails. "You're serious. No bullshit, you wouldn't." Her face broke into a grimace as she choked back a sob. "I have to get out of here."

CHAPTER 12

Jeff and Nancy walked out of the police station together, each reliving their years-long nightmares of Brock Saunders. Nancy had to rest against a wall. Wheezing audibly, she fumbled in her pocketbook. "I need my inhaler." Two puffs later, she still couldn't move. "Oh my God, Jeff—what are we gonna do?" She wiped the tears rolling down her face on the back of her trembling hands.

"Nothing." Jeff's voice sounded octaves deeper. "Don't panic. We rebuilt our lives—no surrender. That piece of shit doesn't get to win. I gotta find out more. Fucking Pete—now I get it." He clenched his fists and almost punched the brick wall before stopping himself.

"I feel like barfing. My blood pressure is through the roof—I'm seeing spots." Nancy panted as she spoke, her eyes closed.

"Damn it, Nance. You can't breathe, your heart's gonna explode, the diabetes, all the meds, the shots, you name it. Jeff propped her up as best he could. She outweighed him by at least forty pounds. "Don't pass out."

Kenny Johnson climbed the stairs near them after parking his Jeep in the lot.

"What's goin' on?" Approaching quickly, he held Nancy's wrist in his hand and took her pulse. "That's not good."

"I'm fine." Nancy shook him off. "Just a big shock."

Jeff nodded. "Thanks, Kenny. If she says she's OK . . ."

Kenny assessed Nancy carefully. "Go sit down on that bench. Do you have a baby aspirin, Ms. Yates? We can get the EMTs out here."

"No."

"Nance, pop an aspirin." Jeff dug into her purse and opened the small bottle. "Take it."

"Kenny, I'm OK now." Nancy chewed the aspirin and tried to smile.

Seeing how she rallied, Kenny started to walk inside. "Call 911 if you feel bad again. Don't wait."

Jeff relaxed as the color returned to Nancy's face. "Alright, I'm driving you home."

Nancy's baggage could break a bull elephant's spine. Cigarettes, sunbathing, stress, booze, and insomnia had aged her so quickly that she didn't even recognize herself at thirty. Divorced with two kids and a boring office job wasn't how she'd pictured her future. Yet she surprised everybody but herself by being a whiz with technology and crawled up the ladder as a tech specialist for an insurance conglomerate. Post-Brock, depression, anxiety and asthma held onto her ankles like dead weights. By forty, a hysterectomy, high cholesterol, dramatic weight gain, and early menopause. Her fifties now featured hypertension, Type-2 diabetes, sleep apnea, and epic hives.

Back in middle school, Nancy and Peter became tight as they sat week after week in detention, busted for having Bad Attitudes. Nancy smoked like a chimney in the bathrooms, chomped gum in class and showed too much skin. Peter never shut up, dropping one-liners like a stand-up comedian and disrupting every class. They hung out when they could, Nancy, an only child, becoming friendly with Jeff, too.

Nancy and Peter had slept together once after she got divorced, about six months before Brock violated her. Curiosity and alcohol fueled whatever sparks led them to the bedroom, and although Nancy thought that this could be the start of something, Peter doused the flame without realizing she wouldn't mind more.

"Wow, let's not do that again. I think that was the tequila talking. Sorry it sucked." Peter, divorced after a brief marriage in his twenties, shook her awake to talk after he got dressed while she was pretend-sleeping. She had been thinking about reaching over to get him hard again when he bolted out of bed.

"Oh, yeah. Wow, no, it's OK. We have like zero sexual

chemistry." Nancy played along. "No offense." She tucked the sheets up over her still-naked body and staged an elaborate yawn.

"None taken. Already checked off on our bucket lists, right? Hey, don't tell Jeff or Tomassi."

"Tell them what—we had lousy drunken sex? Please."

"Sometimes, it's just an itch, you know? We're OK, though, right?"

"Sure. I'm going back to sleep," Nancy said, turning away from Peter and doing a halfway decent job of acting casual. "Close the door on your way out. Catch you later."

CHAPTER 13

JEFF COULD NEVER SHAKE OFF THE SUCKER PUNCH of being utterly ripped off, the heart-stopping moment when he knew he had lost everything. Artie Russo, Jeff and Peter's father farmed the fruit and vegetable fields that his father farmed before him. And, unfortunately, he farmed it exactly the way his father did. Innovations were met with suspicion and derision, but fortunately for the balance sheet, so was debt. Artie ran the farm on a shoe-string budget; he didn't trust bankers as far as he could throw them. When Artie anointed Jeff as his successor at age twenty-three, Jeff couldn't believe the meager cash flow. Neither could the accountant he hired on the sly. In a bad year, plagued by drought or too much rain, the farm fell dangerously into the red. Peter avoided Artie like the plague and made it known that unless Jeff needed help with the crops, Peter wasn't visiting. Jeff shouldered the burden, staying awake nights trying to think of ways to make more money.

"The asshole doesn't get that to make money, you have to spend money." Peter bought another round of beers at their favorite watering hole, nodding as Jeff complained.

"I don't know what to do." Jeff didn't even notice the pretty young woman making eyes at him from across the room until Peter pointed her out.

"She likes your ugly mug. Poor thing needs glasses."

"Fuck off."

The Russo farm's acres of proximity to the Connecticut River brought developers out of the woodwork. Where once schooners, sloops and freight steamboats sailed the river, now jet skis and motorboats dominated the waterways. Fertile alluvial soil, almost rockless, graced the Russo homestead. But with Bridgeville now ranking as the hottest town West of the river for residential and commercial real estate, a day didn't go by without a card in the mail, a phone call, a knock on the door, or an inquiring email.

"Hell, no. We got river water and dirt in our veins," Jeff joked, turning down every offer to sell after consulting with Peter. Artie made his wishes known, too.

"You never sell this farm, you hear me. Never."

Traitors to the hold-out farming community practically had to flee town after inking their deals with developers eager to blow up their fields. No one except the greedy and corrupt got rich off of farming.

"I'm good," Peter said when Jeff agonized for the millionth time about Artie's Byzantine manipulation to divide, conquer and rule. Their mother, an alcoholic by then, did nothing to interfere with Artie's decision. Jeff and Peter hardly expected her to, either. They'd watched her live for as long as they could remember in the shadow of a tyrannical husband who only let her have charge of the kitchen and the washing machine. When she died, they mourned, mostly for what could have been, but she had long ago become a bit player in their lives.

"I've got a great gig at the factory. You keep the headache of dealing with the old man and running the farm. I'll be your right-hand man when you need me."

"Hello, dipshit—I need you. But when he kicks off, you're getting like 25 percent of the farm. The good and the bad." Jeff held out his pinky for Peter to grab with his own. They shook pinkies just like they did when they were boys.

"So make me a deal, boss. What do you need?"

"A deal? Like I pay you in cash money? And don't call me that."

"You can pay me in beer."

"I can't pay you, period. Everything is so run down, it's for shit. But, how 'bout you take a crop and handle it from planting to harvest?" Jeff scratched his head and thought for a minute. "I'll keep Dad away from you, but don't fuck it up. You got the corn."

"OK, but we need new equipment to do it right. The old man hasn't upgraded since the 1950's."

"Yeah, that John Deere is held together by spit and duct tape. Get your ass over to some auctions and get what you need." Jeff never let on to Artie that to get the equipment, he'd have to borrow from the bank. Set up with a generous line of credit, collateralized by the farm, Jeff made changes to improve everything. Slowly, the modernization paid off until Brock Saunders made his pitch, selling Jeff and Artie on the promise of can't miss riches.

"I'll kill him," Jeff vowed angrily to Peter after the Ponzi scheme unraveled. "I'm gonna cut off his balls and stuff them in his lying sonovabitch mouth."

"Yeah, you gotta get in line."

Brock Saunders bolted from his hometown in the dark of night after the implosion of Pioneer Premium Properties' shell game. When the first few irate investors, choking with rage or tears, called him at the office before it shut down, Brock stonewalled.

"I'm as surprised as you are. Call Customer Service. Someone will definitely get back to you." Brock's stock response didn't buy him much time. Customer Service didn't exist now that the shit hit the fan. And just about everybody knew the location of his palatial bachelor pad. He split before Jeff and hundreds of others got to confront him.

Brock laid low. Although advised by legal counsel to stay in the area, it came out in court documents that Brock took up exile in an oceanside condo overlooking the Atlantic in posh Westerly, RI, some two hours away from Bridgeville. Rented under a fake name, he sat on the terrace, drank heavily, avoided his father and gorged on fried clams. Never appearing anywhere without sunglasses and a baseball cap, he finally agreed to meet his lawyer at a rest stop on I-95. Brock had no idea that the prized attorney was wearing a wire.

"Brock, I hear that you're going to be charged with fraud and securities law violations, just like everyone else at PPP. We can probably bargain if you roll over on your bosses. I'm more concerned with the IRS. Did you declare all your income?"

Brock hemmed and hawed. "By all, do you mean everything?" He guzzled his vodka gimlet and signaled for another one.

The lawyer had gotten rich off the billable hours he spent defending Brock's father, always for Saunders Construction's failure to provide or pay for contracted goods and services. But the lawyer's hands got dirty. Busted by the feds, he offered them Brock.

"All, everything—what the hell's the difference?" The lawyer dismissed the inconvenience of semantics.

"What I tell you is private, right?" Brock paused, waiting for a yes. "So, not exactly all. You know, I had some shitty accountants who didn't give me good advice. It's their goddam fault."

"How many?"

"How many accountants or millions?"

CHAPTER 14

NANCY, STILL LABORING TO BREATHE, STRUGGLED to keep from free-falling back to the fateful night that changed her life forever. Fire and Ice, a popular bar in West Hadley, pulsated per usual with loud music and musk that fateful night when Nancy, then thirty-three, decided to go to Brock's place.

"We'll have some fun," he said, and kissed her willing lips again at the end of the long u-shaped bar. It functioned essentially as his lair when he graced the place, and Nancy was happy to be the chosen one for a change.

After her divorce at age thirty-one, Nancy became a Saturday night regular. She dressed her curvy figure to attract attention like every other woman out on the town. Cleavage, big hair, tight miniskirt, black opaque tights. She met up with some girlfriends usually, and they eyed the attractive men who eyed them back. People bought each other drinks, and everyone wanted to get lucky with someone.

Brock Saunders dropped by every now and then. He was making money hand over fist for Pioneer Premium

Properties. Their parties were the stuff of legend on huge chartered yachts and in tricked-out mansions. Food, booze, entertainment; costs upwards of six-figures were nothing. But Brock liked to scout for easy prey outside of work.

"You don't eat where you shit," his boss told him after some complaints about Brock's aggressive trawling of secretaries. "Work the older rich broads whose money we want, otherwise get your pussy elsewhere."

At Fire and Ice, Brock favored the grand entrance. Good-looking, with hard brown eyes and brown hair, he accentuated his muscular physique by dressing like a character straight out of Miami Vice. He even had the shades.

"Drinks for all the ladies." Brock expensed everything, so it was really no skin off his back.

Nancy held her booze well, but she never brought men home; her kids were there. In her pocketbook, she always kept condoms hidden inside a small zippered compartment.

"I don't want my kids finding them," she said, showing her friends where she kept them in case they needed one quick.

Brock's showy visits pissed off more than a few average guys. He just sucked the air out of the room.

"Fucking asshole with house money."

"Watch out, ladies—here it comes again. Bend over."

"I'm gettin' mine, no matter what. Fuck Brock."

Nancy flirted with Brock like she flirted with every guy. Everyone knew Brock prowled with a purpose. He went through women like water, and Nancy didn't see herself with him. But after Nancy and Peter's fizzled one-night stand, and a few lousy lays from the bar, Nancy eyed Brock differently. He became a Maybe.

RIVER RULES

"What do you think about me going after Brock?" she asked one of her friends.

"He's pretty hot. I'd do him."

"Yeah, he's gotta be better than some of the losers around here." Nancy pointed her index finger and made it droop, prompting giggles from everyone at her table. "What do you hear about him in bed?"

Her friend signaled the bartended for another drink. "Check out his hands. He's gotta be hung with a beer bottle."

They laughed, and Nancy looked for him, but she only saw his back, broad shoulders, moussed hair, and hands splayed across the ass of the brunette leaning into him.

"Hey, get a room," someone yelled. Brock grinned, extracting his tongue from the brunette's mouth long enough to flash his teeth. They left together around eleven, Brock's very obvious hard-on tenting his pants. Nancy left alone soon after; none of the available guys still standing at that hour appealed to her, and the sitter needed to get home.

The following month, Nancy sat alone at the bar on a Friday night, a rare occasion for her. Both kids were sleeping over friends' houses, so she indulged her need for a martini and repartee. She even played darts with an old geezer who regaled her with tales about building the Alaska pipeline. Laughing and focused on the game, she was startled when the bartender walked over and set another martini down on the counter.

"From Brock," he said.

Nancy looked to where the bartender had nodded. Brock raised his glass to her and smiled. Nancy strolled over to him, making sure to emphasize her sashaying hips and two inches of exposed cleavage.

"Thanks, Brock."

"My pleasure, Nancy. It is Nancy, right?" He took her hand in his and tickled her palm with his index finger.

"You know my name. Don't forget I was only two years behind you at school, Brock." Nancy sipped at her martini, bringing it to her lips with her free hand.

"Did we ever go out?"

"No, and that's your loss." Nancy took her hand back and reached for a cigarette from her purse. She waited until Brock lit it for her.

"I can see what I missed," he said, getting even closer. "That needs to be fixed. You with someone?"

"Not at the moment. How about you?" Nancy felt his hot breath close to her ear. The smell of his cologne and his obvious interest made her body tingle with excitement.

"Tonight, I'm with you," he said, kissing her on the neck before lightly licking her ear.

"Oh, really? What—" Her words evaporated into his mouth as he kissed her lips. She kissed him back, their tongues getting to know each other.

"Come back to my place," Brock whispered, "You can follow me in your car."

Nancy knew all eyes were on them as he draped his arm over her shoulder and steered her out the door. She hesitated in the parking lot, almost too drunk to navigate.

"Just follow me." Brock drove his Porsche slowly as he lead the way.

Feeling her up as they pawed each other in the elevator up to his river-view penthouse, he placed her hand on his cock. "For you."

He made them both drinks, put on some light rock and patted the couch next to him. After getting her shirt and bra off, he licked and sucked her nipples until she moaned loudly.

"You got me so hard I can't move. Help me, you bad girl," he said, unzipping his pants and pushing her head down so she could take him in her mouth. Nancy obliged him but gagged as he came, his hands holding her head immobile.

"Nice, very nice. Finish your drink." Once she had drained her glass, he offered her the rest of his untouched glass.

Nancy felt the room start spinning. So dizzy, suddenly, she couldn't even stand when Brock tried to pull her up. She sagged against him as he dragged her to his king-size bed.

"I don't feel good," she said, as he took off her skirt and tights, her limbs like foreign objects. "Another time, OK?"

"You let me handle things. You need some Vitamin B, get it? B for Brock."

"I'm gonna go. Just go home." Nancy could hear herself mumbling, her voice going weak as she tasted fear.

"The party's just starting," she heard him say before she lost consciousness

When she woke up, she couldn't figure out anything. No memory of where she was and why she had such a headache. Within seconds, she felt throbbing pain in her pelvis. Brock snored loudly, his foul breath making her retch and realize where she was. She staggered to the bathroom and sat on the toilet, feeling for all the world like she'd just birthed twins out of both ends. Nancy reached for some toilet paper and saw a bunch of used condoms in the garbage can by the sink. She had to wet the paper, it hurt so much when she wiped. Wincing with pain, the blood proof that it wasn't all in her head, she gasped at her perineum bulging purple and puffy, everything swollen, her anatomy almost unrecognizable.

"Bastard, you fucking bastard," she cried. Clutching the wall as she made her way towards Brock, she screamed. "You drugged me, didn't you? And then you raped me." Big, heaving sobs made her almost incoherent.

"News to me," Brock said from the bed. "You begged for it, Nancy. You just don't remember." Brock propped himself up on one elbow and laughed. "You should see yourself."

"How could you? Fuck you—you hurt me."

"Bullshit. You couldn't get enough, always asking for more." He sank back onto the pillows and rolled over. "You should thank me. Instead you're an ungrateful bitch."

Nancy wept now with rage, crawling for her clothes. "I'm gonna make you pay."

"Yeah, right. Get your shit and get out."

CHAPTER 15

OFFICER KENNY JOHNSON COMPLETED HIS MONTHLY required target practice perfectly at the gun range after running into Jeff and Nancy. His hand-eye coordination never failed him. Getting hired right out of the Police Academy by the Bridgeville PD had been Kenny's goal after the rude awakening that baseball didn't love him as much as he loved it. At least not at the Division-1 college level.

"Too many really good outfielders on the team," he explained to his disappointed parents. "And in college, I'm just decent—nothing special."

They didn't seem to grasp that no matter how much Kenny tried, he would never be more than second or third-string, riding the bench for game after game.

"I'm gonna play club ball. It's fun, less pressure and I can actually have a life."

Kenny had a little too much fun freshman year, getting hammered at frat parties and fooling around with lots of pretty young women who found his friendly nature, cute face and jacked body quite appealing. But after getting slapped with academic probation, a humiliating comeuppance for a kid who never got below a B in high school, he hit the books.

Kenny double-majored in Criminal Justice and Sociology, playing club ball the whole time. Now at the Bridgeville PD, he was at the bottom of the totem pole, but he loved being a cop. Tomassi took him under his wing, doling out advice and kicks in the pants when he thought Kenny messed up or could do better.

After Peter asked him to look for the photo of the baseball team, Kenny, who shared an old house with some high school buddies, searched his parent's attic and basement on Saturday. His parents put their modest home on the market, stunned to hear it could fetch three times what they paid for it. Crammed full of moving boxes in every room, Kenny had to walk upstairs to find a giant box filled with all his baseball awards. He rummaged under all the trophies until he found the 5 x 8 picture inside a dog-eared folder.

Kenny stared at the picture, going over faces he hadn't thought about in years. He finally located Marco in the front row, a small kid beaming excitedly with a mouthful of big crooked teeth.

"Damn, Marco. What happened?"

Kenny looked at Peter, husky and strong in his team T-shirt, and at himself, gangly and grinning in the back row with all the tallest boys. With no one home, Kenny drank straight from an open carton of milk from the refrigerator, left a quick note on the table and let himself out the back door. He carefully placed the picture on the passenger seat of his Jeep.

Peter wanted to talk to Marco about the same thing Kenny pondered. He waited until Marco was done conferring with his Legal Aid lawyer. Once he got back, it was recreation time. Peter called him over to stand in the shade of a big oak tree. Paco was sunning himself in the corner of the yard.

"Marco, what're you now, twenty-three?"

"Yeah. Twenty-three and goin' nowhere."

"So, what's up with that?" Peter waited for Marco to respond, but he just kicked the dirt.

"Coach, no offense. I don't wanna talk about it."

"I'm not judging."

"Yo, coach. No disrespect, but for real, why'd you do what you did? Just coz you thought it was ugly? Shit, you got a lot more buildings to do. Come to Hatfield, man."

Peter laughed but stopped when he saw Marco's serious expression. "Well, there's more than meets than eye here, Marco. Really bad blood, for starters."

"Jail bad?" Marco looked at him expectantly. "A guy like you with everything ain't gonna throw it away for nothin'."

"Believe me, I don't have everything."

Marco squared up to face Peter. "Ima call bullshit, no offense. You got family, friends, a nice place to live, right? Probs women, too. What you think most people got?"

Peter sighed and reached out his hand for Marco to slap. "Damn. When you put it like that, I have to tell you. Alright. The fucker who is building that fuel cell is the same piece of shit who ripped off my brother for so much money that we almost lost the farm, and he date-raped one of my best friends. She's never been the same since."

Marco's eyes popped out as he whistled loudly. "And

you just plant flowers? Mess up the motherfucker, Coach. He hurt your people."

"An eye for an eye sounds so good, believe me. But I can't go there. I got a warning to stay away from him long ago or he'd press charges."

"I know a guy who knows a guy. Just say the word."

"No. Now I'm gonna change the subject. When you get out, you're gonna need a job. Call me."

"You got a business? Nobody hires dudes like me."

"Starting a food truck with my brother. You know, the guy who yelled at me non-stop on Saturday."

"Yeah. First I thought you was yelling at yourself coz you got almost the same voice. He's mad pissed. You sure the deal's still on?"

"Yup. Might take a while, but it's on. You know how to drive?"

"Course I do. Even got a license."

"Good man," Peter clapped Marco on the shoulder. "Hey, I think I see Kenny. Maybe he got that picture."

Before Peter could walk across the yard to get Kenny's attention, Officer Billy O'Leary strolled over.

"Tomassi needs to see you. Come with me."

Peter obliged, following O'Leary towards Tomassi's small office.

"Here comes trouble. Hey, jailbird—get over here," Tomassi called out. O'Leary delivered Peter and happily selected one of the chili dogs that sat in a Tupperware container on Tomassi's desk. Tomassi, resplendent in knee-length plaid shorts and a bright yellow shirt that strained against his impressive belly, opened a big bag of potato chips and started munching.

Peter, unsure of how pissed Tomassi still was, waited to be invited. "Beautiful. Donna added hot sauce to the chili, right?"

"Like a gallon. Take one." Tomassi commanded, his mouth full of chips.

Peter took a big bite and smiled, sweat beading on his forehead. "Hot, really hot." His face turned bright red. "You got any water?"

O'Leary reached down into the insulated freezer bag under Tomassi's desk and extracted two bottles. "You want one, Sarge?"

"Yeah, one for you and one for me, right, Billy?"

"Aw, come on, John. Have mercy." Peter took the unopened bottle out of Tomassi's hand and drank it in two gulps. "Thanks. Tell Donna she's the best."

"I tell her that every day." Tomassi smiled broadly and waggled his unibrow.

Kenny knocked on the door frame. "Whoa, is there one for me?"

Tomassi handed him the last one. "Enjoy. What you got?" He nodded at the picture Kenny put down on the desk.

Peter grabbed it and whistled. "Damn, look at that stud of a coach. What a good-looking guy."

"In your dreams," Tomassi said. "So, let's see. Kenny, there's you in the back row looking like a dweeb."

"Sarge, the kid in the front is Marco Torres, the guy from Hatfield on a second bust for weed. We were all on that team together for two seasons."

"Wow, that's crazy," O'Leary said.

"He was a great kid," Peter said. "A pleasure to coach."

"He ran like a deer, so fast. When we had to run around the field, he lapped just about everybody. We had to tell him to slow down; he was making us look bad," Kenny said with a laugh.

"He's young," Tomassi said. "Maybe he can turn it around."

CHAPTER 16

AT HIS LAST GIG ON LOCAL RADIO BEFORE GETTING arrested, Peter entertained listeners for over two hours as a guest on Bridgeville Byway. After playing back-to-back sets of Creedence Clearwater Revival and Allman Brothers tunes, he launched into some stories about Brutus. His favorite one was always about Brutus terrified to get his nails cut at PetSmart.

He'd just told some bird-watchers looking for eagles near the ferry that very story when they asked if Brutus was dangerous.

"This damn dog is a marshmallow, and that's how he gets more bosom action than me. We just pull into the parking lot at PetSmart to get his nails clipped, and he starts crying. We get in the store, and he's bawling and shaking like a leaf. In no time, he's got the buxomest one cradling his head, two extremely well-endowed gals hugging his front legs and another hot babe on his back paws. They're cooing to him and whispering sweet nothings. I swear he looked at me and winked."

Down by the river, Peter enjoyed his reign like a chatty emperor. Walking Brutus, he shot the breeze with just about anyone. He had a special place in his heart for the hopeful eagle watchers who came armed with binoculars and cameras, and who usually left disappointed.

"It's easier to find the eagles in winter because they nest in the trees along the riverbank," Peter consoled. "And if the river doesn't freeze in a hard winter, you'll see some of them just soaring above the water, scouting for food."

Brutus used these chats as opportunities to relieve himself and to reinforce his alpha dog status. He could stare down a Cockapoo or Goldendoodle in less than five seconds, so lots of dog-walkers waved at Peter but gave Brutus a wide berth.

"You might see a few Great Blue Herons today—they love it here in spring and summer," Peter would say to people imploring him for help in spotting eagles. "The biggest one around here is Big Daddy, you can't miss him. He cruises the river looking for prey—fish, frogs, reptiles. They all go crazy when the shad migrate upriver. But you'll definitely spot a few Belted Kingfishers, and you can't miss hearing the racket they make."

"Is that a woodpecker?" Someone inevitably asked, pointing to a big bird with a bright red crest and black and white markings tapping away at a tree.

"Yeah, of course. That's a pileated beauty, an absolute workhorse. He makes holes other species like to live in, like owls, bats and pine martens. Right now, he's chowing down on insects who live in dead trees. Check out his size. Just huge."

"Are you like the mayor of the river and the wildlife down here?" A well-meaning idiot always asked Peter some variation of this question.

"Man, the river takes care of *me* and the wildlife. This river goes 400 miles through four states. And no one rules the river. The native Americans and early settlers fought over the river. And I don't need to tell you how that turned out. Then, the river turned into a water highway. It carried more traffic than the railroads. But industry used it as a dump. Pollution of all kind— pick your poison. They damn near killed it and all the wildlife that depends on a healthy river like the bald eagles you're trying to find."

Peter could talk about the river for hours. But when people asked about his scholarly credentials, he laughed.

"I'm a graduate of the school of life. College wasn't my thing. I'd rather poke out my eyes than sit in a big lecture hall. I worked third shift at Pratt long enough to support my vices: rescuing dogs, hanging out with my buddies and giving Mother Nature the good lovin' she deserves."

After Jeff gave him the corn, Peter took his responsibilities very seriously. He brought in great harvests, thanks to all the upgrades and his own sweat. Once he caught some corn thieves trying to stuff burlap bags full of his prize Silver Queen variety, the one that fetched the highest price. He charged at them, and sicced Brutus's much-loved predecessor, Angus, a rescue Rottweiler mix, on the culprits. They ran for their lives and dropped the sacks in their hurry to get away. Peter never got tired of telling the story.

Artie lost his way after his wife died, and he complied with Jeff's dictate to give Peter a wide berth. But the gut-wrenching loss of the $50,000 that he urged Jeff to invest in Pioneer's real estate scam after hearing his buddies talk it up, sent Artie to an early grave. It also brought the farm close to bankruptcy when the loan payments were due and couldn't be paid. After a lot of tense back-and-forth, including coming very close to filing for Chapter 12 bankruptcy, the bank a long-time agricultural lender and, itself, a victim of the swindle, agreed to renegotiate the terms.

When the Great Recession hastened the decimation of what was left of the manufacturing industry in New England, Peter got downsized.

"I can't believe it," he told Jeff. "Like twenty-five years is gone in a puff of smoke."

The middling severance package couldn't support the mortgage on his riverside condo when he ran the numbers. Always a realist, Peter sold his pride and joy and moved to a small outbuilding catty-corner to the farm's main house, now a happy home with Jeff and Annie, his wife, and his kids, Rachel and Sean.

Peter really put his back into renovating the old dwelling. After a lot of help from his fishing buddies, Jeff and John Tomassi, to put in a decent bathroom, kitchen and rear deck, he had a great place to enjoy the sunsets over a cold beer. Less than a tenth of a mile from the river, he could fish, hike and bullshit with Jeff whenever he wanted.

As soon as Jeff's son, Sean, finished the ag-sci program at the state university, Peter crowned him the Corn King. Sean planted Butter and Sugar, Early Sunglow and Snowcrest, and revamped the irrigation system.

After Peter's doctor read him the riot act about his weight and his drinking, Peter upped his rambles and started working out at BIG, using the personal training sessions he'd won in a fundraiser auction. Ian and Andre quickly took to him while they made him laugh with their messianic zeal to reduce his body fat.

"You lunatics measure and weigh me like a 4-H cow. Don't you have something better to do?" Peter definitely had a gut but his broad shoulders and sturdy limbs hid a lot of sins. He drove Ian and Andre crazy because his hiking boots were always encrusted with dirt which he tracked into their gym.

"You are my punishment for having been very bad in a previous life," Ian sighed. "Why can't you at least hose off or buy a pair of cheap sneakers?"

"Nope, I refuse to support the swoosh. I'm old-school; it's either this or my old smelly feet, guys."

"Dude, you are like Pigpen from Charlie Brown," Andre scolded, nipping at Peter's heels with a Dirt Devil hand-vacuum. "And either you've been hitting MacDonald's again or you have 6 pounds of dirt in your damn boots."

"For Pete's sake, Peter." Ian chuckled and patted Peter on the belly. "Would a carrot kill you? Even if it is dirt, you haven't lost an ounce and your body fat is higher than ever. And has anyone ever told you that you've got a face for radio?"

"I love being on the radio. You ever listen to me?"

In fact, whenever Peter was announced as a guest, people tuned in for his rich baritone, Brutus stories, and musical stylings. He milked it for all it was worth and felt a responsibility to conjure up the heyday of beloved FM deejays when they spun great rock music and held a generation together.

But the last time he appeared, just before his arrest, the free-spirited radio station had changed. Peter started to launch into the Brutus at PetSmart story, but the producer wouldn't let him.

"Peter," the host leaned over and covered the microphone. "You can't say 'bosom' on the air. Last time you told this story, we got some angry emails and calls."

"So, what am I supposed to say? Tits?"

"No, don't say that either. Also, don't say buxom, well-endowed, chick, or hot babe. Maybe go with something new . . ."

"Man, this political correctness crap makes it impossible to tell a good story."

"Peter," the host sighed and held up his hands imploringly. "Tell a different story or wrap it up."

So, Peter, after a quick whispered lecture on the difficulties of finding tit synonyms, announced his lucky eagle feather catch, which he altered on the fly to feature Brutus more prominently.

"Two weeks ago, and this is true, by the way, I caught a huge eagle feather drifting down from the sky. I knew it was a blessing from Mother Nature, so I raised my baseball cap in salute to that magnificent bird. I thanked her for bringing me good luck. I turn around to show Brutus and he's gone. Suddenly, from the middle of the river, comes a loud voice through a megaphone. 'We've got Brutus.' I look around to see if he was dognapped, but it's the high school crew team. Son-of-a-gun Brutus was pursuing some beaver and swam like halfway across the river before he gave out. They haul him out of the water, all panting and exhausted. They save his damn life. So, the spirits have smiled upon me and Brutus. And they can smile upon you. Find us down by the river, and I'll gladly show you my epic plume."

The host moaned audibly as Peter winked at him. Before the producer could cut Peter's mic, he said, "Step right up, ladies and gents. I'll be taking names and kicking butt, so no cutting in line."

CHAPTER 17

In the weeks leading up to Peter's arrest, Zenergy topped the most wanted list, dead or alive, and it would have surprised almost no one to learn Zenergy and Satan were joined at the hip. Plus, it turned out Zenergy benefitted from major financial incentives and tax credits courtesy of the shadowy New England Consortium Council, a quasi-governmental regional authority.

But no one in town government even peeped about Saunders Construction's contract from Zenergy. Saunders Construction went belly-up in the Great Recession, mourned by few. Brock pleaded guilty to tax evasion after being charged by a federal grand jury working with the IRS and FBI.

"Brock didn't get prison, I can't fucking believe it." Jeff fumed as he watched the proceedings unfold.

"Greased palms, baby." Peter threw the newspaper on the floor. "He gets probation and community service? What a joke."

"I'm gonna find him and beat the shit out of him, like in the old days."

"Don't. It'll just blow back on you. He's protected, the bastard. We got such a corrupt state."

Brock never set foot in Bridgeville again as far as anyone could tell. But Saunders Construction did. Its faltering steps to reinvent itself after the Great Recession crashed and burned at least twice.

When Jeff brought Peter a change of clothes and some pictures of Brutus, which Peter proudly showed off to Marco and Paco, he floated his latest theory about Saunders and Zenergy's unholy alliance.

"I been thinking. Saunders pulled strings to get Zenergy that land. I know it."

Peter took off his T-shirt and gasped after he smelled it. "Hey, this is rag material. It stinks—what am I, a goddam skunk?"

"Yup—switched at birth. I got a skunk brother. Let's get back to the land question."

"Gotta be something under the table. There's no way they got that land on the up and up."

Zenergy, a darling of Wall Street, nonetheless had a glaring weakness. Its vulnerability, its kryptonite, was land, particularly in the densely populated and highly profitable East Coast corridor between Washington and Boston.

Zenergy had no problem wooing federal, state and local officials or entering intricate deals with pipeline, utility and natural gas conglomerates. They hired a platoon of lobbyists to schmooze, cajole and threaten. But the problem remained getting hold of land.

Bridgeville endured a terrible winter that year. Blizzard followed blizzard, the polar vortex moved in and wouldn't leave. When Bridgevillians finally staggered out of their homes at the end of April, they rubbed their eyes like blinking moles. Spring's tentative arrival seemed miraculous until Zenergy's brutalist fuel cell on Maple Street blindsided them. Rising high above the tarps in which it had been cocooned during the winter, the massive structure caused traffic jams, accusations and fury.

The Bridgeville Gazette thundered its disapproval in a front-page editorial in the May 4 edition. "Neighborhood desecrated by fuel cell facility."

The next day, at the first hastily called meeting of concerned citizens in the town library's auxiliary wing, shouting and yelling about firing the Town Council escalated out of control.

"Not in Bridgewater Backyards! NIBBY!"

"It's NIMBY, you morons," Nancy corrected loudly. "What about 'Leave Our Land Alone?' LOLA."

"The cat's out of the bag, people. Too little too late," Peter said. "Let's get names and then vote out their asses."

"What do we want?" The call and response echoed. "No fuel cell!"

The following week, Bridgeville's mayor attended a town forum that kicked off with a beloved elderly gadfly proclaiming loudly from the stage at the Senior Center's main meeting room.

"Zenergy stole Bridgeville's heritage right out from under us. We need to kick the bastards out."

The overflow audience didn't need much prompting to rev up to full fury. Copies of the *Bridgeville Gazette*'s editorial hung from the back of each folding chair, some of which were still covered with crumbs from the featured lunch of breaded cod.

In a community where everything seemed to be debated forever in committees on public-access TV, the secrecy surrounding the fuel cell stoked every kind of conspiracy theory from the Illuminati to imminent thermonuclear warfare. But Peter, who knew more about the fuel cell than he let on, voiced the big question once the old man finally yielded the floor, grinning happily as two strapping firemen helped him off the stage.

"Who sold out Bridgeville? We deserve answers." Peter motioned for the yelling and clapping to get louder.

"People, please. Allow me to speak," said the mayor, a nondescript middle-aged man with a receding hairline and a severe underbite. "The New England Council Consortium and Zenergy submitted a document to the town zoning committee through a subsidiary about two years ago. All they applied for was a ruling on whether the land had any wetlands issues that would make it an unbuildable property. The gas company owned the land."

The audience buzzed as people tried to puzzle out the request. Nancy stood up and demanded to be recognized by the mayor.

"Nancy," he sighed.

"Clearly, Zenergy and the Consortium had ulterior motives. So, three years ago, let's say, the gas company owns this land and is never going to build on it. How and when did the Consortium and Zenergy buy it?"

"It might be too complicated to explain." The mayor hedged, looking at his watch.

"Try me." Nancy crossed her arms and remained standing.

"Well, please sit down. There may have been an intermediary. And the ruling just slipped through without any red flags being raised because there was no wetlands impingement. Just a yes or no vote." The mayor looked quite chagrined. "That was it. We had no idea this ruling was the tip of the iceberg."

"Well, we're on the Titanic," Peter said loudly. "And we're going down."

Someone yelled out from the back of the room. "Corruption or stupidity?"

"How dare you?" the mayor responded indignantly. "Quite frankly, I resent your remarks. We work hard for the greater good of Bridgeville."

"I am beyond done with incompetent men explaining and running the world," Nancy, still standing, shouted. "This is a slap in the face to everyone who loves Bridgeville."

CHAPTER 18

AT 5:55, ANDRE EXCUSED HIMSELF FOR A MOMENT from monitoring a client on the lat pulldown machine. He motioned for Ian, who had just strolled in.

"Lori's stopping by for a quickie. Can you take her?"

"What? You know I'm celibate."

"Ha ha. Just help her work out the kinks. She carries

her stress in her shoulders and neck. Make sure to give them a quick going over." After Ian gave him a long look, Andre added, "I'm just saying . . ."

"Andre, focus on your client—her form is deteriorating."

Lori dashed through the doorway at precisely 6:05, a vision in neon orange spandex. Once again, a topknot swept up her hair.

"Lori, you smell like vodka. Am I right?" Ian stared at her reproachfully.

"Just one vodka gimlet. What're you a bloodhound?"

"Brings back memories. Right—playtime's over. I am now in charge of this fitness intervention. Please walk across the room as fast as you can."

"Andre—I thought you were going to help me got the knots out. I don't want to exercise. And especially not with this character." Lori complied with Ian's instructions while beseeching Andre.

"I see the problem," Ian announced.

"What problem? Andre, tell him. I don't have any problems walking."

Andre choked back laughter and shrugged.

"Yes, you do. Now tell me, how tight are your hamstrings?"

"Ian, I don't want—wait, actually they're pretty tight."

"Your hamstrings are thrusting your pelvis forward like a cheap tart. Between your waist and your knees, your body is terribly unorganized."

"What! Andre—are you paying him to mess with me?" Lori grinned but her hands were firmly planted on her hips in a very defiant stance.

"Hey, I told you I had a client." Andre adjusted the woman's arm so that she didn't swing the dumbbell and hit herself in the face.

"But, I didn't think he'd be so critical."

"Uh-hem," Ian said loudly. "He, as in me, is very much in this room. Now Lori, we are going to take a walk outside to the park across the street. Look, the light is still lovely. Let's go." He shooed her out the door and onto the park's green lawn before she could muster a sustained protest.

"Seriously, you think walking with you is going to help my stress?"

"Just listen and watch me for a second. You need to tighten your butt cheeks, really feel purposeful clenching."

Lori roared. "Oh, my God. Is this as opposed to casual clenching? You're too much."

"Maybe so, but I want you to walk alongside me, feeling the angle of your pelvis shift as you tighten up your arse. Now, keep squeezing your cheeks and walk ahead of me," he instructed. "Faster. Zoom, Lori—zoom."

Surging ahead, Lori was up the small incline in no time. "Wow, pretty fast."

"Yes, well if you don't squeeze your cheeks when you move, no one will ever want to squeeze them, either. Ouch." He rubbed his arm where Lori smacked him.

"You got what was coming."

"Fine. Now let's zoom over to that hill." Ian pointed to his left. "Stride with stiff arms as you go. Left arm moves forward with right leg and so on." Admiring his pupil's form as she conquered the hill, he encouraged her by shouting, "Take it with your butt, Lori. Feel it in your ass—in the ass!"

Lori flipped him off while charging up the hill. When he rocketed up the hill to join her, she unleashed. "Do you even hear yourself? I have a certain professional respectability I'd like to maintain, if you don't mind."

"Yes, but your glute power is a thing of beauty. You were magnificent down there."

"Shut up, you idiot. My point is not registering with your brain. And you need to go see Carmen tomorrow morning."

"I don't understand why she wants to meet me if you and Vic have already given me marching orders."

They walked back so fast Lori barely got to explain why. "That's just how she is."

"Just so long as she pays the bills. I'm not doing it pro bono. I already discussed this with Vic. Much as Peter is a good mate, I don't do free."

"Understood. Hey, when we get inside, can you actually help me loosen up my neck and shoulders?"

As they re-entered the gym, Andre looked at them to see if blood had been drawn. Surprised to find Lori and Ian bantering good-naturedly, Andre offered Lori a cup of water.

"Not now, Andre," Ian said. "She's going to work on some rotation to loosen up her neck and shoulders."

Lori reached for the cup and took a big gulp. "Geez, who knew Ian was such a dictator?"

"You don't know the half of what I put up with, Lor. He's impossible."

"Well, unkinking your neck and shoulders is going to be mission impossible, Lori, if you don't get down on this mat right away and get into the child's play pose."

"Hey, sounds pretty good." Andre, free for five minutes between clients, squatted next to Lori.

Ian surrendered to the moment and knelt next to Andre. Side-by-side on the mat, like three ducks in a row, they elongated their spines in ever deeper stretches. As they breathed in unison, Ian felt a shift in the air, as if the earth had just started spinning a little more interestingly.

• • •

CHAPTER 19

WHEN IAN AND CARMEN FINALLY MET FACE-TO-FACE Saturday morning at the orchard, Carmen didn't seem very friendly. Ian, still surprised at the extent of her micro-management to exonerate Peter, considering she had cut him off like a gangrenous limb, played the Brit card while trying to break the ice. In his experience, the sooner women heard his accent and then gazed into his baby blues, the sooner he got what he wanted.

"This is a lovely orchard, Carmen. Breathtaking—I would love to meditate here." Ian peered at her, taking in her poker face. "What is your favorite view from here? Your favorite apple?" Finally, he noticed Carmen staring at his feet. Sporting his favorite minimalist sneakers, the toe-separating Vibram Five-Fingers, he offered her the opportunity to try them on.

Cracking a smile, Carmen demurred. "You have to be kidding. First of all, eew. Second of all, those are the ugliest things I've ever seen."

"Are you sure? You shouldn't judge a book by its cover. These will literally change your life."

"My life is going fine without them, thank you very much. Now let's talk turkey. What are you going to do to get Pete off the hook?"

"Well, it's your loss; I'll have to convince you another time." Ian dictated a text to himself. "Get Carmen to try toe shoes." He ignored her derisive snort. "Shall we walk?"

"No. Lori warned me about walking with you. I don't like being told to take it in the ass."

Ian gestured as if he were shooing away a buzzing fly. "Merely trying to help Lori get her pelvis under control."

Carmen cackled. "You. Are. Insane."

"Hardly. Now this is what I'm going to do." Outlining his plan to her, she nodded approvingly.

After Carmen and Ian shook on it, she texted Lori her approval. Seeing Ian still standing in front of her, she said, "What are you waiting for? Go straighten out this mess. Like by Monday."

Returning to the gym, Ian knew he needed some help to get it all accomplished in the compressed timeframe Carmen laid out.

"Andre—"

"Hell, yeah. I'm in."

"How did you know what I was going to say?"

"I know what you're thinking before you do. I'm in your head," Andre teased.

"That's a scary place. Better you than me."

They started by compiling a quick dossier on the security guard. Ian insisted on documenting everything carefully.

"It's important to be methodical so you don't wind up reinventing the wheel each time you construct the scenario."

"Come on, we need to haul ass. This security guard might could be a dead-end."

"Right. Work your contacts in the community, Andre. The security guard is key; we just need to find how the dots connect to him. The cops have more than enough circumstantial evidence to implicate Peter. We need to find the hidden links they won't bother investigating, and that's typical by the way. They'll just want to close the case and move on."

Three hours later, Andre called with exciting news. "Guess what I found out from my cousin's neighbor's ex-boyfriend? This skanky guard's a real player, and lately he's been banging a married babe whose got a psycho for a husband. Let's see the police get hold of that juicy fact as quick as me. Skanko's making time with another man's woman could be a big lead, dude."

"I'm not going to say I told you so."

"You just did."

"Imagine that. So, what's her name, and who's she still married to?"

"Kimmy La-something. And he's Skippy La-something."

"Skippy Lafford? This is unbelievable—I once investigated him for something entirely different, but he's a known piece of shite. Arrests on possession, drunk driving, theft, and brawling."

"Wow—talk about coincidence. I got goosebumps, man."

"There's no such thing as coincidence, Andre. How many times do we have to go over this."

"I can't hear you."

"Look, stay on the guard and Kimmy. I'll do Skippy and known associates."

"Got it."

They worked non-stop over the long weekend, fueled by caffeine and adrenaline. Andre didn't have the kids, so he was glad to have something to keep him busy.

"Brain power needs fuel. It's a scientific fact," Andre said. "Come over for dinner."

Ian waved a baggy full of celery and carrots in the air. "I'm all set."

"Give me that." Andre grabbed the bag from him. "This is fine if you're a guinea pig. What, you think black people don't know how to make salad?"

"Really, Andre. How am I supposed to respond?"

"You're supposed to graciously accept my extremely generous invitation." Andre did his best imitation of WASP-y nasal intonation.

When Ian arrived at Andre's house, bearing a basil plant for his host, Andre had just finished garnishing a platter of sliced beefsteak tomatoes overlaid with thin cucumber slices.

"Mmm, parsley," Ian said, reaching for a stalk. "I'll do the vinaigrette. Do you like garlic?"

"Bring it."

Andre set the table, putting a glass full of water by Ian's plate and a big glass of red wine by his own. "For the antioxidants."

"Right."

Ian demolished his half of the tomato salad after bowing his head over the food, sopping up the dressing with a whole wheat roll. Once Andre finished his broiled chicken and salad, they put together the case, bit by bit.

"Skippy is a piece of shit, no doubt about it." Andre pointed to a threatening tweet as they examined his social media posts. "Look, he called her a cunt."

According to Andre's sources, Skippy's fury at being cuckolded by the security guard boiled over by the beginning of May. Ian found his previous file on Skippy, and they decided to concentrate on Skippy's merry band of thugs and Kimmy Lafford.

"I've got to say Skippy had motive. What was he doing Thursday night? There's his opportunity," Ian mused. "Does he have an alibi? I mean it's quite easy to attack someone at night with a metal object if you lie in wait or sneak up, and, voila—we've got means. Now all we have to do is get some proof."

Ian and Andre searched database after database to track Skippy and his crew's movements. They scoured public records that tracked everything under the sun.

"Look at these pictures of her and Stulow together. The dates work, too. You can see when Kimmy and Skippy broke up, and when Kimmy starts up with Stulow."

"Hey, I saw Brock Saunders at the nursing home in West Hadley the other day. I meant to tell you." Andre taught senior yoga and a chair exercise class at Wood Haven, the local skilled nursing facility, two afternoons per week.

"Don't tell Peter or Jeff," Ian said. "Last thing they need is to confront him."

Brock visited his mother every other day, usually after Bingo, now that he was back in the area. He brought her favorite salty snacks, either a small bag of potato chips or a few slices of salami, both on her doctor's list of absolute no-no's.

Brock showered the nurses with donuts and chocolates. They looked forward to his visits.

"Such a nice son."

Mrs. Saunders rarely got a visit from her husband. Her poor prognosis due to congestive heart failure and emphysema meant her days were numbered, but he occupied his time with the business and a series of widows and divorcees.

When Brock's father summoned him back to Bridgeville, it wasn't because he missed Brock. Saunders Construction, limping along as the region's prospects dimmed, needed a shot of marketing pizzazz. Brock had been living in Wilmington, North Carolina, playing golf and dabbling successfully in real estate. But the combination of his mother's poor health and his father's badgering brought him home.

"We need to get in with the Consortium," his father said. "They're the only thing growing around here."

Brock nosed around and learned on the down-low about Zenergy's dealings with the Consortium. Saunders Construction undercut every bid to get the Zenergy contract.

"We're not going to make any money on this," Brock said.

"No shit, Sherlock. But we'll cut some corners on material and labor to sock something away."

"Yeah, but that could be dangerous."

"Not our problem. You in or out? I don't want any whining bullshit. Either you man up or hit the road. And your name is on the line of credit, so if you go all pussy on me, this is gonna bite you in the ass big-time."

Saunders senior specialized in acrimony with most of his peers. This certainly included Aldo Fiori. In fact, Aldo spat whenever the name came up.

"Pieces of shit, the lot of 'em."

Carmen never mentioned Brock, in particular, without shuddering. Peter hadn't asked her point blank if Brock had tried something with her because he was pretty sure Carmen would have killed him, but she and her friends didn't hide their contempt for Brock. When Vic took on Peter's case, he shed more light on the particulars of Aldo's latest anti-Saunders campaign.

"I can't believe Carm didn't fill you in," Vic said with surprise.

"Yeah, well there's that little detail of her not speaking to me."

The Fiori's orchard abutted disputed land that Brock's father had won in a marathon booze-soaked gambling weekend with his regular crew of liars and cheats. The state claimed the land as compensation for non-payment of taxes and other financial shenanigans.

Aldo Fiori had nothing but contempt for his new next-door neighbor. Old farm boys never forgot the bad blood that seeped down through generations. Yet when some of Aldo's field hands began telling about dynamite blasting, dying timber rattlesnakes and exploded dinosaur fossils, or at least that's what he thought they were saying as he listened to their agitated descriptions in a combination of Spanish, English, and Italian, he didn't hesitate to act.

Vic's keen nose for threats to Fiori interests was key, and Aldo scored first blood.

"It's cause you got a crush on Carm," Aldo rasped, casting a knowing eye at Vic. "You Baldini's."

"Oh, get off it, Aldo. Carm's my brother's ex-wife, and she's old enough to be my mother." Vic laughed and jumped back when Aldo dropped a bocce ball about a centimeter away from his foot.

"You're dog meat, she hears you saying that. Now go check this shit out."

Vic reported back quickly. "Looks like he's clearing land for some high-end houses—without the necessary permits."

"Yeah, well that ain't his land. It's the state's. I don't want no development up here sucking the aquifer dry. Let's shut him down. We need a little birdie. You got any ideas?"

"Plenty, Aldo. First, he's counting on the state being too broke and broken. But guess what? If it's state land, you can't blow up dinosaur fossils and bones; you can only do that on your own land."

"Yeah."

"What do ya mean yeah? That's important."

"Eh, everyone does it. Dinosaurs. You remember when they built the mall? They found more dinosaur bones and, you know, footprints than you got hair, more than anywhere in New England. But, you're right. On private land, the state can't do squat. You go to Home Depot or Target, and you're standing on dinosaurs from like a million years ago."

"Aldo, focus. Saunders is breaking the law. Plus he's blowing up and killing timber rattlesnakes; they're endangered and protected."

"Oh big whoop. Who's gonna care? I mean, I like'em; they eat all the varmints. But I don't get too cozy when they're around."

"I just gave you two ways to shut him down and piss him off big-time."

"Do it. I fucking hate that guy."

State officials responded immediately. They didn't find any dead rattlesnakes but they found plenty of damaged fossils.

It didn't take long for Saunders to retaliate. First, he informed the town that Fiori's wells were contaminated with radon, lead and all sorts of agricultural waste. The health inspectors showed up quickly if apologetically. Then Saunders somehow dumped a dozen dead timber rattlers right by Aldo's primary apple storage facility and sent his own alert to the Department of Environmental Protection. The officials converged on Fiori Orchards before Aldo even know what was happening.

Vic couldn't keep them at bay. "Are you serious?" He implored the DEEP inspector who imposed fines of $2,000 per dead timber rattlesnake and threatened imprisonment for up to 180 days if one more got "molested."

Aldo seethed. "It's on, baby. This ain't over."

• • •

CHAPTER 20

BY NOON ON MONDAY, IAN SAT IN VIC'S OFFICE WITH Lori on speakerphone and confidently sketched out what he considered the real story.

"Here's how I see it. Can you hear me OK, Lori?"

"Loud and clear."

"Dazzle us," Vic said, leaning back in his chair, motioning for Ian to get going.

"The gist of it is this: Skippy Lafford wanted revenge for Kimmy dumping him and shacking up with Stulow aka sleazeball Zenergy security guard. Skippy stalked Stulow night and day until he knew everything about his routines. He carefully planned—and this is premeditated, so I'm thinking attempted murder is the right charge."

"Leave that to us, Ian," Lori said. "Play on your ballfield."

"Yeah," Vic chimed in. "Think less. Don't hurt yourself."

"Fine. Skippy and his crew decided that a nighttime head thrashing up at the fuel cell facility would do the trick. Hard enough and it would kill him or at least drop him unconscious into a bloody heap so animals could eat his face. Or at least that's what Tank LaBois told me when I threatened to go to the police about a certain parole violation."

Ian knew where Tank hung with his buddies, getting high and drunk—not too far from where Becky Fiori died. The terrain, steep and rocky, stunned in the late afternoon sun as Ian searched for Tank. Skippy Lafford used him as muscle on the previous case Ian worked, so Tank had to know what Skippy was up to these days.

"Tank's the weak link," Ian said out loud while floating on his back in Small Lake after Andre discovered Kimmy Lafford's involvement. Small Lake, a beautiful body of water near Devil's Falls, officially lacked a name. No one in Bridgeville agreed on whether it should be called Big Pond or Small Lake, but Ian was firmly in the lake camp. When he needed to think unfettered thoughts and let them soar beyond gravity, Ian loved to float. He walked out chest-high before flipping onto his back. The towering pine trees scented the air and framed a cloudless sky. He gave himself twenty minutes in the bracingly cold water, checking his waterproof watch every now and then. As he drifted pleasantly weightless, a strategy came to him.

An hour later, dressed in dry clothes, Ian searched for Tank. The softening light filtered in rays through the canopy of leaves, illuminating floating particles and swarms of tiny insects. Loud crickets chirped ceaselessly, and Ian cocked his head to listen to trilling bird songs and occasional owl hoots.

The smell of weed and cigarettes beckoned Ian closer to Tank's lair. Someone was pissing like a racehorse in the woods to Ian's right, and he saw the enormous hulk of a man who could only be Tank. Ian hurried to catch Tank shaking out the last few drops of yeasty urine; any advantage over the 6 foot 8, 350 pound giant needed to be used.

"Oh, shit," Tank yelled as Ian materialized in his line of vision.

"Hullo, Tank. Long time no see."

"What the fuck? You still hungry for my meat?" Tank patted his quickly zipped-in junk.

"Funny. Sorry I didn't knock. Still on parole, are we Tank?"

"You know I am. Stop busting my ass and get lost." Tank turned back to the trail, but Ian followed closely at his heels.

"Oh, I thought we could get reacquainted, a reunion of sorts to remember old times." Ian spoke to Tank's broad flabby back, but he knew Tank was all ears.

"I got nothin' to say to you."

"I think you do," Ian said confidently. "So, Tank. I hear you're up to some old tricks with Skippy Lafford. Your parole officer know?"

Tank turned around and looked down at Ian through bleary eyes. His breath heavy with beer and years of neglected dental hygiene, Tank spat at Ian's feet. "Fuck you."

"Now, now. Here's how it's going to go down, Tank. Skippy's a risk for you to be seen with, yet I somehow found many photos of your escapades on social media. Here's you both at a strip club; did you think those tatas were real? And here's a really good one of you two sharing a bong." Ian scrolled through his phone, holding up pictures for Tank to see. "I can send these to the West Hadley police and the parole office with one little tap." Ian wiggled his index finger in the air and then hovered it over his phone.

Tank's shoulders slumped. "I will fuck you up," he said somewhat dejectedly, his demeanor now more house cat than king of the jungle.

"Tell me about Skippy and Kimmy. What he did when she left him."

"Oh, man. You know about that? I'm not ratting out nobody, but I'm not going back inside neither."

"So, just between us—no need for your parole officer to know—did you help Skippy take down the guard at the Zenergy plant? I mean, Kimmy shagging the guard had to sting, right?"

"Hell, yeah, if shagging means fucking. You want your snatch cheatin' on you? I didn't do nothin' to that guard, it was all Skip. He slugged him in the head with a hammer wrench. I just helped with, you know, logistics. We did a couple practice runs, like getting ready for the big game. That's it."

"Good lad. Tell me more."

Vic chortled with glee at Ian's reenactment of the conversation. "Told you to find the weak link. Just gotta have a nose for the jugular."

"Of course, it helped immensely that I knew Tank from previous successful work," Ian sniffed, unwilling to shower Vic with all the credit.

"True, so true." Lori murmured her assent.

Ian, soothed by her acknowledgement of his ingenuity, launched back into the story. "Skippy takes a trial run one night in mid-May at the Zenergy facility. The boys drop him off on a side street, and Skippy times the assault. But Tank said Skippy was worried about how close the neighborhood houses were to the fuel cell. Someone might be able to see him."

"Yeah, those older ranches are so close that the neighbors can flush each other's toilets and a lot more, if you get my drift." Vic smirked and shrugged. "I get a couple of voyeurism clients every year. If they don't use recording devices, I can get it kicked out."

"That's why you have a reputation as a sleazebag, Vic," Lori said. "Lose those clients. You don't need them."

"Money's money."

Ian rotated his neck right and left before tenting the tips of his outstretched middle fingers and bowing his head. "A prayer," he told Vic. He could hear Lori laughing.

"Stop with the prissy shit. Human cesspools furnished this place." Vic gestured proudly at the elaborate crown molding and animal heads adorning his walls. "Where I come from, you gotta be willing to tear somebody's face off."

"Vic, you're from West Hadley." Lori's voice crackled with amusement over the speaker.

"The wrong side of West Hadley. Cut to the chase already, Ian."

"OK. Now, it's D-Day, the Thursday night before Memorial Day weekend. Skippy sends Kimmy a batch of threatening texts, dons his all- black outfit, including gloves and a balaclava, grabs his weapon, and mobilizes the troops."

"We can guess the rest," Lori said. "So—"

"Let me finish the narrative," Vic interrupted. "Skippy sneaks up on Stulow and clobbers him. Bam, bam! Stulow drops like a dead weight onto his panic button and Skippy fades into the night."

"Exactly," Lori said. "Peter winds up taking the fall for Skippy's attack. This is great."

"Gotta love it. BPD, here comes a gift-wrapped present. You're welcome," Vic crowed.

Ian walked over to one of the deer heads on the wall and patted it solemnly.

"They're dead." Vic pointed to an impressively antlered buck that Ian couldn't reach. "This whole hunting and safari vibe costs plenty, lemme tell you."

"Nobody hunts deer on safari, Vic," Lori laughed. "Just shoot through your kitchen window. Ian, take a bow. It would've taken BPD a lot longer to do the investigation, so you've basically sprung Peter."

Ian couldn't let it go. "How are you going to get the cops to look beyond Peter?"

Vic cracked his knuckles loudly. "Probable cause. Actually, they need to *want* to look at probable cause beyond Peter. Tomassi's not gonna give his buddy any obvious special favors. BPD's running squeaky clean after that captain with all the hard-core porn on his work computer. I always knew he was a scumbag. Everything by the book, now. You gotta get a compliance check if you fart over there. So, we'll throw down a line of breadcrumbs for them. You good, Lor?"

"Absolutely. Vic, take it from here, and we'll talk tonight. Ian, terrific work. Marti's about ready to shoot me for not paying enough attention to her. God, women are demanding, aren't they?"

Vic and Ian nodded, catching each other's eyes as they smiled.

"Hey, I thought you were a monk or something," Vic said. "What do you know about women?"

"More than you ever will. Now, in a perfect world, the one I pray for," Ian said as Vic rolled his eyes, "the cops see the love triangle because you serve it to them on a gleaming silver platter. They get off their arses to search Skippy's place, look for the weapon and have a chat with Miss Kimmy. Are you going to subpoena cellphone records?"

"I got this, Jessica Jones. You did good. Now, it's my turn."

CHAPTER 21

PETER GOT OUT OF JAIL TUESDAY MORNING AFTER LORI and Vic wheeled and dealed with the prosecutor to reduce the charges to misdemeanor trespassing, a $500 fine, a two-year probationary period, and four months of community service. Marco and Paco had already been taken to the courthouse, so Peter didn't get to say good-bye.

Waiting for Jeff to pick him up, Peter saw Kenny Johnson looking glum.

"What's the matter? You gonna miss me and Marco so much?"

"Yeah, right—that's it."

"So, tell me."

"Girlfriend problems. She dumped me." Kenny kicked the garbage can as he spoke.

"A great-looking guy like you? C'mon, Kenny. Plenty of fish in the sea."

"Whatever." Kenny clenched his jaw and busied himself with paperwork before looking up. "Peter, I'm glad you're getting out of here. And don't even think of messing up your probation."

"OK, chief." Peter saluted.

"You really thinking of hiring Marco when he gets out if you get the food truck going?"

"Yeah. And we're gonna get it going. Why is everyone doubting me and Jeff?"

"No one's doubting Jeff," Kenny said with a grin, his dark mood lifting momentarily.

Vic told Peter to forget about Marco and Paco when Jeff brought him to his office for a wrap-up. "They'll do some time. You should stay away from jailbirds. You're lucky you got a fairy godmother."

"What?"

"Never mind." But, Peter couldn't get Paco and Marco out of his head. The marijuana bust that landed them in the Bridgeville jail was a second offense for each of them.

"I want to do something for them. Try to wrap your mind around this bullshit: second possession of just over an ounce of weed, a pipe and a bong is getting them a minimum of ninety days of jail time and a big-time fine," he said to Jeff Wednesday morning. They sat in Jeff's kitchen, having coffee and home-made muffins while Brutus slept at Peter's feet. Jeff motioned for him to shut up.

"Hey, the law's the law. Thanks, hon," Jeff said to his daughter, Rachel, doe-eyed and lively, as she refreshed their mugs.

"Do you like the muffins? I put more cinnamon and walnuts in than normal because I know you love them, Pete." Rachel, a little too lean for Jeff's comfort level, looked exactly like Annie did as a young woman. After being arrested on heroin possession, Rachel had enrolled in culinary school five months ago as a condition of her court-mandated rehab program.

"Jeff, Annie—I'm gonna tell it to you straight. If you can call getting lucky to be busted for heroin anywhere, it's good it was here in town," Tomassi said to her stunned parents. "This is a huge fucking problem everywhere. Don't think it's only your kid. Plus, she didn't overdose, so get down on your knees, thank God and then do it a hundred more times."

Rachel had been clean for six months, but the shock of her heroin use and how well she concealed it pulled the rug out from under Jeff and Annie. They fretted constantly about a relapse.

"Normal," Jeff snorted. "There's nothing normal about your uncle."

"Awesome, Rach," Peter said, waving off Jeff's comment. "When are you done with the program?"

Jeff shot him a look. "Which one?"

"Oh, come on. Look, your dad and I are looking for a baking partner in the food truck, but now he wants it gluten-free. Right up your alley, kiddo. Any thoughts?"

"Again," Jeff said, "read my lips. Who are you talking to—me or her?"

Rachel put a hand on her father's shoulder. "How about both of us, Dad. Stop being so grouchy. It would be perfect for me. I'm gluten-free and I can really focus on specialty baking. But it'll only work if you fund my share. I'll pay you back once we make some money—and we will, like crazy."

Jeff sighed. "Rach, it could put too much pressure on you. Start-ups are risky and, being honest here, I don't know if you could handle having to bake on a deadline. Maybe just hire a more experienced baker and be an assistant."

"Way to believe in me, Dad. Thanks a lot for your vote of confidence." Rachel turned her back on him and walked behind Peter's chair, gripping the back tightly, almost using Peter as a shield. "I'm ready for this. I need this," she said, her voice tightening.

Peter tried to get Jeff to lighten up. "Hey, moron. We want your wallet not your opinion. What the hell do you know about start-ups or baking?"

Rachel stomped her foot. "You don't have faith in me. What kind of father expects his daughter to fail? Well, it's not gonna happen." She appealed to Peter to back her up as Annie came in from the garage holding two bags of groceries. "Mom, Dad won't help me." Rachel's eyes welled with tears and her bottom lip quivered.

"What the hell is going on here?" Annie asked. She kissed Peter on the cheek and looked back and forth between her husband and daughter. "Tell me why you're spoiling Pete's first real morning of freedom. And why my daughter is crying." Her eyes harpooned Jeff's, and he squirmed, his face already flushed with emotion.

Annie had kept the same blonde shag hairdo for years. Although she had put on weight, just like Jeff, she looked ready to shed her cardigan, kick off her clogs and whip his ass if he said one more word to upset Rachel.

"Easy now, everyone." Peter held up his hands. "I

didn't come here to rock the boat. I just want to make this a Russo family enterprise. And, truth be told, I'd love for Rachel to be an equal partner in this project. You," he said to Jeff, "might think of being one who takes a vow of silence."

Rachel barked a laugh. "Exactly."

"Of course we'll do it as three equal partners," Annie said. "This could work out for everyone. We need a baker, a truck and product. Rachel is a baker. Jeff can barter for the truck, and Pete can be chief driver. This'll be great."

"Annie," Jeff began. "Not—"

She stopped him cold. "I don't want to hear it. Let's sketch out a rough plan." Annie never met a problem she couldn't pound into submission; she could have run the country from the back of a napkin. With a velvet fist, she resolved dilemmas that King Solomon would have abandoned as hopeless. The only one she couldn't decipher was the one that caused her the most pain, Rachel's drug use.

Rachel poured her mother a cup of coffee and sat down by her side. Rachel's purple pixie cut and multiple ear-piercings contrasted with Annie's head-to-toe LL Bean. Jeff regarded them anxiously and rolled his eyes at Peter who smiled and looked away, reaching down to stroke Brutus as he snored.

CHAPTER 22

JOHN TOMASSI TEXTED PETER TO COME OVER FOR A beer the next day. Peter showed up at the Tomassi's small but well-maintained colonial-style home to find Donna, sweating and surrounded by a cloud of bugs, kneeling on a rolled-up towel and weeding her vegetable garden.

"Hey, Donna. Want some help?"

"Peter, hi." She waved her dirt-covered hand at him. "Oh my God. The rabbits are eating all my lettuce. I'm so annoyed. And you, Johnny wanted to wring your neck. You're in for a big lecture; you deserve it, too."

"Yeah, he isn't my biggest fan right now. Listen, I can put up some rabbit-proof fencing and raise the railroad ties higher. It's not like John's gonna do it. Scoot over," he said, bending down next to her and pulling up several handfuls of nasty weeds.

"Please? Johnny goes deaf when I ask him. I know it's his hip and because he hates to eat salad."

"Very true. He likes to call ketchup a vegetable. How are the kids?" Peter got a real kick out of the two Tomassi offspring because they read their gruff dad like a children's book and could bend him to their will. "My god-daughter better be staying out of trouble."

"Knock on wood, no problems. Cath is coming back for the fundraiser for Becky Fiori's scholarship. She got a promotion. I'm sure she'll say hi. I think Mike will be here Saturday, but he'll be hanging out with Josh Richardson. They were always thick as thieves, but Mike says Josh could be moving to California. I hope not."

"You done good. Cath and Mike are great."

"Hey, Donna," Tomassi yelled, coming outside. "Dirtbag bothering you?" Without waiting for an answer, he handed Peter a cold beer and guided him by the scruff of his neck to the rear deck. "Sit."

"Is this the big lecture? I already know what you're gonna say."

"Tough titties." Tomassi drained his beer and leaned against the railing. "You got really lucky. No more childish bullshit, you hear me? You gotta avoid any trouble, and I mean any. Someone's got road rage because they don't like how you drive? Ignore 'em, even if they're flipping you off with both hands. Someone bumps into you and wants to mix it up? Walk away. You got me? Any violation of the agreement lands you in massive shit."

"Loud and clear. And thanks again for looking out for me."

"What? I couldn't and didn't do anything special even though I knew the assault charge was bullshit."

"Exactly my point, Sergeant. I could be in jail until doomsday for all the help you gave me."

"Yeah, right. Lori and Vic were on it from the beginning. Even that whack job PI did solid work. But without Carmen? Good thing she still gives a shit. Oops—I wasn't supposed to say that."

"Carmen? You gotta tell me. What do you mean she gives a shit? Oh, wait. No. She didn't, no way."

"Yeah, no—she bankrolled your defense team. You never heard this from me. Swear? She'll have my balls."

"John, no worries. Donna's already got 'em framed and mounted on the wall. And you better not be yanking my chain about Carmen."

"What chain, douchebag."

Peter called Lori as he peeled out of Tomassi's driveway. Getting no answer, he drove over to Vic's office and barged in after hurriedly parking his truck across two spaces. He wanted to find out if Tomassi had it right. He stopped dead in his tracks at the sight of Carmen. She jumped up like she had been stung by a swarm of bees, recovered and then regarded him coolly as she resumed her perch on the rollback arm of Vic's burnished Corinthian leather couch. Vic turned around from his well-stocked cocktail bar, clutching an ice cube in gleaming silver tongs, and chuckled.

"Look at what the cat dragged in."

"Carmen, Vic. If I'd known this was a party, I'd have brought my world-famous onion dip and put on my fancy clothes." Peter's jeans and hands were smeared with dirt from Donna's garden.

"Tell you what, I've got some calls to make. I'll catch up with you in a few minutes." Vic grabbed a handful of nuts and left the room.

"I need to talk to you," Peter said to his back before he closed the door.

"Call me next time. I don't do drop-ins. Better yet, lose my number—call Lori."

Carmen and Peter stared at each other. Neither one blinked until Peter walked over to her and offered his hand.

"What's this for?" Carmen asked. "Do you want me to wash it?"

"Ha. It's just a hand, my hand. A little dirt won't kill you."

"Yeah, I'm aware. I grow apples."

"Look, I just want to thank you for everything, Carm. A little birdie told me." Peter kept his hand outstretched. "Shaking my hand won't get you pregnant, despite what the nuns said."

"I never believed them. But I didn't do anything. I don't know what you're talking about."

Peter gently took her hand. "Right. Is that the story we're going with? Well then, thank you for doing nothing. I'm grateful from the bottom of my heart."

"You're welcome." Carmen reclaimed her hand and took a step back.

"I'm still hoping we can talk. I mean, it's been way too long."

"Yeah, well, no. There's really nothing left to say. How about we just take a raincheck."

"Come on. We're not getting any younger. I could drop dead tomorrow."

"Look, Pete—no. And you're not going to kick off any time soon. I'm not going there. No offense."

"Some taken. You look fantastic, by the way." His eyes scoped down her body and, immediately, he flashed back to how much he loved to hold her hips when they made it doggy-style. She smoothed her hair, and the movement drew his gaze to her breasts.

"Thank you. Eyes here," she said pointing to her face. "Look, we might as well try to act like somewhat normal people. Maybe set up some boundaries so things aren't so awkward."

"Awkward doesn't even begin to define whatever this is," he said, gesturing at the two of them. "Let me guess— you get to define the boundaries. Are we going to sign an official peace treaty, too?"

"Here's how it's going to be. We keep it light. A 'hello,' a 'wow can you believe this humidity.' Easy. Nothing deep or heavy. And I want to make this beyond clear—no going out together and definitely no sex." She crossed her arms across her chest and waited for his reaction.

"Geez, you've thought about this. You miss me." He reached over to give her a hug.

"No touching!"

Peter held his hands up. "Come on, you know I'm a hugger. These are some strict rules. So no make big whoopee soon?"

"Cut it out." But she couldn't suppress a low chuckle.

"Carm, I always meant to tell you this—you've got a filthy laugh, dirty as hell."

"Boundaries, Pete."

"OK, boundaries. If I see you, I can wave. If we happen to be going to the movies at the same time, at the same movie theater, I should sit a few rows away. And if you've stopped breathing and need mouth-to-mouth and I'm the only living soul around, I should call 911 and wait for the ambulance. Is that it?"

"Exactly right. You're getting much less feebleminded. A miracle."

"Aw shucks, it was nothing."

They stood face to face, neither of them saying anything. Peter knew he had to make an exit before he prostrated himself at her feet and either clung to her ankles like a toddler or tried to pleasure her right then and there.

"Hallelujah—it's a new day." He blew her a kiss and walked towards the door.

"Wait. I thought you came here to see Vic."

"And spoil this moment? Not a chance. I'll call him tomorrow."

Carmen opened the door for him. "Good thinking. Vic doesn't do drop-ins."

PART 2

PRESENT TIME

CHAPTER 23

PETER HIKED UP A ROCKY TRAIL ALONG THE horseshoe-shaped perimeter of the old dam when suddenly Brutus started pawing frantically in the wood.

"Easy, boy," Peter said to Brutus, who in no time, had excavated a crater.

Peter used his walking stick to investigate and poked some daylight into the mass of dirt, sticks and leaves.

"What the hell?"

He stared in disbelief at what looked like a festering bundle of black leather tied up tight with rope like a bulky parcel.

"Jesus." Peter crouched close enough to eyeball his discovery, still poking with his stick. "Ugh, it stinks like something dead." Peter covered his nose and mouth with his bandana and squatted down even closer.

Peter unearthed the jacket, but he couldn't pull it out of the hole. He got down on his knees and leaned into the hole until he tugged it free. Brutus drooled puddles onto the putrid leather jacket.

Breathing heavily, Peter took out his pocket knife and cut the rope attached to the cinder block. He held the package gingerly by the remaining rope that still encircled it like a present. "Now, let's get out of here, B. You never know who's watching."

They walked to the trailhead where Peter parked his pickup.

Peter rummaged on the truck's floor for some old newspapers and spread them out on the Jeep's hood. He cut the remaining rope after putting on his ancient work gloves and untied the black bomber jacket's sleeves to get at what lay inside

"What the—?" Peter tossed the jacket to the ground and held up a carefully taped plastic garbage bag wrapped around something rectangular and hard. Peter ripped open the garbage bag and extracted a 9 x 12 cardboard mailing envelope bulging with papers and a small zippered pouch.

"Brutus, we're not far from Nancy's. Let's drop by and try the flash drive on her laptop. She's nosy."

Peter picked up the jacket with a stick and threw it in the open back of the pickup.

"Let's go."

They drove away from the dilapidated dam, known as Devil's Falls, once vital to Bridgeville's textile industry. It had turned into a costly and practically useless eyesore that the state pressured Bridgeville to repair after almost a century of damage to the rivers it fed. Some of them had trickled to a halt, bled dry by overuse, others were hopelessly befouled by pollutants. A few had been repurposed, like the heavily used dry riverbed racing track, fought over by dirt bikers and BMXers.

Town Council after Town Council town balked repeatedly at the state's demands; suits and counter-suits created stalemate. Even the most litigious environmental organizations were thwarted by bureaucratic inertia. They didn't give up, but they did move on to more newsworthy disasters like the Colorado River practically running dry, and the Wikileaks revelation of underground nuclear bombing in New Mexico to access natural gas during the 1960's by the Department of Energy.

Bridgeville didn't have gas; it had land and water. And soon it had a big natural gas pipeline running through it. The easy money of the 1980's fueled a feeding frenzy that almost transformed the town from rural farm country to suburban hotspot. It became a coveted place to raise a family or do business. But the metamorphosis created a whole new array of problems. Bridgeville's amazingly fertile farmland and open space disappeared by over one-half.

CHAPTER 24

NANCY WAVED PETER AND BRUTUS INTO THE KITCHEN, a steaming mug of black coffee by her pile of papers on the table.

"Give Brutus some water on the porch." Nancy pointed to an empty bowl she had set aside after getting Peter's call.

"Nance, damn that coffee smells good." Peter took a cup out of a cabinet, very familiar with the layout of Nancy's kitchen.

"There's a couple of packages of cream and sugar from Dunkin Donuts over there. Long time no see. How come? Don't tell me it's your busy love life."

"Busy alright, just not with love. The food truck takes up like half my day, plus Rachel is maxed out—baking like mad. I gotta help."

Rachel also ran the commissary like a four-star general. She'd inherited her mother's need for order—alphabetized, labelled, color-coded, and entered on Excel spreadsheets kind of order.

Once Rachel won over Peter and Annie to start the food truck, Annie staggered Jeff with just how obsessed she was with helping Rachel. Their guilt about Rachel's addiction had created a painful dialogue that never seemed to get anywhere until they settled on the food truck.

"I know everyone screws up their kids somehow, but we gave Rachel and Sean the best, most loving child-hoods. But somewhere we must've done something wrong with Rachel. I still can't get over it—heroin?" Annie choked on a sob and shook off Jeff's attempt at a hug. They stood with Peter on the farmhouse's front porch, the breeze from the ceiling fan barely cooling the humid air.

"Annie, it's nothing you did or didn't do. You're awe-some parents. It's the times." Peter stepped in as Jeff bit his lips hard and teared up.

"Bullshit." Annie inhaled shakily. "I mean, I started working full-time at Park and Rec way back when the kids were little so we'd get great benefits and I'd be home when they came home from school. I volunteered for everything. But look what happened."

"That fucking dentist giving her oxy." Jeff balled his hands into fists, ready for a fight.

"Exactly. It wasn't you. Tomassi says it's like an out-of-control freight train, getting faster and faster. First the pain pills get prescribed, then they hijack people's lives. Prescriptions dry up but the addiction's got con-trol. That's what happened with Rach. She had to get it from the street." Peter stopped talking as he heard Brutus barking ferociously. Craning his neck, he saw the Fed-Ex driver drop off a package and toss Brutus a biscuit before taking off.

Jeff kicked a plastic deck chair over onto its side with

a resounding thud. "My sweet baby got stuck between a rock and a hard place. All alone, at least in her head. Why didn't she tell us?" He wiped his blood-shot eyes roughly on his sleeve. "And don't get me going on her so-called friends who got her on the shit."

Annie, composed now, her puffy eyelids obscuring her pale blue eyes, scoffed. "Tell you? Please. You're not exactly warm and fuzzy, Mister Tough Guy. You both lock it down so tight. I blame your sorry excuses for parents. A selfish, bitter mother who put her kids last, dead last. Booze and being your father's doormat came first."

"Annie, cut it out. You think reliving the past does any good? Like hell." Peter stepped in close to her, Jeff picking up the chair he sent flying.

"Oh, I'm saying the truth. And I'm not done. Your father was the nastiest piece of work, the exact opposite of what a dad should be. He treated you like shit, especially you, Pete. You boys were beasts of burden. If he said jump, you jumped or else."

"Look, this conversation is over." Jeff took two big strides and held onto Annie's shoulder. "Pete and I had each other, and that got us through. Did it suck? Yeah, absolutely. It double-sucked. But parents aren't everything. You were lucky, your mom and dad are terrific. And I'm so lucky because I have you. And we've got two great kids." He hugged her tight as she stepped into his arms, leaning hard against him.

"I should've picked up on her signals that she was so desperate," Annie said into his barrel chest. "Maybe she tried to tell me; I just missed the hints."

"No, she hid them. She always liked her secrets, tucking her dolls under her bed and stashing her make-up under a pillow even though we said no. Like we wouldn't notice our ten-year-old sporting bright green eyeshadow and red lipstick. Plus, she's a great little actress. Remember all those plays she did in school?" Jeff planted small kisses on Annie's forehead.

"Oscar-worthy. Good with accents, too. Her southern belle slayed me." Peter patted them both on the back. "Maybe Rach had the bad luck to get some of Mom's alcoholism gene plus our amazing acting chops. Of course, ours were survival skills. Who the fuck knows?"

Annie straightened up and pointed at Jeff. "We need to show her how much we love and trust her. Sean got the farm. It's time for Rachel. She's a baker now—you have to do the food truck with her."

"Yeah, honey. I'm almost there." He pinched some air between his forefinger and thumb. "This close. What's holding me back isn't the truck. It's the gamble on Rach. You gotta keep your eyes peeled. If we do it, me and Pete'll be really busy."

Annie nodded, revved up with new energy. "Yup. The Three Musketeers. I'll keep chugging at Park and Rec, but count on me behind the scenes, watching and helping. She'll be terrific. I know it like I know my own name."

"Hey, Igor Russo—just so me and him don't turn it into the Three Stooges." Peter got a smile from Annie, her fierce expression relaxing momentarily, and a throaty chuckle from Jeff.

When the commissary was finally ready to get off the ground some four months after the tearful porch session, Annie and Rachel put out a red alert for help with production and stockpiling some frozen inventory. Sean had his hands full with the farm, Annie had a nagging sinus infection, and Donna Tomassi was visiting her mother in North Carolina. Jeff showed up ready to go, but Rachel, running the show, exiled him to clean-up.

"Stop hovering, Dad. You're pissing me off."

John Tomassi answered the call, sporting a frilly apron

of Donna's, and swore that his son, Mike, on break from law school, would be there in a heartbeat. Tomassi was elbow deep in dough when Mike and his old pal, Josh Richardson, clattered downstairs.

"Nice look, Sergeant T," Josh said, laughing. Josh, as lean as Mike was stocky, had spent many hours at the Tomassi household after his father died and his mother lost her connection with reality. Now finishing up his MBA at a middling local university, Josh hated his job as an assistant guidance counselor at West Hadley High School and was counting the days until he could leave for something better. Josh's mother, still fragile and clingy, was the biggest impediment to that plan.

"You wish you had the balls to wear this, Josh. Only real men can pull this off." Tomassi pranced in a circle to loud cat-calls.

"Dad, you look like Fred Flintstone in drag as Julia Child. Only worse, and in real life." Mike ducked when his father flicked a ball of dough at him.

"No food fights," Rachel yelled. "We have a time dead-line, people. Where's Pete?"

"Town council meeting." Jeff rolled his eyes. "This time, he's speaking for the piping plovers. Some kind of problem with Bridgeville's hospitality."

"I thought it was shad migration. Can you believe they want to build another gas pipeline across the river? I told Pete to give 'em hell." Tomassi turned very seri-ous and pounded the mound of dough into submission. "Enough's enough."

"So, Dad, why don't you go support him at the meet-ing? He could use a few soldiers."

"Nah, no can do, Mikey. Too political. I gotta be Switzerland to the public."

"Yeah, but maybe you could catch them doing some-thing illegal."

"My son, the almost-lawyer. Lemme tell you, those morons couldn't catch a cold. Every word is a lie."

"Whoa." Josh feigned shock and staggered under the weight of Tomassi's truth.

"Get to work, people," Rachel said as she approached Josh. "Do you remember me at all?"

Josh knew all about Rachel's drug bust, but he didn't go there. "Your name's on the tip of my tongue. Gertrude?" Josh had a winning streak with women that was a running joke in the Tomassi household, but his current girlfriend, Emmie, usually had a pleasing grip on his mind and body. Plus she bought into his California dream. The only hitch remained his mother.

"That better be the only thing of hers at the tip of your tongue," Mike muttered. "Her boyfriend could shred you like a carrot."

Josh guffawed as Rachel swatted Mike with a dish towel, and then swerved as she came after him with a big grin on her face. The joy of child's play helped Josh forgot about the fight he'd had with Emmie about getting his mother out of their business.

Jeff hadn't wanted Rachel to handle all the baking. He reinforced his point one night sitting outside on Peter's deck, putting a big dent into some frozen margaritas. They sat quietly and spellbound in the dark, watching the fireflies' magic show.

"I never get tired of this," Peter said.

"What—you, me and the fireflies?"

"And the margaritas." Peter looked over at Jeff when he exhaled loudly. "Tell me."

Jeff spoke haltingly. "So, Rach is all-or-nothing about doing the baking. Nobody else. Pressure like that on her scares the shit out of me, you know. It could backfire and then what?"

"She'll have help from all of us. Me, you, Annie,

Marco, probably a couple of friends. Plus, she's still getting counseling."

"Yeah. You're chief dishwasher, more like it. Listen, I can't put her in a position to fail." Jeff laid his cards on the table. "I'm trusting you that Marco is a good guy who's done with the fuck-ups. Fine for working on the truck, but not near Rachel too much. I don't want to put my baby into a situation where she's got easy access again to, you know—easy access to drugs."

"Hate to break it to you, but Rach probably knows more eager-beaver dealers than you can count. Scary people, too." Peter poured more margaritas for himself and Jeff. "She's into a new chapter of her life. Are you saying Marco's going to corrupt her? Get real, all due respect to Rach."

"Hey, you know what I mean."

"No, I don't." Peter sat up straight and jabbed his finger in Jeff's face. "Marco is not your problem. He's good people. He and Kenny Johnson have been hanging out; try that on for size. Marco talked him into doing some part-time coaching for the youth baseball team that Marco's cousin manages."

"Huh, Marco and Kenny? I didn't see that coming."

CHAPTER 25

NANCY HAD BEEN HANGING BY A THREAD FOR TOO long, the insurance company having dicked her around endlessly.

Some days she could barely breathe and rarely slept at night for longer than one hour. Impatient at the delay, Nancy's anger and blood pressure surged. Anything on the floor got kicked into a corner until she could corral it with long plastic tongs. Putting on socks was as likely as climbing Everest.

Inspirational magnets and pictures from magazines covered every inch of Nancy's white refrigerator door. The big red paper stop sign taped to her snack drawer had started to curl at the edges. Finally, after fits and starts, insurance agreed to pay every penny for her pending gastric sleeve surgery.

Nancy's psychologist, not her regular one, but one assigned to the hospital's gastric sleeve team, worked with her on getting mentally strong, ready for the obstacles she needed to overcome pre- and post-surgery. Nancy fired the first one for stupidity after one session.

"How do you cope?" Shrink Number One posed the question while sucking noisily on the end of his pen. His feet, clad in worn Birkenstocks, smelled awful.

"With what?"

"With life," he said, seemingly stunned at her dim-wittedness.

"How do you think? I'm a morbidly obese woman who's single."

"Hmmm. I'd like to hear you articulate how you handle life's complications, the stresses that come from personhood in our time. What are your strategies?

"Are you fucking kidding me? It should be beyond obvious that I have exactly one coping mechanism. Eating. Don't even try to psychoanalyze me."

"Aha."

After Nancy cut the session short, she called her surgeon's office manager and demanded to be set up with a competent and female therapist. Assigned to a younger woman who dressed very formally—pencil skirts, blazers, pumps, and pearls—Nancy tried to be patient with the process. Part of their work centered on locating here-and-now Nancy and taking her pulse. The rage bubbled up surprisingly quickly once she found the trapdoor into caverns of anger at just about everyone, especially her sons, her ex-husband, Brock Saunders, and Peter.

"I don't even know why I'm angry with Peter."

"You do realize that the people you are most angry with are the men in your life's arc. Let's sit with that for a few minutes."

"I don't need to waste our time on the obvious answer. Men suck."

"All of them?"

"Every single last one. Can we move on to something actually important, like how to keep the weight off?"

When Peter came over with the cache of documents and the flash drive, Nancy tried to pour cold water on his curiosity.

"Why do you care about this—it's not your business."

"Why wouldn't you care? Someone went to a ridiculous amount of trouble to bury everything."

Nancy plugged in her laptop. "Give it to me. But I want to refresh the security software first. The drive could be corrupted or loaded with a virus." She checked her cellphone. "I've got a doctor's appointment in an hour; this one's with the pulmonologist. They have to be confident I can make it through anesthesia."

"You better."

"Saying good riddance to all the fat clothes will make my day. I hate them, and I hate this." Nancy gestured disgustedly at her body.

"Stop." Peter patted her arm. "Ian says your body can hear you. Don't talk smack to it."

"Ian is a blockhead."

Peter reached for a pair of Nancy's omnipresent bifocals from the countertop and removed the documents from the envelope, being careful not to spill his coffee.

"Holy moly." Nancy whistled softly. "I've seen zillions of spreadsheets, but these are some big calculations. This could be like some kind of revenue projections for manufacturing and production runs."

"Are those New England Council Consortium watermarks? Look: N-E-C-C. Bastards. I wonder who made these documents." Peter reached for the laptop to check on its progress, but Nancy grabbed it from him.

"Don't even sneeze near it. You have some weird paralyzing effect on electronics. They malfunction immediately."

"Geez, I'm hurt."

"Yeah, the truth stings. Hey, this flash drive is password protected, and the financials were probably stolen from the Consortium. I don't want to mess with it and neither do you." She gave him a very pointed look over her leopard-print bifocals.

"Come on, Nance. Quick party game—we get one guess for the password, and then we give up. You go first."

"Danger." Nancy typed it in on the keyboard. "No, not it. I'm out."

"Try: Fuck the Consortium."

"Is that one word or three?" Nancy tried both versions. "Nope."

"Where there's smoke there's fire. Something's happening, and the timeframe is the key." Peter slurped the remainder of his coffee. "I mean, my mother, not the brightest crayon in the box by a long shot, actually created those stupid blankets with sleeves that ended up being such a big thing. She could have made millions if the timing was right. Sometimes you don't know the world has been waiting for something so simple."

"As simple as water?" Nancy asked.

"What are you talking about?"

"I keep seeing 'H2o' on these projections. That's water."

"I don't get it. They're making water?"

"Whatever." Nancy started to clear the mugs from the table. "I have to go. We're done here."

"So how do we unlock the password?" Peter drummed his fingers impatiently.

"We don't. Just stop this wild goose chase."

"If the Consortium is involved, it's sketchy. I can smell it."

"Let's talk about me for a change. I'm getting nervous. I'm only a month out from surgery. God, I hope my numbers are decent. Can we sacrifice a goat or something?" Nancy motioned for him to get moving.

"Alright, alright."

"Take all this stuff with you. I don't know why you think some gigantic earth-shattering revelation is hidden there." Nancy slicked her lips with pink lip gloss in front of her hallway mirror. "Just don't let it bring any bad luck my way."

Peter whistled for Brutus as Nancy hurried out of the house.

"Just close the door tight behind you when you leave. Or maybe I should ask Brutus to do it. Pay attention. Sometimes it doesn't click shut so really give it a pull."

"Sure. No problemo."

CHAPTER 26

PETER WASN'T THE ONLY PERSON THINKING ABOUT THE Consortium and its activities. The Consortium now dominated Josh Richardson's life, too. Back before he and Mike helped Rachel build inventory, his mother sent his resume into the Consortium, along with ten other regional companies in a massive blitz, unbeknownst to him. Desperate to keep him from leaving, she pulled a rabbit out of the hat when Human Resources at the Consortium plowed double-time through their file folder of resumes and settled on Josh's. That same day, the last day of the school year, the Consortium requested an immediate interview.

"What the hell?" Josh read the email from HR while eating jello at his mother's kitchen table. "How does the Consortium know I exist?"

His mother squealed with joy. "I sent them your resume months ago. Look at the opportunity, Joshy." she said, beaming with pride.

"Mom. No." Josh put down his spoon and started pacing.

"The Consortium protects our natural resources and the environment," she read to him from its website. "You love the environment, Joshy."

"Mom, I asked you to stop calling me by that stupid nickname like twenty years ago." Josh really did like to snowboard, hike, and swim. But in his mind, he was already gone to California. "The Consortium is not a place I want to work. Nobody does."

"You could be making great money in no time. You could be an executive. Come on, Emmie told me all about you helping Sean Russo's sister bake bread. That's ridiculous."

"I was doing Sean and her a favor like months ago. And I went with Mike. Emmie's got a big mouth." Josh hated when the two women talked about him. Besides, Rachel Russo, hot and a little too daring for a typical Josh woman, still occupied a space in Josh's brain.

"Just go in for the interview. If you take the job, I'll sign the papers to give you control of the money your father left when you turn thirty instead of thirty-five."

"Can I get that in writing and notarized?"

"Cross my heart. Oh, I just know they're going to hire you. Wear the navy blazer and the red tie. You look even more handsome when you get dressed up."

After meeting two days later with the CFO and several underwhelming sidekicks for a position billed as strategic business analyst, Josh found himself fast-tracked through Human Resources. Pamphlets for dental, health and 401-k in hand, he signed a standard contract. Going from $30,000 to $85,000 practically overnight made him and Emmie postpone their plans for just a little longer.

"When do I start?"

"Yesterday," his immediate boss said. "Get up to speed fast." He dumped a mountain of files into Josh's arms. "From now on, you eat, drink and breathe this deal."

Josh found his way to his small bare office, little more than a desktop computer, printer, desk, chair, file cabinet, and a mountain of folders. He got a paper cut when he opened the top folder and sucked on his bleeding finger.

"You got half a window?" a grumpy co-worker asked, suddenly walking into Josh's office. "I'm still in a cubicle after four years. Not fair. What did they hire you for?"

Josh closed the door so he could concentrate. Shifting uncomfortably in the stiff desk chair, he pulled out his calculator, flash drive, phone, and Tic-Tacs. He started going over his copy of the deal with a yellow highlighter, affixing sticky notes and wishing he had a band-aid.

"Two million gallons of water daily?" Josh stopped writing, put down the report and popped two Tic-Tacs. "That's a lot of water."

He started searching through online documents and spreadsheets to find an essential study that should have been conducted.

"Where's the basic supply-demand analysis? This could place a big strain on the available water supply." He tapped his pen against his cheek and read everything that might answer the question until his eyes felt like they were hemorrhaging.

CHAPTER 27

MARCO FRIENDED KENNY ON FACEBOOK WHEN HE GOT out after only serving half his jail sentence due to good behavior and over-crowding. Kenny started following him on Instagram. They bonded over Peter and their shared love of baseball. Marco bemoaned his cousin's weak-hitting youth baseball team.

"Dude, there's tons of hitting videos online," Kenny said. "Just start schooling them."

"Nah, I got a better idea. You the school." Marco and Kenny stood side by side, watching batting practice at the minor league stadium in Hatfield. Every spring, the team offered cheap tickets to the earliest pre-season games, and Kenny had nabbed two from the break room at the police department.

On a whim, he called Marco to see if he wanted to go. Marco, uncharacteristically, fell silent.

"Hey, don't do me any favors," Kenny said. "Just thought it would fun, something different, man. I mean who doesn't like the Hatfield Herrings?"

"Fucking stupid name." Marco paused for a few beats. "Ok, sounds good, bro. But I gotta say, you got cop written all over you. Gonna mess up my street cred."

"Oh, yeah? I won't even say what you're gonna do to my reputation."

They both started to laugh. "We gonna blow some minds, Officer KJ."

"Damn straight."

Marco's cousin, Jose, pot-bellied and short, stared at Kenny for a long time when Marco brought him to the ball field. Jose, his muscular legs and arms testifying to his strength, barely lightened up when Kenny offered a handshake. Jose's reservations about bringing Kenny on board could not have been more clear.

"What're you 6' 3", 190? You play in college?" Jose evaluated Kenny without emotion. Kenny's fit and muscular physique in his T-shirt and jeans attracted a lot of attention from onlookers.

"Club ball. You know, intercollegiate. I was good, but at a D-1 university, you gotta be great. Me—average stick, average arm, average everything. They would have kept me around, you know—for emergencies, but collecting splinters on the bench didn't do it for me." Kenny took off his sunglasses, so he could look Jose directly in the eye.

"He can teach 'em how to hit better. You got like no nothin'," Marco said. "How many games you been shut out already?"

"I don't know," Jose finally said. "But stick around if you want. Back there is good." He pointed to some empty rusty bleachers baking in the sun.

"Dude, everybody gonna think you like Immigration or FBI." Marco laughed and gestured at all the anxious and cold stares from the crowd.

"Yeah," Jose said, shaking his head. "I won't have no team on the field. Everybody gonna clear out."

Kenny shook his head. "It's all about baseball. Just tell them it's about hitting dingers. Hey, the field's not looking too good." He gestured at the crumbly rock-strewn infield.

"I just raked it for like a half hour," Jose said, wiping his sweaty face. "That's lookin' good, man. You wanna do it?"

"Sorry, my bad."

Marco and Jose looked at each other and cracked up. "You so white," Marco said. "Ima stand next to you, give you some protection."

"It's a shitty field, but it's all we got." Jose walked away and whistled for his team to gather. Within minutes, boys and young teens in bright orange T-shirts surrounded him. When Kenny squinted, he could see the Dollar General patch on each shirt.

"Wait 'til you hear the cheer. Something lame like, 'Go, shopping.'" Marco wiped his sunglasses off on his shirt and leaned his back against the rickety metal bleachers, so he could face Kenny. "You gonna do it?"

"I don't think he wants me to." Kenny mirrored Marco's sunglasses cleaning.

"He just don't want you to show up once and don't come back no more. Kids never met no one like you. A cop who's a regular dude—some kinda white unicorn. You know, a alien from a distant planet."

"You're so full of shit." Kenny grinned at Marco and shrugged. "If I do it, you do it."

"Duh. But how come you not some hot-shot coach in Bridgeville?" Marco waved at a giggling group of pretty young women and shouted greetings in Spanish.

"Bridgeville overload, dude. I'm fried."

"I feel you." Marco nodded and whistled shrilly through his teeth as Jose's team took the field. "Play ball!"

CHAPTER 28

DURING PETER'S REGULAR EVENING WALK WITH Brutus, Lori Welles called. "So, I'm at a meeting today, representing a client, and who do I see? Brock Fucking Saunders. You will not believe this. He's on the Water Board at the New England Council Consortium."

"Wait. Brock is what? And there's something called the Water Board? This is a shitty practical joke, Lori."

"Swear to God. He's some kind of permanent consultant. Not finance, obviously. I think he's barred for life from anything involving investments."

"What the fuck does Brock know about water? I thought the scuzzbag was busy running his old man's company into the ground."

"Looks like Brock's got something going on with the Consortium. My client says Brock went from like six months on the Zoning Board in Old Bridge to a political appointment with the Consortium."

"Unbelievable." Peter yelled so loud that Brutus turned around to see if he was all right.

"Don't kill the messenger. Hey, you were supposed to come over for a drink last week and you weaseled out."

"So tired, Lor. Like to the bone. I'm working my ass off. Thank God for Marco."

After hanging up with Lori, Peter thought about all the changes he'd seen in the past few years in Bridgeville.

"Brutus, first the goddam builders buy up all the river views. Then they grease the palms of the greedy pigs in town government. And that includes looking the other way on just about everything. Think of all those ridiculous mansions up by Devil's Falls."

For generations, kids bent on getting high, drinking and having sex hung out at Devil's Falls Dam. The beautiful reservoir surrounded by tall pine trees stood far enough away from the dam that most of the partying took place down the hill. Its pristine depths supplied water for surrounding towns and fell under the Consortium's jurisdiction. It set rates and billed residents for their water consumption. New neighborhoods sprouting near the dam boasted starter homes at $500,000.

Marti got the call to set up a tasting of California wines for one of those new neighborhood's ritzy summer block party, right up on the ridge near Devil's Falls. The homeowners bitched at her non-stop about the ignorant old-timers who didn't understand the importance of protecting the newcomers' expensive appraisals and tranquility.

"I don't get how anti-townie these people are," Marti said to Lori as they cuddled on their bed after making love.

"Yeah, there's always been some tension between new and old, but never as bad as now. It's downright nasty."

"So, what's that about?"

"Is this like tell me a story?" When Marti closed her eyes and nodded, Lori tenderly stroked the lion tattoo on her chest before launching into an explanation.

"OK. It's almost a cliché, like old versus new. The new families moving here are pretty worldly and know what they want: great schools, good retail, a pretty downtown, safe neighborhoods."

"Sounds reasonable to me."

"But think about just how much their wants butt up against being frugal, saving money, not being showy, not being greedy—you know, traditional New England values."

"Yeah, but whatever happened to live and let live?"

"Stop being so naïve. Change is guaranteed to be expensive. Plus, the message ends up being insulting: what was good enough for you and your kids isn't good enough for me and mine."

Marti got up on one elbow to make her point. "If you have young well-off families moving into new neighborhoods, you have to change. Build new schools, pass expensive education budgets. It's obvious. The town approved these developments so of course they had to know the infrastructure costs."

"Please. Peter's right about most of the town officials."

"They're not very good at running things."

"To quote the famous Mr. Russo, half of those clowns couldn't run a race."

Marti laughed. "Wow, get over here, you. Open space preservation is at least getting to the top of the to-do list."

"Big bucks, baby girl. And all those new neighborhoods use so much fertilizer, pesticide, insecticide, whatever, for their precious emerald lawns. I mean, that land is ledge."

"I like our weeds. They're kind of neon."

"Let me finish my rant. All the underground sprinkler systems they've installed are gonna run the reservoir dry if this drought lasts much longer."

Bridgeville's small farmers had PhD's in water management and utilization. At the Russo farm, Jeff and Sean enlarged the ponds to capture and store rainwater. He also added micro-irrigation techniques to conserve even more water. But, agricultural interests didn't carry the same weight any more.

"We're an endangered species. Where's our protections?" Jeff's loud complaints found traction. People who loved the rural vistas and cherished the classic New England landscape sought him out. They listened attentively to farmer after farmer who, voices sometimes cracking from the pressure, demanded lower taxes and urgent action.

Jeff and Peter organized potluck dinners to get the farmers to agree on an agenda.

"We can bitch and moan forever. But the fact is John and Jane Q. Public need to get educated about farmland's importance in New England's history and economy," Peter said. "If we don't do it, who will?"

"Just from talking to people we know, about 40 percent of farm owners around here are over sixty. The big question is what happens next?" Jeff addressed the roomful of anxious faces. "Does the farm go to the next generation to work the land or do they sell for beaucoup bucks? We need more protection from developers and banks just waiting like vultures." Jeff waited for dissenting views. There were none.

Town politics grew uglier. The property tax rate climbed steadily, prompting the farmers by the river to petition to secede from Bridgeville.

"Didn't we fight the American revolution about taxation without representation?" Jeff asked.

"Don't you have anything else to do? Get a life," the head of the Zoning Commission demanded after a particularly contentious meeting about approving a right-of-way for yet another gas pipeline.

"Why are you so blind? How many gas pipelines do we need? Mother Nature isn't making any more of what we got. The river used to be a toilet. Now it's clean, and you want to kill it with natural gas." Peter grew so agitated that his spittle sprayed onto the other man's shirt.

But after the Zenergy debacle, which the Hatfield Gazette called, "A spectacular failure of town officials to protect Bridgeville from "corporatocracy," Peter tried to lower his profile.

CHAPTER 29

THE NEW ENGLAND COUNCIL CONSORTIUM FACED an imminent threat unlike any other in its long history. Money, or more accurately, lack of it. The executive board dithered, procrastinated and kicked the can around the table until it was no more than a little nub of metal. But the problem only grew more acute.

Revenue from its core businesses—water and land—had started rolling downhill so fast that they were practically in a freefall.

The Consortium had been approached from time to time by other water and power companies about selling tracts of land or water rights, but nothing ever materialized until Eautopia knocked on the door. When Eautopia decided to jump into the New England water market, it came first to the Consortium, which, uncharacteristically, listened to the pitch. But true to form, the protracted pre-negotiation rituals barely inched forward until Brock Saunders came on board.

Brock now looked like a game show host in a hotly contested battle with Father Time. His brownish-orange sprayed-on tan gleamed. His skin looked smooth and unwrinkled, his thinning hair glossily shellacked like an apricot helmet.

Brock's three failed marriages disemboweled his finances. After resurfacing as the face of Saunders Construction around the time of Peter's Zenergy caper, he made a splash in local Old Bridge politics, running for the Town Council on a platform of cost-cutting and belt-tightening. His narrow loss resulted in a pity appointment to the Zoning Board. Within months, the old-boy political machinery, desperate to make the Hatfield metro region a natural resource player, got him an appointment to the Consortium. His marching orders were clear; bring home the bacon.

Eautopia's patience had been sorely tested by the Consortium's inertia. When Brock learned Eautopia was being courted by a rival for a multi-million dollar bottling deal, he saw his moment.

"Talk to us," Brock urged. "Come back to the table. How can we sweeten the pot?"

"Are you for real?" Brock's Eautopia contact asked.

"Present your plan to the full Board. I guarantee you won't be sorry," Brock said.

Within a few days, Eautopia's senior vice president of Marketing spoke to a specially scheduled meeting of the Consortium's upper echelon of management. Not a single woman or minority graced the room.

"Gentlemen, we have a great opportunity in front of us, a mutually beneficial one. For Eautopia, the deal has obvious benefits. For you, with water usage falling, and lower profits for water, this deal smooths out your revenue stream and expands your product line. I'll leave you now to discuss this among yourselves." With a head nod at Brock, he exited.

"Those goddam energy efficient washers and dryers. They don't just use less electricity, they use less water. And then there's the dishwashers, the toilets, the showerheads. They're a threat to our very survival." The Consortium's Chief Finance Officer snapped his monogramed cufflinks and surveyed the room.

"Don't forget wastewater treatment, sewers, EPA

compliance, and all the thousands of other things we need to stay on top of. Money is getting tight." The Chief Operations Officer played tag-team. "We need to float bonds to upgrade everything. Our rating is going to be in the crapper. We need this cash infusion, or we don't have a chance with all the new state, regional and federal requirements. The penalties for non-compliance are catastrophic."

"Raising prices won't cut it," the now florid-faced CFO declaimed the obvious. "Not this time. The problem is our current business model doesn't work anymore. And we don't have the manpower to fully analyze the deal. It's complicated, and we're short-staffed."

Member towns balked at the rates. The State Legislature had no less than three bills in the House and Senate about oversight and opening up the Consortium's books for scrutiny. The Great Recession had body-slammed the big aerospace companies, their contractors and their subcontractors all the way down to the small mom-and-pop businesses. Consumers still barely had a pulse. Add the evisceration of the submarine base plus an outflux bordering on stampede of high-net worth residents. Palliative care and a fire sale of assets beckoned unless the Consortium struck a bold deal.

Brock spoke up. "Pretty soon, our member towns are going to get it through their thick skulls that they don't need us. Our contracts aren't locked into perpetuity. They're not completely stupid."

"We need this deal. I move for a vote. Eautopia could sign an agreement with another entity; we have to be careful and act fast," the CFO said. "We need to hire someone to run the numbers every which way from Sunday."

The Consortium never enticed any first-tier MBA graduates despite using the top fifty schools as the generous benchmark. Nor did the second-tier, charitably categorized as the next fifty on the US News and World Reports rankings, submit resumes. Although once in a blue moon, in a trend completely opposite to the region's prevailing brain drain, a local newly minted MBA came to the Consortium's attention. They rarely got an interview, but their resumes were printed and kept in a giant file. And that's where the Consortium found Josh, courtesy of his mother.

CHAPTER 30

CLIMBING THE STEEP HILL OF CHURCH MOUNTAIN, Peter saw a feather wafting down from the sky, and had a flashback to the eagle feather he caught before his Zenergy arrest.

"It fell from a sick eagle; the king of the flock was dying. I should've known what it really meant, Brutus." The mossy rock face had sent more than a few people to their deaths, so they kept a healthy distance from the edge. "It was a cry for help."

After Rachel issued her own cry for help getting the food truck up and running, figuring out who to bring on board for helping on the truck still generated some controversy.

"I'd like to give Paco a try, too. Not just Marco." Peter knew he was pushing his luck with Jeff.

"You can get tax credits for hiring ex-cons, you know," Rachel said.

"You mean like your uncle?"

"Or me." Rachel glared at Jeff.

"You don't have a record, sweetie," Jeff said evenly. "We start with Marco. He's got to have a valid driver's license, obviously. Still not comfortable with this, I gotta say."

"C'mon, Jeff. Do you know how hard it is for these guys to get a decent job? We can make drug testing part of hiring him." Peter knew Marco would agree. "Think about it. You write up a contract and he signs it as a condition of employment."

"Yeah, but I'm not just talking about one test. He's got to agree to random testing. I'm not doing it otherwise. And if he fucks up, he's gone. Zero tolerance." Jeff felt his daughter stiffen. "Not you, Rach."

"Oh, yes me. I want the same deal. You can't discriminate."

"Let me try to get this through my thick skull. You want random drug testing?" He looked from Peter to Rachel incredulously.

"Yup. There are like a hundred companies around here who test. Plus, it will help me stay straight. It's pretty common, Dad."

Jeff flinched. "Staying straight is the goal. Whatever helps, I'm in."

Rachel also received the honor of naming the business.

"It's only fair," Peter said. "You're baking the product. The business doesn't exist without you."

"Grate Full Bread," she said over and over. But after reading about her favorite band's notoriety for suing for trademark and copyright infringement, she tried some different permutations on Grateful Dead.

"I've got it. We're calling it Great Full Bread. And I'm betting that the 'G F' in front of Bread will also make people remember that we're gluten-free."

"Hey, did Ben and Jerry's get sued for Cherry Garcia?" Peter idly sketched logos for the truck as they talked.

Rachel showed him some mock-ups she'd done on her laptop. "Check out the groovy flower-power lettering. I'm feeling very late sixties, early seventies, so bright funky colors. I want the truck to be sunshine yellow with big psychedelic flowers, maybe some butterflies and birds."

Rachel's new boyfriend, Zack, the handsome mid-thirties owner of Bridge, a popular bar and restaurant, had set them up with one of his suppliers who was building a kosher catering facility at the old matzo factory in the basement of Temple Beth Shalom. The more they spoke, the more the builder liked the idea of adding a gluten-free dedicated baking facility with the proviso that it had to be kosher. Great Full Bread piggy-backed onto the new facility, with a small commissary for production and handling. Once they got certified as kosher and gluten-free, they were in business.

But it took Rachel night and day to complete the bureaucratic legwork to get the commissary and truck legal. She doggedly shouldered the compliance burden since Jeff made it crystal clear that if he was bankrolling it, she had to be at the top of her game as a baker and co-owner. Peter got Paco a shot in production, helping with the bake.

"Why you call it 'the bake?' Even I know that ain't good English." Paco regarded Rachel with the utmost seriousness.

"That's just what bakers say. It's cool. Don't worry."

"Failure is not an option," Jeff said one too many times. Meeting in his kitchen late in the afternoon with Peter, Zack and Rachel as the brain trust tried to move forward, he repeated his demand for A+ compliance. "Everything by the book; otherwise we're in a deep hellhole with the state."

"Yup, we got reams of paperwork," Rachel said. "And

I'm on it. Listen to this: a plan to present to the Department of Health, what's going to be made on the truck and what's going to be made in a commercial kitchen, background check, a catering commissary license, a food safety manager certificate, a food truck license, a retail sales license, and something called a victualling license. I don't know what the hell that is."

"Vittles, yee-ha." Peter banged a teaspoon against his beer can.

"This dadgum critter stew sure tastes good, Pa." Jeff got in the spirit by shooting imaginary pistols in the air.

"Guys, chill." Rachel stuck two fingers in her mouth and whistled loudly to get their attention. "This is serious. We're using as much locally sourced stuff as possible. Remember, we're doing cheese, so we can't do meat to stay kosher. Cheese and dairy, fruit and veggies—think healthy and trendy. What about a little store?"

"I'll give you a good deal on the produce," Jeff said. "Just 50 percent over cost."

"You're a real sport." Peter tossed a crumpled piece of paper at him but managed to hit Rachel in the forehead.

Tossing the paper back at Peter, Zack read them the riot act against over-extending. "I want you to listen to me since I'm the only one with food business experience. Don't do a store; it will end up being a fucking nightmare. Do farmers markets, the truck and a website where people can order online. You can always get shelf space at local shops."

"He speaks." Peter aimed the crumpled paper at the garbage can and missed. "Do-over, the big kahuna distracted me."

"Hey, I mean it," Zack said, slapping the table with his palms. "The food business is a money pit, and you can lose your shirt. Don't half-ass it."

CHAPTER 31

PETER HADN'T LACKED FOR ACTION AT ANY POINT IN his life, and somehow women were even more attracted to him after Carmen stomped on his heart. He indulged selectively—no brunettes, they reminded him too much of Carmen—but never seriously.

"I'm just having adult fun," he told Nancy when she called him out about being friends with benefits with a woman she loathed.

"You're just as much of a slut as she is. Can't you at least have some taste?"

"What—I need your approval for who I fool around with?"

"I just don't see you with one woman your own age. And why on earth are they so attracted to you?"

"Thanks a lot. Look, nobody's got any expectations about the future. No one's thinking about long-term whatever. A fun evening, some decent sex, sharing a laugh. What's not to like?"

Nancy glared at him and downed her Chardonnay, still enjoying alcohol at that time. Now, she glared at him over a vile protein liquid.

"Men have it so easy. You disgust me."

After Peter let himself back in the house, he checked in with Rachel to see how the bake for tomorrow shaped up.

"We're doing the rosemary olive bread, onion focaccia, strawberry rhubarb tarts, and the usual basics," she said, sounding tired. "I need more help, Pete. Mom sprained her wrist and she can't do the packaging for a while. Paco tries, but he has no patience."

"Sorry, you're carrying the load right now. Paco should be more helpful."

"He needs to be out on the truck with you or Dad. What about that program for wounded vets? Did you find anyone?"

"Maybe, I'm interviewing two tomorrow. If I think they might be decent, I'll bring them over to the commissary."

"Awesome."

"You doing OK, though?" Jeff's words about putting too much pressure on Rachel came back to him.

"Yeah. Just pooped." Rachel hung up, leaving Peter to wander around his house deep in thought.

On a whim, he called Lori to see if she had heard anything about the Consortium doing any new projects in the area. He also wanted more details about what the hell Brock Saunders and his cronies were up to.

"Hey, this water thing with Count Brockula has got me thinking about if the Consortium is doing something fishy. Did you actually talk to him?"

"Yeah. He asked me if I was still playing for the other team, his usual smarmy lounge lizard shtick."

"Asshole."

"There's more. But it'll piss you off."

"Now I gotta hear it. Come on."

"OK, but you asked for it. He wanted to know if I was still your lawyer."

"What's it to him? Like how did he say it?"

"Just like," Lori lowered her voice into a deep range, "looks like your smarts finally caught up with your good looks; representing better clients now, no pathetic losers, no more low-rent trash like Russo."

"I'd like to punch his lights out, the piece of shit."

"Stay away. Don't let him goad you into jeopardizing your probation. It's almost over."

"True. So what do you hear about the Consortium—any buzz?"

"Right, like they would broadcast their intentions. Come on, they play it so close to the vest. You know, using shell companies. There's no way to find out anything unless they did a large land purchase or sale."

"Where would I check?"

"Don't poke the hornet's nest; so not smart."

"I may be dumb but I'm not stupid. I find an envelope full of financial statements and a flash drive inside of a garbage bag inside of a bloody leather jacket tied up with string? In a deep hole weighted down by a cement block and covered by leaves and sticks? Tell me that doesn't set off bells in your brain."

"Hey, it's a turducken. You know, the chicken stuffed into a duck and then stuffed into a turkey."

"Yeah, yeah. So, where do I look, Lor?"

"That's just it. If you don't have any knowledge about where, who and what, it's a total crapshoot. Maybe start searching by town."

"Yeah, but for what? That's the kicker."

"Listen, not to change the subject, but Marti wants some shade-loving perennials by the pond. Can you plant some? And I'll check some databases in the next day or so."

Peter grabbed a handful of peanuts and plopped down on the couch with his laptop. Google yielded nothing of interest when he typed in a few searches about the Consortium. Frustrated, he whistled for Brutus and set off on a walk. The beauty of the trees silhouetted in the starlight took his breath away. Songbirds settled in for the evening, their melodies yielding to the crickets' thrum.

The river twinkled magically, practically bringing him to his knees with its vulnerability.

Back in his kitchen, scratching at some itchy mosquito bites, Peter made a ham sandwich but pushed it away after one unsatisfying bite. Brutus looked at it longingly and got a Milk Bone instead. Peter stalked the piles of his dirty laundry and put on a load, tossing stray socks in the washing machine as he found them. But everything kept dragging him back to how the Consortium snuck the Zenergy fuel cell facility into Bridgeville due to the absolute stupidity of town officials. If the Consortium's ugly agenda had Bridgeville in its rifle scope again, Peter needed to act fast or at least sound the alarm. He fell into an uneasy sleep in the den, tossing and turning so much that Brutus plunked a paw on his face.

CHAPTER 32

PETER CALLED IAN THAT NEXT MORNING AND launched into the saga about finding the mysterious package.

"Why haven't you been working out?" Ian interrupted Peter in mid-sentence. "You won another ten sessions in the library fundraiser auction. Do you rig these things?"

"I'm just a lucky fella. But I really need you to look at this."

"Luck is a fantasy for idiots. Get over here around 3:00; be ready to work hard." Minutes later, Ian followed up with a text message. STAY OUT OF TROUBLE.

When Peter got to BIG just before 3:00, Ian pulled a face as Peter explained about the folder full of documents and showed him the flash drive.

"How is this your business?"

"Look, just try to get the flash drive to work. Nancy says it's password-protected. There's evil in the air, don't you feel it?"

Ian set conditions. "Work out first or no deal. I'm thinking lots of core and Pilates."

"No way. I'm not in the mood to stay cooped up inside. How about a hike up at the reservoir instead?" Peter motioned towards the open door.

"I'm listening. Low-impact cardio could work so long as you tuck your abs. Who's driving, you or me?" Ian grabbed his keys without waiting for a response.

They parked near the dam, stepping over discarded water and energy drink bottles.

"Assholes can't even hold onto their own trash," Peter said with disgust, kicking a pile out of his path and vowing to dispose of it on their way back.

"Terrible—Bridgeville's version of the Three Monkeys. They don't see the evil, they don't hear it, yet they spread it. Unbelievable lack of consciousness. This mess needs picking up."

"Hey, you sound like me. I finally rubbed off on you."

"Please, you unsexy beast; I'm off the market, remember? Celibacy and PARSLEY go together like, I dunno, tea and scones. If you came up with me for a weekend or bothered to listen to anything I say, you'd know this."

Prana and Self-Realization Love Energy Yoga (PARSLEY) exerted a magnetic hold on Ian for the past six years. Meditating with fellow travelers and toiling like a mule pushed all his buttons. At PARSLEY's mosquito-ridden Catskill retreat, he felled trees, dragged them through thick woods and chopped them for firewood. He julienned mounds of carrots and potatoes for giant vats of soup that he stirred with an oar. But he could never talk any of his friends into visiting.

"Ian, all due respect and everything, but there's gotta be a few good-looking women up there who'd like to jump your bones. Lonely, horny and all hot and bothered about world peace just screams 'fuck me,' doesn't it?"

"Only because you think with your cock. Try using the big head instead of the one in your pants for a change. Sex is a distraction, a diversion of important energy. And, I'm hardly lonely. How could I be lonely with you lot in my life? Ian halted abruptly and pointed to a red blanket hanging off a tree. "What's that over there?"

Peter motioned for Ian to wait. "Hold up. I got this. Hey, Sherry," he yelled. "It's Peter Russo. You decent?"

A blondish-gray cloud of hair appeared at the corner of the blanket. "Wait a minute!" A woman's voice yelled hoarsely, and after a few minutes, Sherry Nicholas stepped past the blanket, arms outstretched to Peter. Clad in layers of worn and dirty garments, it was almost impossible to tell if she was fat or slim, male or female.

"Keep your distance," Peter muttered to Ian. "She's living rough and smells to high heaven." Changing his tone immediately, he said, "Sherry, how the hell are you this fine day?" As she got close, he stiff-armed her and patted her on the shoulder. Ian gagged at the whiff of shit and piss.

"Petey, there's weird stuff happening out here, man," Sherry said, her missing teeth showing as she gave a big fetid yawn. "Who's this?" She pointed to Ian.

"Sherry, we've met before, not sure if you remember. When Peter was arrested two years ago?"

Sherry had joined the demonstrations protesting Peter's arrest. She marched enthusiastically, shouting and yelling incoherent phrases. Nancy had taken her into the town hall to clean up in the bathroom and cool down in the air conditioning.

"No." Turning to Peter, she said, "There's bombs here and big yellow tanks. You got anything to drink?"

"Here," Ian said, offering her the metal water flask he brought everywhere.

Sherry cast a disparaging eye at the bottle. "I mean anything good."

"This is good. This is water."

Peter shot him a glance. "You're never going to get it back."

"Not a problem."

Sherry grabbed the flask and drank thirstily. Wiping her dripping chin on her sleeve exposed a streak of weathered skin under the grime on her face. "Come on," she said, motioning to Ian and Peter to follow her.

She took them around the blanket where she proudly pointed to a small tattered pup tent and a rusted metal shopping cart loaded with bulging plastic bags. "I gotta pick up more bottles and cans. Then I'm gonna get some cash."

She carefully put Ian's gift into her tent. After rummaging in her pockets, she extracted some sticks connected together by brightly colored yarn and offered it to Ian. "For you. Now we're even-steven."

"Thank you. It's a lovely, um, dream catcher, isn't it?" He showed it to Peter who nodded. Sherry grabbed it back suddenly and crawled into her tent. Ian and Peter exchanged glances.

"Sherry?" Peter waited and held a finger for Ian to stay put. "Don't go in there."

Sherry wriggled out, ass-backwards, and handed Ian the dream catcher, which now sported two small white feathers. "Ta-da!"

"It's absolutely perfect."

"How 'bout me, Sherry—what am I, chopped liver?" Peter pretended to be hurt.

"Yum, liver. I'm hungry." Sherry rubbed her tummy like a child.

"I'll drop off some muffins and sandwiches from the truck by our usual rock, OK?"

"But no butterscotch. I hate butterscotch." Sherry pouted and whispered, "There's bad things happening by the water, but I'm watching them. I'm keeping an eye on them." She reached into the recesses of her baggy jacket and pulled out a battered pair of glasses.

"OK, you do that." Peter patted her on the back. "I'll see you soon."

"Not if I see you first!"

"Sherry," said Ian. "Let's celebrate this moment near the beautiful pink clover." He led her to a clump of flowering weeds, raised his arms to the sky and encouraged her to do the same. "That's it. In and out, cleansing breaths."

Sherry coughed in harsh rasps and ugly wheezes. Tears streamed from her eyes after the first deep inhalation. Her chest heaved visibly despite being under so many layers, and she pounded her solar plexus.

"Whoa, you don't sound good, Sher." Peter eyed her with concern. "I'll leave you some tea and honey, too." Sotto voce to Ian, he said, "I don't trust her with a bottle of Robitussin."

As Sherry wiped her cheeks with the back of her hands, Ian mulled the situation. "What about these little green men?"

"Blue meanies," Sherry said. "With yellow tanks."

"All right—we're gonna go." Peter started shuffling his feet. He shot Ian a warning glance and quickly drew a finger across his throat to get him to shut up. "See ya soon, Sherry baby." Peter blew her a kiss that she caught and tucked in her pocket.

137

Ian held up the dream catcher and touched his heart.

Walking back to the car, Peter and Ian fell silent. The pleasant scent of pine trees filled the cool air.

"Goddammit. She's really hallucinating."

"She could be a seer." Ian mused thoughtfully as he tested a low hanging branch with his weight, stretching his back and shoulders. "Feels so good. Try it."

"No. Hey, Sherry didn't give you the dream catcher for nothing. Use the spiritual energy, brother, and aim it at the flash drive."

"Oh, I will. Even if I can't crack the password, I'm going to put the dream catcher on it overnight, let the power swirl."

"Go for it. Shit, I don't like the way her cough sounded."

CHAPTER 33

NANCY ANXIOUSLY INTERROGATED PETER OVER THE phone.

"Did you pull the front door shut really tight like I asked you to? You swear you didn't forget?"

"No, of course not. I'm not an idiot. Why?"

"Someone was in my house. I'm sure of it. I'm totally freaked out."

"No way. Maybe one of your kids dropped over. Or it could have been a big gust of wind." Peter tried to recall if he actually had shut the door firmly and settled on a definite maybe.

"Did the wind turn my closet light on and open my desk drawers? And you know Justin or Alex would never just drop by. The only time they ever reach out is when they need money, and right now we're not speaking. Someone was in my house, I'm telling you."

"Come on. You probably just don't remember doing those things. You've got a lot on your mind what with the surgery coming up. Stop being so jumpy."

"Peter whatever you're doing with those damn documents—leave me the hell out of it. I really don't want to get on the wrong side of the Consortium. I don't want to be even a blip on their radar."

"Message received loud and clear." Peter didn't mention his sneaking suspicion that somehow Brock's sudden appearance on the Water Board and the baffling documents were connected. In fact, he didn't mention Brock at all.

"Good, they're worse than the KGB. Let it go. Not one drop of blowback on me."

"Nance, are you turning into a chicken in your old age?"

"Who you calling old? Absolutely nothing can screw up my surgery. I would blow the devil right now, down on my knees in broad daylight, to keep it from going off the rails."

"Take it easy. Just kidding."

"You don't get it. Getting the loose skin cut off after the gastric sleeve is on my dime. I'll have to borrow against my house unless I get a miracle. I'll take a bad one or a good one."

"What's a bad miracle? All miracles are good, aren't they? Come on, Nance. Lighten up."

Nancy bulldozed over his voice. "Like maybe I almost die, and when I wake up, I'm completely fine and down a hundred pounds, and they've cut off all the excess skin while I was in a coma. That's a bad miracle."

"Stop it. That's sick. And not like the kids mean it."

"No shit."

"Look, just chill out. I'm going to work with Paco to see how he does on the truck. You know, kind of a trial basis with the eating public. Jeff's not too sure about him—he's got a short fuse, almost as bad as yours. There's nothing to worry about."

CHAPTER 34

JOHN TOMASSI, OF ALL PEOPLE, GAVE PETER A CLUE about why the Consortium could be projecting massive profits from selling water.

Peter had asked just about everyone if they'd heard anything new about the local water. He still didn't know anything more than Nancy's insight from the first day. Peter decided to keep Jeff out of it, just like Zenergy. Copping to paranoia, he kept the documents and flash drive inside a small lockbox under his doomsday larder of canned tuna, beans, dog food, and soup. He kept the key close, adding it to his jingly omnipresent key chain.

After stopping at the library with some fresh strawberries for Miss Pampuro, the elderly reference librarian who never tired of answering his questions, Peter saw Tomassi browsing in the large-print New Arrivals section.

"John," he said, clapping Tomassi on the back. "I didn't know you could read."

"Funny. So funny, I forgot to laugh."

"For your mom?"

"Yeah, now that I took away her car—remember when she drove into the roundabout the wrong way and caused all kinds of mayhem?" He didn't wait for Peter's response. "So now, I'm paying for my good deeds. Look at this romance shit I gotta look through. If it's got sex, she doesn't want it. And no technology, either. Just heaving bosoms in corsets."

"Hey, you like those. So, you hear anything about new plans for water around here?"

"You mean like drinking water?"

"Yeah. I heard something interesting might be happening." Peter deliberately kept his voice light and his inquiry vague.

Tomassi shifted his weight from one foot to the other and put the books down on an empty shelf. "Maybe. You ever heard of the outfit called Eautopia?"

"Oh-what?"

"Yeah, I kid you not. Eautopia." Tomassi spelled it for Peter. "You know Donna's on Patty Lennon's real estate team or whatever the hell it's called. Donna does a lot of legwork with potential clients, so Patty can take home the bacon."

"Patty rakes it in, she's not shy, no doubt about it. So, what the hell does this have to do with water?" Peter waved to the librarian at the checkout desk who made shushing noises. "Hey. inside voice, loudmouth."

"Like you should talk. Didn't you pay attention back in French class? Eau is water." Tomassi punched it into his Google app and showed Peter the translation.

"Eautopia is a water company? A water utopia company? I don't get it. What's the tie-in?"

"I don't know, but what I'm trying to tell you, moron, is Donna's been showing some houses in Bridgeville to some Eautopia honchos who are relocating for business purposes, and the referral to Team Patty came from the Consortium."

"Well, now. Very interesting."

"I wouldn't read much into it. People move all the time."

Peter whipped out his phone and searched for Eautopia. "Shit. They're a big water-bottling company. Ginormous. Listen to what Wikipedia says, 'the company is expansion-minded and flush with cash . . . looking to expand operations to New England.' Like what—they're gonna bottle the water from here?"

Tomassi let out a low whistle. "That's crazy. Don't go jumping to cockamamie conclusions. It's not like the Consortium can sell our water to a bottling company."

"They damn well better not. I gotta tell Ian. This could be the key."

"The key to what? And how come you're so hot to trot about this in the first place?"

Peter hemmed and hawed. Finally, he said, "John, I really can't share that with you."

"Don't fuck with me. Why not?"

"Because then I'd have to kill you."

"What. Did. You. Do?" Tomassi loomed larger than life, directly in Peter's face.

Peter shook his head. "Nothing. Take it easy, I'm just kidding. Hey, listen, off the record," Peter lowered his voice, "what happens if a person picks up property that might be stolen? I mean literally picks it up from the ground."

Tomassi glowered at him. "Possession of stolen goods is a crime, asshole. What the hell are we talking about?"

"Nothing. Just shootin' the breeze."

"So help me God, I find out you're violating your agreement and poking your nose where it don't belong— your ass is mine."

"Relax, I'm not violating anything."

Tomassi snorted. "Tomorrow's my day off. After I get done with all the 'Honey-do's' that Donna's been saving for me, then you and me are going to have a little sit-down."

"John, you're getting all hot and bothered over nothing." He patted Tomassi's shoulder in parting. "Stick to the bosoms."

CHAPTER 35

AFTER HUSTLING OUT OF THE LIBRARY, PETER DROVE to the Dairy Queen in West Hadley, the opposite direction Tomassi would be going.

Peter always ordered his favorite, a chocolate M & M Blizzard, which made him think about Marco. He'd come a long way, and Peter couldn't imagine Great Full Bread working without him. Marco had bonded with Rachel and pitched in to help whenever he could.

Peter licked the last traces of his Blizzard from the red plastic spoon and resolved to give Marco a raise. He called Jeff, who didn't pick up until the fifth ring.

"Hey, I'm just finishing up the lunch at Hatfield Medical Center. We sold out of everything, practically. What's up?"

"Just thinking—we need to pay Marco more. You on board?"

"Yeah, definitely. I gotta say I was wrong. Can't talk now. Paco needs me."

Still sitting in his car, Peter searched on his phone using every combination of Eautopia, Bridgeville, water bottling, and the Consortium that he could think of. He came up empty-handed except for a chart of Eautopia's water bottling operations in the Midwest and a recent press release for a big national deal with Walmart.

"We better not be part of that."

Peter called Marco but went straight to voicemail. Shrugging, he decided the coast was clear enough to head home.

"So, how come you start messin' around with dope?" Marco casually asked Rachel that afternoon at the commissary when they were making an extra batch of bread to freeze.

"Wow, you're pretty direct. And nosy." Rachel scowled, her tone gone cold. She took off her sanitary gloves and threw them on the floor.

"No disrespect. I know it ain't my business, but we workin' together, and we cool. I see you so smart, a real hard worker. It just don't add up. A guy get you started, someone you hung with?

Rachel challenged his eyes as she leaned forward. "Yeah, a guy. A fucking middle-aged dentist if you really want to know."

"Oh, man. Oxy from the tooth fairy? No fuckin' way."

"Way." Rachel checked on her ear piercings, twisting each one back and forth, a process she repeated three times. "How you like me now? A poster girl for stupid."

"Don't say that; it ain't true. What—you get hooked from your wisdom teeth and then no more oxy?" Marco folded his arms and leaned back against the wall, watching her closely.

"Yeah, I got a really bad infection that went on forever, and the only thing that worked on the pain—" Rachel shrugged. "Then I couldn't get any more, and people I knew got me some dope. Plus I failed two science classes at community college, so everything sucked."

"Except gettin' high. I feel you."

Rachel picked at her cuticles. "We're never gonna have this conversation again."

"Deal. Busted twice and doin' time ain't somethin' I wanna talk about no more. So stop bringin' it up."

Rachel burst out laughing and clapped her hands. "I wanted to be a veterinary tech so bad, but I bite at bio and chem." Rachel looked at Marco ruefully as he picked up her gloves and put them in the trash. "Thanks. Sorry about the hissy fit. You know, it's a big stupid joke—just loving animals doesn't help."

"Who laughin' now? Baking's chemistry, dude."

"Yup, chemistry I care about. I want to kick ass on Great Full Bread. Please don't say everything happens for a reason. So help me, I'll scream if I hear it one more time."

"Yeah, that's some bullshit."

CHAPTER 36

ANNIE SURPRISED PETER BY SHOWING UP FOR JEFF'S Saturday morning shift after Peter beeped the horn twice outside the farmhouse's side door.

"Hey, those hormones are kicking in, bro." He peered at her through the pre-dawn darkness and laughed.

"Yeah, you want some?" Annie grinned as she pointed to the tight neon-green Great Full Bread T-shirt stretching to accommodate her ample curves before climbing into his truck. "Sean's got a stomach bug so Jeff's a farmer again, at least for the day."

"Sucks for Sean. We got lots of ball fields today. Your wrist gonna be OK? Just follow my lead."

"Uh, you're only talking to the concession-stand queen of the universe. I can sell upside down, blindfolded and hanging over the Grand Canyon. C'mon, let's get this show on the road." She turned on the radio, scanning through stations until she found Bon Jovi's *It's My Life*. Cranking up the volume, she sang surprisingly tunefully at top volume, punching Peter in the arm to join her on the chorus.

They bellowed in unison on the drive to the commissary to pick up the freshly loaded food truck. Grabbing steaming hot cups of coffee provided by Aaron, the very capable preparation worker Peter hired from the wounded vets program, they went over the day's specials. The Great Full Bread truck, its neon hues immaculately buffed and shiny, attracted crowds at hour-long stops in West Hadley and Bridgeville, finally arriving at the Hatfield ball field where Kenny and Marco were co-coaching the Dollar General team.

"I gotta take a wicked whizz. Can you handle things by yourself for a minute?" Peter shifted uncomfortably, his bladder bursting.

"If I take off my shoes and count on my toes, maybe I'll be able to make change. Go pee before you embarrass yourself." Annie moved over to the counter and greeted the people waiting in line. "Men."

"Ay, por favor," the woman closest to the front said with a chuckle. "Men."

Annie sold out all the churros and arepas by the time Peter hustled back.

"Wow," he said. "You're good."

"Duh. Hey, I like this. Put me in, coach."

"Talk to your lesser half. I bet he'll even let you keep the tips." Peter pointed admiringly at the cup brimming with dollar bills and quarters.

The crowd cheered and chanted loudly for their teams, banging on the bleachers and razzing the home plate umpire. Relatives and friends of every age monitored toddlers who trundled behind the backstop, seeking shelter from the hot sun and release from their sweaty strollers.

Kenny, eyes inscrutable behind mirrored cop glasses and under a Herrings baseball cap, jotted down notes on a clipboard as Dollar General batted in the bottom of the second inning. They had one out, with runners on first and second. Jose stood by third base and clapped his hands.

Marco, coaching on the first-base side, kept up a running stream of encouragement. "Good eye. You got this, dude." Getting the attention of the runner on second base and shouting into the ear of the kid on first, he yelled, "Rapido—on contact."

The batter hit a sizzling ground ball straight to the shortstop who tossed it to the second baseman. After a slight bobble during the transfer from his mitt to his throwing arm, the second baseman executed a balletic pivot and crisp throw to first base.

"Next time, man," Marco said to the dejected batter whose lunge to the bag had no chance to prevent the double play.

As Dollar General prepared to take the field, Kenny called the batter over to him.

"Sweet swing, Ricardo. You waited for your pitch." Kenny held out his fist for a bump. The upset youngster brightened at Kenny's praise.

"I keep hitting into double plays. I'm sorry, Coach Kenny."

"Hey, no sorry. You're due, buddy. Just gotta find you a bat with a hit in it." Kenny selected a bright silver and green bat from the pile near him and handed it to Ricardo.

"Use this one next time. Now grab your mitt, get out to right field and catch us some fly balls."

Marco crouched over the third-baseman's cleats, quickly tying triple knots. Sending him on his way with a tap on the head, Marco walked over to Kenny and complained. "Kids these days. You see him lose his shoe last inning?"

Peter and Annie sold out completely, while the adjacent Mister Softee ice cream truck, hot dog vendor, and kids' lemonade stands enjoyed brisk business. The smell of grilled meat and red-hot charcoal briquettes wafted through the air. Salsa, reggaeton, and hip hop thumped in competing rhythms.

Peter got out to watch his proteges coach their team to a bases-loaded walk-off double by none other than Ricardo. Mobbed by jubilant teammates, he glowed with excitement. Kenny, Jose, and Marco gathered the team to slap hands with the opposing players, and then they all got in a circle and jumped up and down, with Marco leading the hollering and Kenny bouncing around, low-fiving each kid.

"God, I love seeing this." Peter almost got teary as he and Annie clapped for the team until their hands stung.

"Your boys, Pete. You must've done something right."

Peter walked over to congratulate them, but Marco, now happily making out with his latest girlfriend, and Kenny, swarmed by his players who begged him to stay for a post-game party, weren't close enough for more than a smiling thumbs-up.

Nancy burst Peter's bubble that night when he dropped by for a beer.

"Carmen said to say hi when I saw her the other day."

"Do tell?" Peter's face lit up.

"She looks terrific and very happy in love."

"Good to hear. Wait, what?" Peter grabbed his not quite empty beer bottle to protect it from Nancy's brandishing of the recycling bin. "Hey, I'm not done yet."

"She's hot to trot with this rich financial advisor. They've been an item for like three months now." She saw Peter's face fall and paused. "Oh, come on. You two are never ever getting back together. Be honest with yourself for a change."

Peter put his beer down abruptly and glared at her. Nancy and Carmen had never warmed up to each other, despite Peter's eagerness for everyone to be friends.

"I don't know, there's something about her I don't trust at all," Carmen said. "She plays the percentages, very what's-in-it-for-me."

Nancy, for her part, didn't like Carmen's self-confidence. "She is so used to male approval, she doesn't doubt herself for a second. Nobody should be so convinced they rule the world just because they're good-looking."

But for Peter's sake, they tried to make nice. After Becky died, Nancy made an effort to be friendlier. It felt easier without Peter between them.

Peter looked over at the TV. Pamela Anderson in an old Baywatch episode pranced sexily on the beach. If he closed his eyes, he could almost picture Carmen strutting naked towards him.

"Hey, Earth to Major Tom. Move on, already. Not just casual sex, either. You know—a life partner, someone who really gets you."

"Just thinking about the food truck. We're going gangbusters. Best decision me and Jeff ever made. I should go get things ready for tomorrow." Peter felt a chill up his spine at Nancy's words. She dropped the occasional hint, but Peter made a point of ignoring them. This one felt too much like a baited fishhook.

"It's taking up like all your time. Get more help if you can."

"Already on the to-do list. Marco's going great, and there's hope for Paco."

"Have Marco tell Paco to smile more at least. You'd think he could manage that, especially since you did a big favor by hiring him."

"Look, he runs hot and cold. Paco's a good guy."

Ian hadn't gotten back to Peter about the flash drive. Peter called him a few times but went straight to voice-mail with no response, irritating the hell out of him.

"Listen," Peter said after the beep. "Just tell me if you got the flash drive to work. And if you don't want to do it, man up and say so." Finally, on Sunday, Peter called Andre to see what he knew about Ian's radio silence.

"Up at the retreat, again," Andre said. "It's a no-phone zone. But, if I didn't know any better, I'd swear he met someone."

"Like a woman, you mean? Come on."

"I'm just saying. So what can I do you for? You wanna train?"

"Nah, I just wanted to pick Ian's brain about how to get hard-to-find information."

"I'll help you—things are slow today. Who's this for?"

Peter had no problem trusting Andre's search skills. Ian relied on Andre's creative problem solving more and more after tasting victory with Zenergy.

"You loved it, admit it, man. Let's roll out a side hustle. You got the license, so you're the face of the business. A butt-ugly face, but whatever." Andre sense of purpose was palpable. "I'll do back-office ops."

They had to overcome a high hurdle first because of Ian's big mouth. When he publicly questioned the Bridgeville PD's commitment to getting things right instead of finished, he pissed off more than a few people.

"The Bridgeville police were lazy, quick to implicate and content with circumstantial evidence," Ian said to a gathering in Peter's honor at BIG. "Just because the attack happened the night Peter finished planting does not make him guilty Yes, he had blood on his hands and the shovel, but it was his own blood from being such a clod."

Peter winced. "Ian, no. Don't say stuff like that."

"What, you're a clumsy oaf?"

Vic, who surprised everyone by showing up, cautioned him. "Hey, you ever heard of not biting the hand that feeds you?"

"They don't feed me anything," Ian said.

"Look, genius. You gotta get along to go along." Vic jabbed a carrot stick loaded with ranch dip in Ian's face. "If you want to work around here, you gotta get with the program. You just popped your cherry. Not exactly a track record, so don't go thinking you're such hot shit."

"I feel you," Andre jumped in. "We could do some clinics for kids and Special Olympics that the cops organize. But," he said, pulling a visibly annoyed Ian into a corner of the gym away from Vic, "we should take on some more cases."

"What a total wanker. Wait, we?"

"We, you heard right. C'mon—it's a guaranteed money-maker. And we did something good by getting Skippy put away."

"True." Ian thought for a few minutes. "Right, why not? Let's give it a go."

By year-end, Believe Investigations Group (BIG) came to life.

"Hold on," Peter said after hearing the name. "You guys are already BIG. Won't that confuse people?"

"Nah," Andre said. "We already own the name and we gave ourselves permission to use it."

"Yeah." Ian slapped Andre's waiting hand. "We promised not to sue."

CHAPTER 37

WHEN IAN FINALLY RETURNED FROM THE CATSKILLS that Sunday night after Tomassi set things in motion about Eautopia, he stopped by Andre's. Finding Andre sitting with Peter at the dining room table, typing on his laptop and printing documents, Ian did a double-take and then lay down on the floor to do his favorite lateral rotation stretches.

"Sorry, I was going to call you back, Peter."

"Yeah, well, Andre's on it. Although, I still feel like this is more up your alley."

"Why?"

"It's kind of an unusual client—Mother Nature."

Andre chuckled at Peter's phrasing. "Be good to mama and mama'll be good to you."

"Right. How's her net worth looking these days?" Ian asked.

"Ha ha. Listen, I heard some water-bottling company called Eautopia is expanding into our area, and the Consortium is cozy with them. Basically, I want to find out if they've got a secret deal." Peter pointed at Ian. "It's probably on the flash drive, you know—the one you were allegedly working on."

"And I've been telling Peter no way in hell is there a deal to sell water from here. We're in the middle of a big-ass drought. I can't find anything. Your source is wrong or at least he better be."

"I don't think so. This is a pretty solid lead."

Ian leaned his legs against the wall and sighed content-edly. "Great hamstring stretch. Nothing like it."

Andre and Peter looked at each other and then looked at Ian.

"Who the hell are you, man?" Andre asked.

"Yeah." Peter threw up his hands. "The world's going to shit and you're happily stretching?"

"Maybe he's finally right," Andre said to Peter. "It's the apocalypse."

Lori left a message for Peter on his cellphone. Then she texted him twice and sent an email. They all said the same thing: Call me—it's important.

Peter and Marco worked like dogs in the hellish heat. They grilled non-stop to give the long line of customers what they wanted. The steamy late-June weather created misery, with temperatures in the nineties and high humidity.

"Glad I hit up Twitter last night to let everyone know we at the park today. Did Spanish and English shout-outs, so I'm like head of the United Nations and all."

"Mad skills, Marco."

"'bout time you knew that." Marco took a rag and wiped down the countertop, trying to get rid of all the condensation.

When they ran out of almost everything except for the ice-cold bottles of water and iced tea that the kids from the playground lined up for, Marco made another pitch for adding a Latin frozen treat called paletas.

"What's a paleta again?" Peter's sweat ran in rivers down his face and arms. He couldn't mop it up fast enough.

"Like ice pops but a million times better. Not so sweet and got like real fruit not some high fructose corn syrup shit. Bridgeville's got fruit everywhere. It fits nice with the whole local angle. You gotta give it a shot. Big fan favorite."

Marco still had some bounce in his step, but Peter leaned wearily against a tree. He couldn't take it any more in the truck, so they parked in the shade at Abigail Adams Park. Some people approached the truck, but Marco had hand-printed a sign that said Sold Out and, below it in Spanish, No Mas. Peter hated seeing them walk away disappointed.

"They got some crazy good flavors like piña colada, strawberry pineapple, blackberry orange, mango—you name it. Ima bring you one tomorrow."

"I could use a dozen of those right now." Peter finally managed to reach into his pocket for his buzzing phone, and he quickly called Lori.

"What's up?"

"It took you long enough. I texted you yesterday."

"Sorry, just finished the lunch. It's so fucking hot that I can barely move."

"So take a shower when you get home, and plan on staying for dinner. We want to talk to you."

"Am I in trouble?"

"Yes, no, maybe."

CHAPTER 38

MARCO AND PETER HOSED DOWN THE TRUCK IN THE shade by the commissary. Aaron scrubbed it from top to bottom after they finished.

By the time Peter got home, Brutus was waiting impatiently to play tug-of-war with his favorite rope toy. Peter tried to oblige but even Brutus could tell that he had nothing in the tank.

The long cold shower he took felt like a gift from the gods. Peter donned clean shorts and a T-shirt. Uncharacteristically for him, he gulped two glasses of water instead of beer.

He drove over to Lori's and Marti's house, with Brutus half out the window. Brutus bounded in first to see if Murphy, their standard-sized schnauzer, wanted to wrassle.

Marti ushered him onto the screened-in porch overlooking the fields, and Peter gratefully accepted a refreshingly cold and highly potent gin and bitter lemon, a cocktail they introduced him to.

"OK, I'm practically human now. What's happening?" Peter chewed on the slice of lime from his drink and kept it between his teeth, flashing a smile like Marlon Brando in Godfather Part 1.

The women scooched together on the rattan wicker sofa and started to do what looked like a hula dance. When Peter couldn't puzzle out what the hell they were doing, Marti and Lori beamed at him, holding up their left hands. "We're getting married!" They waved their matching diamond engagement rings under his nose.

"Hey, I get it now. Fantastic. Mazel tov—it's about time, you two." After kissing each one on the cheek, he sat up more attentively. "Tell me, when's the wedding?"

"I think you're going to love this," Lori said excitedly. "Try September 23, the night of the Harvest Moon."

"Don't forget the Blood-Red moon and the eclipse." Marti grabbed a chip out of Peter's hand and ate it.

"Oh, man—all at once? That's perfect for the wedding of the century."

"Peter, we really want Great Full Bread to bake lots of gluten-free goodies for the wedding," Marti said, going over to the table and grabbing a notebook. "Yeah, I'm in warrior planning mode." Lori rolled her eyes. "Hey, I saw that. So, 'no' is not an option."

"Are you kidding? Y-E-S." He looked at her spreadsheet carefully. "We'll get all hands on deck."

"Terrific." Marti wrote GFB at the left side of the catering tab. She had printed something else on the right side, but Peter couldn't read it. "So, this is what we're thinking: enough gluten-free bread, cookies, and apple pies for 150 people."

"What? All of your guests?"

"No, I just meant that's how many are invited. Figure 25 percent of them will go for the gluten-free option." Marti used her phone calculator and said, "So 37.5."

"You're inviting half a person? This I'd like to see. Who's your caterer?"

"Carmen." Lori let the information sink in for a beat. "We're doing it up at Fiori Orchards."

"Carm's a helluva cook. Does she know about you asking me?"

"She'll be fine with it."

"OK, I better wear something loose because she's so good that just thinking about this makes my pants too tight. What?" Marti and Lori cackled. "Grow up, you two. Talk about immature."

"Sooo, that's settled." They linked arms and moved closer to Peter.

"Now what? I promise to behave. Carm and I are on decent terms even though I hear she's dating some tycoon."

"That's not it," Lori said. "We want you to do the wedding ceremony. We would be thrilled if you would officiate. I checked; you can become a Universal Life Minister so it's legal. Will you do it?" They hovered near him, waiting for his response.

"In a heartbeat, absolutely. I'm so honored. Wow— maybe I can start my own religion, too. The right Reverend Russo. It's got a nice shake, rattle and roll to it, don't you think?"

A few days later, Peter asked to sit down with them to discuss what they wanted in the sermon.

"I really like calling it a sermon. Do you have any objections, my child?"

"Whatever you want to call it, just make it good," Lori said.

"I love the whole Harvest Moon connection. It's like a big valentine to the past. Farmers always depended on a good harvest moon." Peter showed them a well-worn photo album his mother had made. "Look at my pops and uncles bringing in the harvest by the light of the moon."

"I know, we used to celebrate the Harvest Moon, too. It was like a ritual." Lori tried to explain to Marti. "We'd go out into the backyard after dinner, build a small bonfire and just watch the sun and the moon in nature's magic show. We could see the sun setting in the west while the moon was rising in the east. We pretended we were drinking moonshine."

"In Jersey, we celebrated not being killed in Newark or mugged in New York," Marti said. "You guys had such charmed lives."

"Yes and no," Peter said. "All the kids helped out with the harvest, and it took every ounce of energy and then some. When the moon came out Dad and the uncles would let us have beer. I bet your moonshine was ginger ale."

"So, since we're committed to the Harvest Moon and Carmen's orchard, apples are the theme." Marti laced her fingers through Lori's.

"Fiori's is a perfect place for an apple wedding." Peter nodded appreciatively. "Tell me more. Are you guys gonna hyphenate your names or invent one? I love this stuff."

"If you are so into wedding plans, you've gotta get back up into the saddle, Pete." Lori arched an eyebrow at him. "You *are* going to bring a special someone to the wedding, right?"

"Yeah, Brutus. He's my plus one—I'm in a committed relationship with him."

"Why not?" Marti shrugged. "It's outdoors. What's the worst he can do?"

"You're talking about a dog who thinks licking his balls is the ultimate. His life is all about a good bone, a good nap and a good dump."

"Don't all males think that way?" Lori asked, squeezing Marti's knee.

CHAPTER 39

FIORI ORCHARDS HOSTED A FEW WEDDINGS EVERY summer, and Lori had her heart set on getting married there. Yankee Bride Guide called the location, "an authentic and magnificent venue for a classic New England summer wedding." With a bewitching charm, the orchard's acres of mature apple trees graced the rolling hills overlooking the river and valley.

Lori and Carmen had a mutual admiration society Marti happily joined when she and Lori got serious. Carmen's benevolent dictatorship of Fiori Orchards extended to her idiot brothers. She paid them small salaries and basic benefits on the condition they butt out. After her divorce, she double-downed on improving the orchard's profitability and community service outreach.

Lori and Marti didn't dare interrupt the epic Scrabble match between Aldo and Jimmy. With a wave, they made themselves comfortable on the patio under the big shade umbrella and waited for Carmen to finish a phone conversation.

Carmen sighed after she hung up but rallied as she turned her attention to her friends.

"We've got something to cheer you up," Lori said. "Here's the date we want. Tell me you don't get the total greatness of our plan." She handed Carmen a spiral-bound calendar from the golf course and pointed to a red circle.

"I love it. September 23 is perfect for your wedding—the Harvest Moon. And it's perfect for us, too. We stop booking after the 15th, but for you two, we're wide open. Thank God, I scheduled the Bocce-b-que before Labor Day. I'll have time to recover. Some of those old-timers can barely walk, but they play all-out bocce, booze it up and chow down like starving wolves. I'll save you some grappa."

"Do they still do the whole roast pig plus every kind of pasta?" Lori, a veteran of Fiori family dinners, still could recall overeating to the point of nausea.

"Yeah, we do the pig, brisket, turkey, lasagna, manicotti, calzone, eggplant parm; it's insane, total gluttony. I would die if I ate a quarter of what they eat."

Carmen started to talk in a stream of consciousness monologue about what she envisioned as the most kick-ass wedding for Lori and Marti.

"I see a huge white tent up on the ridge, a dance floor, a stage for the band, strings of twinkling lights, stunning floral arrangements, passed hors d'oeuvres, a three-course meal, and plenty of booze."

"Is that all?" Lori joked

"No, just for you I'm making sure all of the toilets are working in the pavilion."

"Now that's the ultimate wedding present," Marti said, offering Carmen a high-five. "I've got the wine and bar covered."

"I made some dishes for you to try." Carmen placed small plates in front of Marti and Lori. "Taste."

"Don't tell me—stuffed zucchini flowers from the gardens? They're gorgeous," Lori dug into a plump blossom and moaned with pleasure.

"Sinful." Marti stole some off Lori's plate. "I can't decide if I like the cheese or meat filling better."

Carmen listened carefully as Lori shared what she and Marti wanted.

"A rustic chic vibe," Lori said, laughing as Carmen rolled her eyes. "Come on, you know what I mean. No fancy lace table linens and gold-plated settings. Picture this: long wooden farm tables set simply but with beautifully arranged white flowers in glass vases."

"Absolutely no pretentious bullshit. And a huge bonfire after the eclipse," Marti added.

"Terrific." Carmen took notes on her iPad. "People could make their own s'mores or just sit. What about music?"

"Astral Plane, our friend Sam's cover band. They're amazing."

"Yeah, terrific choice. Now, since you're going with the apple theme, I want to do a signature cocktail, like an Appletini, but better. Then, I'm thinking a basic field green salad with ripe tomatoes and local goat cheese for the first course. For entrees, a choice of either grilled chicken or pork with apple salsa, chilled string beans vinaigrette and garlic roasted potatoes. Any vegans? And I came up with a great sour apple sorbet for a palate cleanser before you guys cut the cake. What do you think?"

"Love it," Lori and Marti said together. Then Lori brought up the baked goods. "You know Great Full Bread is baking all of the gluten-free bread and cookies. I already arranged it with Peter. He said it won't be a problem on his end. What about for you?"

"Of course not. We're OK-ish. Rachel or Jeff will probably do the coordinating, anyway."

"He knows you're seeing someone. Nancy told him, but I haven't said boo. What about you, Marti?"

"No, nothing. You two are grown-ups, so I don't get the big deal."

"Let's talk about the cake." Carmen gestured dismissively at the conversation's detour.

"Yeah, some kind of salute to apples and mythology," Marti said. "Like the opposite of the usual Eve and the apple symbolizing the fall of mankind, blah, blah, blah— everything's all the woman's fault. Let's bring in some cool references to apples and their love powers."

"So, my guys could blast out a few apple ice sculptures with a chainsaw." Carmen started to sketch apples on a piece of paper. "We could make the cake look like an apple or use marzipan and icing to decorate apple images along the top and up the sides." She furrowed her brow in concentration as her pencil danced along the paper. "Like this."

"Yes, perfect." Lori hugged herself with excitement. "Marti, that'll work so great with Peter's ideas. I can't wait to hear the rough draft of his sermon."

"Oh my God," Carmen laughed. "Pete's marrying you? You've got to be kidding me."

"He's totally into it. He's going to be great," Marti said. "But don't ask Reverend Russo to do you and your honey."

"Never happening." After Lori and Marti left, Carmen found herself chuckling randomly throughout the day. "Reverend Russo. Please."

CHAPTER 40

IAN AND PETER SETTLED IN AT PETER'S TO WATCH the lightweight boxing match between Mikey Garcia and Dejan Zlaticanin on pay-per-view. It was over after Round Three on a technical knockout.

"Boy, talk about a bust," Ian said as he lay back on the pillows. "Imagine if you paid full price for those outrageous tickets."

"For a Brahmin or whatever, you sure like violence. Zlaticanin looked too lean, I think he dropped down too many weight classes."

"He didn't have it. Sometimes we should just be what we are."

"True. Say, the flash drive still bugs me. I know you explained it, but what's an encrypted drive, again?"

"It's a pricey item that has a self-destruct mechanism built into it. There's software that's called write-protection and by using third-party tools—"

"So it's a doomsday scenario. It goes nuclear on itself."

"Yes, sort of. Basically, yes."

"So why the hell didn't you say so? What it means is we'll never be able to access what's on the drive, right?"

"Yup. You still have the documents, though. Not that they'll get you anywhere. The universe doesn't want you involved. Listen to what it's telling you."

"That's not how I roll."

"Unfortunately." Ian sighed. "Tell me more about Sherry. She seems so out of place here, yet it's her hometown."

"It's not a good bedtime story." Peter poured himself another brandy.

"Yeah, but I'm all grown up now, Mum. I think I can hear the scary story. And go easy on the alcohol."

"Sure I can't tempt you?" Peter held the bottle of Remy Martin in the air. "It puts hair on your balls."

Ian chuckled. "Tell me her story." He settled comfortably, curling his legs under a red fleece Red Sox blanket.

"You gotta get yourself one of these babies. Look how cozy you are."

"Sod off and tell me about Sherry."

"OK." Peter took a long pull on his drink. "She got fucked in the—what is it Warren Buffett calls it? Right, the uterine lottery. With an alcoholic mother and an evil sonofabitch for a father, she had no chance. She's the youngest of four or five kids, the only girl. We didn't know jack back then, and nobody talked, but Sherry no doubt was a punching bag and sex toy for her old man, the piece of shit. I can't remember all of her brothers, but I know at least one died in 'Nam. Maybe two."

"Poor Sherry. There's no justice—just awful."

"Wait, there's more. Sherry was really pretty, I know—hard to believe. She knew her way around men, let me tell you. Makes sense, unfortunately. Male teachers drooled over her, and she used it. She could get out of anything—cutting class, failing a test. She split as soon as she graduated high school, I mean she rocketed outta here. But then she comes back after like thirty years, a complete basket case."

"But, she comes back and she's homeless, demented even. Why didn't someone take her in?"

"She doesn't want 'in.' Carmen offered her a small cottage that some of the field-hands used back when immigration wasn't such a big deal, and they brought their families. Sherry said no like a million times. I mean, people tried to help her."

For a while, Sherry took Carmen up on an offer to sort apples at the orchard. Fiori's specialized in Macintosh, Maccouns, Winesap, and Ginger Golds. Carmen didn't trust her at the retail operation just down the hill from the old cider mill, where people lined up for apple every-thing: apple fritters, candied apples, apple pie, apple but-ter, apple cider, apple crisp, and applesauce. Aldo Fiori held court as he sat by the cash register, and even though he felt sorry for Sherry, he wanted her gone after finding her drunk and passed out more than a few times. Aldo wanted to keep his regulars happy and coming back for more. He loved greeting them like long-lost relatives who owed him money. Everyone knew that beneath that jok-ing exterior still beat an aching heart grieving for his wife and granddaughter.

"So Sherry chooses to live rough out in the woods. What about winter?" Ian asked.

"She goes into the shelters. I know, I know it sounds heartless, but that's how she wants it. She always was stubborn. The booze and drugs and whatever didn't kill that part of her."

"Living off her wits and the kindness of old friends. Not a good story at all." Ian motioned for Peter to pass over the brandy. "I just want to smell it."

"Wait." Peter moved the bottle away from Ian's

outstretched hand. "Are you sure? I mean, don't trigger anything."

Ian wiggled his fingers impatiently. "Just a sniff is all I want and all I'll do."

"Fine. Here."

Ian sat up straight while he held the bottle and read the label. "Forty percent alcohol and produced for 300 years." He removed the corked top and inhaled the aroma. His abdomen expanded visibly. After one inhalation he passed the bottle back to Peter. "Tibetan breathing—*prana*. Not what you're supposed to do with alcoholic vapors, but . . ."

Peter cracked a smile. "Gotcha. When in Rome . . ."

"Precisely. Now tell me, when are you and Carmen getting back together?"

Peter closed his eyes and leaned back on the couch cushion. "Fuck off. Don't even bring it up. She's all involved with some rich ex-jock banker. Nancy told me."

"Just passing time until you're both ready. Trust me." Ian nestled into the couch and patted Brutus on the snout. "I'll give you a pep talk tomorrow."

CHAPTER 41

IAN SQUIRRELED AWAY A LOT OF SECRETS. IF anyone had asked, he would've described his strengths and weaknesses the same way: compartmentalizing, avoiding, rising above, and ignoring.

"I might hate people," Ian confided to Andre as they stretched together after an exasperating day.

"Duh." Andre rolled on a foam cylinder to loosen his hamstrings. "How's that go along with being a point of light, again?"

"There is a bit of overlap, you tosser. I love humanity but am not attached to any one person. Certainly no family ties. It doesn't make me a complete hypocrite, but I might be complicit in this madness."

"Honestly—since when do you care? Maybe you're getting sick. Do one of those cleanses you love, flush out all the toxins." Andre peered at Ian closely. "You look like shit, man. Stay away from me."

"That's just my face, arsehole." Ian half-heartedly flicked a towel at Andre.

Andre got up to fill two plastic bags with ice and tried to prop them on his aching knees. "Getting old's a bitch." He leaned back against the wall to get comfortable before sneezing violently. "Get your damn germs outta here," he grumbled as one of the bags tumbled to the ground.

Ian picked it up. "Here." He rolled a yoga mat for Andre to put under his legs. "You need at least two high colonics, maybe three."

"Nobody's sticking any hose up my ass."

"Your loss," Ian said, sitting down next to him. "You know, for some reason, I keep remembering all the violence that was normal growing up—my brother, sister, parents. Punching, slaps, kicks. And, mind you, this is at home."

"Always for your own good, right? Man, I never lay a finger on my kids. I had AJ at eighteen, but I already knew I was gonna use words and motivation to get him to be his best self."

Ian offered an approving fist bump. "So, being a beat cop, well, violence and mayhem behind every corner. And all we had were these nightsticks and batons—no

guns. They scared me then and they scare me now. Here—
perps, cops, grannies; everyone's got one."

"You're preaching to the choir. Driving, walking, shopping—hell, just being a black man in America. Some cops
here, man. I keep Tomassi's card in my wallet in case
something goes south." Andre's voice got more high-
pitched. "I got it planned. 'Call Sergeant Tomassi, please,
sir.' Don't even get me started on my kids."

"Yeah, but school's not a safe place for anyone, either.
All these young male shooters, they're armed to the teeth
and stone-cold killers. I can't wrap my head around what
passes for normal now."

"Don't. Just don't." Andre fell silent. "But, you being a
cop—you must got some karma comin' back at you. Just
sayin'."

"How did we get on this conversation?"

"Talking, just talkin' some heavy shit." Andre got off
the floor slowly and dumped the melting ice into the sink.

When Ian checked his voicemail, he was bowled over
by a message to call his yogi's personal assistant as soon
as possible.

"This has to be a joke," he muttered and considered
ignoring it. Andre had already left to go grocery shopping. Ian hesitated as he locked up the gym. If he offended
Baba, as the titular head of PARSLEY liked to be called,
there could be serious repercussions.

The personal assistant took his call right away.

"Ian, Baba has been thinking about you very deeply.
He will be so happy you are calling."

Baba spoke non-stop for several minutes during
which time Ian's normally regal posture dissolved into a
hunchback.

"I am honored to be selected for this committee," he
said. "But I know nothing about recruiting. I'm not good

with people. I would much prefer to be on the building committee."

Brooding after he hung up, his preference shot down, Ian munched slowly on a pear. Its sugary over-ripeness felt sublime. But recruiting new worker bees felt like a punishment. For what, he didn't know.

Ian could have taken lessons from Marco, whose deft recruitment of Kenny as the hitting guru for his cousin's team, found them both waiting for the kids to show up for extra batting practice.

"You gotta help these kids hit more. They're sucking it up." Marco handed Kenny a water saved from the food truck and tilted his sideways baseball cap lower.

"Dude, I already told them to shorten up their swings like a million times. Make contact, even go for the bunt. But, no. They want to look good for the TV cameras." Kenny mimicked a long loopy swing that looked like it belonged in a ballet or on a golf course.

"True dat. Let's give 'em candy if they get a single or keep the line goin'. Snickers got magic powers." Marco angled the brim even lower over the left side of his face. This time, Kenny noticed.

"Jesus, what happened to you?" Kenny tried to peer closer, but Marco moved back before doffing his cap.

"This ain't nothin'. You should see the other guy." Marco's swollen and bruised cheekbone almost forced his eye shut.

"Nasty." Kenny whistled his admiration. "You can take a punch, that's for sure. But, what the fuck? You got something to lose now, so come on—stay out of trouble." Kenny stared at him hard.

"Easy for you to say, man. Ain't self-defense my right, officer?"

"Yeah, it is." Kenny remembered Marco, short and fast, being the first out on the field to protect a fighting teammate. And Kenny charged right behind him if he wasn't on base or on deck. "But you can't afford another bust." And Peter went out on a limb for you. Don't screw it up."

"So, I'm the bad guy? Bullshit. I spot you five seconds in the 'hood before you in a fight. And I don't mean in your blues. Just a dude trying to get home or catch the bus."

Kenny shifted uneasily as he nodded. "I hear you, but you read me?"

"Like my Miranda Rights, homie. Hey, how 'bout them Yankees?" Marco pointed to the logo on his cap.

"Anyone but the Yankees. Go, Herrings." Kenny backed off. "The kids need more practice with live pitching. Face it, getting a hit is the greatest feeling in the world. Well, I mean the best thing you can do with your clothes on, asshole," Kenny added after Marco howled.

"You gettin' any, KJ? I can set you up with some sweet Latinas. Just say the word."

"Like I need your help with the ladies." Kenny crumpled the empty water bottle and aimed it at a nearby garbage can. When it missed wide of the mark, he took his time retrieving it.

"Hey—recycle, litterbug. Planet's polluted enough." Marco tipped his hat at two attractive twenty-something women walking by. Noting their interest, he yelled, "Hey, you wanna go out with this stud?"

Kenny turned every shade of red. "Shut the fuck up, Marco." He walked away, acknowledging the hooting and cat-calling women with a wave.

"Man, you got no game aside from baseball. Aight, got my hands full here, I can see that." He ambled alongside Kenny who had picked up a bag full of bats and balls. "All business."

Kenny ignored him, striding purposefully towards the backstop.

CHAPTER 42

WHEN JOSH RICHARDSON REALLY SCRUTINIZED THE Eautopia deal, making money didn't look remotely like a problem.

"This can't be right." Josh got up and walked over to the wall where he had hung a calendar called Fish of the Connecticut River. He loved the color photo of the solemn shad.

"The poor man's salmon," he read out loud. The shad looked like a patient saint awaiting certain doom, its knowing eyes and tight lips acknowledging cruel fate.

Josh enjoyed shad fishing with his father, a top-ten memory. Learning how to cast from shore, his father the picture of patience and encouragement, Josh could practically hear his voice in his ear urging him on.

Emmie kept asking him to give up animal protein, especially fish if he thought they were so special. She'd been a vegan for ten months and kept trying to convert Josh. He humored her at first, but Emmie was no slouch. She quickly caught on that an all-or-nothing approach would backfire. She started by showing him articles about the toxins that decimated river fish like shad decades ago.

"Watch this documentary, babe. Poisoned, they were poisoned by contaminants like fertilizers, PCBs, dioxin, DDT, and mercury."

"Those poor shad." Josh absorbed the news mournfully. "I might have eaten them if my dad didn't know better." He managed to give up fish; he didn't miss eating it too much. But he refused to give up meat, no matter how hard she pushed.

"One step at a time, babe. I can't do it all at once." He staked out his position as they shopped at Whole Foods.

"Well, I'm not buying it or cooking it. Have it for lunch when you're at work. I don't even want it in the house." She reached into their cart and jettisoned the artisanal pork sausages marinated in hard apple cider. "These are history."

"Wow, way harsh." Josh's light blue eyes darkened with annoyance. He stopped pushing the cart and gestured toward the cheese counter. "Is cheese banned, too?"

"One day, you'll get it. And harsh is how these animals are treated. They are living, breathing creatures with feelings."

Josh rolled his eyes. He'd heard this too many times. "Yeah, I know. They had a mother and a face. I'm not a criminal, Em. I just like meat."

"Promise me you won't eat meat except at work, and I swear we can split for California whenever you feel ready." She put her hand on his chest and scooted close to whisper in his ear. "I'll even throw in a BJ every day."

Josh titled his head and smiled winningly. "Sounds like a plan."

Back at his desk, after a juicy burger for lunch, Josh deconstructed the deal, trying to see if he had miscalculated the venture's potential net profit. The figures, if correct, would yield astronomical riches. He thought there had to be an error, a misplaced decimal. But he had strict instructions to get moving on the double, so he ran some quick scenarios.

Josh projected revenue using increases of 10, 15, and 20 percent. The millions of single-serve plastic bottles would come out of the massive 500,000 square foot plant located at the reservoir in Bridgeville. Josh frowned again at the location. Why Bridgeville? Josh made a mental note to hike at the reservoir; he remembered it as a beautiful pastoral panorama. Endless clear water, pine trees, steep banks.

"Focus, come on," he said to himself. "Back to the spreadsheet, asshole."

Once production at the bottling plant ramped up to four lines, full capacity, everything looked golden. Profitability went through the roof for Eautopia, and the Consortium pocketed a boatload of money.

The water bottles would be packaged into cases, loaded onto trucks and sold at the big chains like Costco and Walmart. Eautopia's deal built in a discounted price based on volume and premium access to the reservoir's water as well as tax credits and abatements with the town and state.

"Wow. There are like no downsides to this deal."

Josh ran the numbers for one bottling line, two, three, and four. The number of workers Eautopia needed didn't increase by much once they had two lines going, and the minimum wage jobs would be very easy to fill given Hatfield's lousy economy.

"They'd pay us $5 million each year for the first three years, assuming at least three lines and water use over 500,000 gallons. They pay Bridgeville zero taxes except for property taxes since they have a 100 percent tax abatement. So, the major expenditures are for equipment, and they'll use whatever depreciation technique they want."

The Consortium assumed no risk and it received a very straight-forward cash payment for water, with built-in incentives for Eautopia to use more and more.

"Eautopia purifies the water, bottles it and then sells it. Fucking great business model—no complications. We get the guaranteed annual payment, so we can cover existing bond payments and modernize. Our financials will look great. We could even lower rates to residential customers."

Josh looked at his watch. "Not bad for four days of work." He got up to present his findings to his boss.

"Hey," Josh knocked on the semi-closed door. "Oh, sorry." Brock Saunders sat in a big leather and teak armchair, his tasseled loafers kicked off to the side. Josh's boss waved him in.

"I've got some forecasts that I'd like to discuss. Here's a copy of the spreadsheet."

"Make a copy for Brock. Meantime, we'll share."

Brock looked Josh up and down. "You play golf?"

"Uh, yes. About a ten handicap."

"Good, we'll get you out on the links with clients. So," Brock asked. "Is it a winner?"

"Hell, yeah." Josh's boss took a highlighter and made some marks on the spreadsheet.

"Nice. Let's get this baby zooming through Bridgeville's approval process."

"Actually, that's the biggest what-if and my major concern. What if Bridgeville says no to building the facility?" Josh looked at both men expectantly.

His boss laughed "Funny."

"A real rookie comment," Brock said. He leaned closer and enunciated very clearly. "It's just for show; they don't get a say."

"I don't get it. Doesn't all this need to go through like a thousand committees and hearings?"

Brock brushed Josh's words aside. "What are you, a boy scout? It's already a done deal. It's our land and our water. We can do what we want, but that's not how we play it to the public."

"Oh, OK—that's not what I expected. So, what do you want me to do next?" Josh's palms began to sweat.

The project had just gone from proposal to fait accompli in a matter of seconds, definitely not how he saw it playing out.

"How about you project Eautopia's production costs and profit, so we can see where to squeeze them. Do it tomorrow, you did enough for today, kiddo."

Brock nodded. "I see big things for you, Jim."

"Josh."

"We should hit some bars sometime soon. Bet the ladies love you. I want you as my wingman."

Excusing himself, Josh knocked off for the day. He took off his tie and unbuttoned his collar before climbing into his car and made it across the river in decent time, considering the afternoon rush hour started at 3:00 P.M. and lasted until 6:00. With a nearly cloudless late afternoon enticing him, Josh decided to check out the reservoir. He changed quickly into shorts and made it up to Devil's Falls by 5:00 P.M.

Emmie's Group Groove classes were back-to-back that evening, so Josh had time to explore. It had been a while since he got to hike impulsively, following wherever a trail might lead him. Once he got past the trash carelessly strewn near the dam, the beauty and tranquility of the reservoir took his breath away. Josh snapped pictures with his phone, framing the landscape with artful shots of trees and rocks. Dogs splashed near the reservoir's banks, chasing sticks thrown by their owners. Officially on the list of no-no's, dogs had been swimming in the reservoir forever. He waved at a woman paddling a canoe, another forbidden activity.

Josh decided to wade in up to his knees. The water, cool and crystal clear, invigorated him. He found some flat rocks perfect for skipping across the water and played like a kid. After he got one to skim the surface four times in a row, he moved on. Squinting into the setting sun, he tried to imagine a 500,000 square foot water bottling plant along the reservoir's shores. He couldn't do it; all he could envision was a brutally industrial facade like the fuel cell facility on Maple Street. It felt as disconnected as scotch-taping together two halves of different people's faces from his mother's old magazines, a long-forgotten way he'd passed time at home while his father lay sick and dying.

After Emmie came home, and they made love until they couldn't even move, Josh voiced his doubts. "I'm not sure I can do it, babe." She lay on his chest, his arms wrapped around her fit body.

Emmie kissed his shoulder. "Just do the projections or whatever. It's not like you're responsible for what happens to the reservoir. They'll do it with or without you."

"Yeah, but maybe I'm on the wrong side of this. I mean the land and the reservoir are fucking awesome."

"So's the money you're being paid. That's our move to California." She teased him with her fingers until he got hard again. Josh forgot about everything as she eased him into her.

The next day, Josh went to work and downloaded copies of all his forecasts and spreadsheets. After printing and tucking them into a folder, he uploaded all his calculations onto the official IT flash drive just in case he had time to work on them from home. But he and Emmie landed a last-minute invite to stay with some friends on Cape Cod, so he barely touched his laptop.

Surprisingly, it took him the better part of the next week to generate ways the Consortium could wring more money out of the deal. The biggest problem ended up being Eautopia's secrecy.

Josh requested more information about Eautopia's production costs from an analyst at Eautopia who hedged about giving him real numbers.

"Until the deal is signed, they're proprietary. So, you're going to have to work off guesstimates."

"That's not very helpful," Josh said. "What if I come up with some projections and you give me guidance, like if I'm too low or high."

"Yeah, I should be able to do that." The analyst ended the conversation abruptly.

Josh hunkered down to research historical and current water-bottling industry averages. He plugged in percentage increases based on the sheer size of the facility to approximate Eautopia's profit margins. When he had gotten as far as he could without guidance, he reached out to the analyst at Eautopia.

He hadn't heard a thing back by the weekend, so he re-sent his request by email and left two more voicemails. Josh's boss kept pressuring him for projections, so he went with what he had.

"I can't get through to Eautopia. The guy I was working with just disappeared. Like he vanished."

"Alright, we need to circulate the deal to the board. Who knows what shit's going down at Eautopia. You believe in your numbers?"

"Without guidance, it's hard to be 100 percent certain. But, even my worst-case scenario for us shows good wiggling room to maximize more profit."

"Terrific. Write a formal report but, in the meantime, send me the numbers. I'll present them to the Board ASAP. And don't forget charts and graphs—they love visuals, the bigger the better."

Josh did as told but again he made a copy for himself and downloaded the work onto the corporate flash drive. He had a weirdly unsettled feeling, but he reminded himself of what Emmie said. The deal would happen with or without him, so he might as well bank the Consortium's money.

When he went for a run along the river, the first one he'd taken in a long while, he saw Kenny Johnson jogging in the opposite direction. He had dated Kenny's sister in high school, so Josh crossed the street to Kenny's side, and they chatted briefly, running in place and dripping sweat.

"Hey, Kenny. Catch any bad guys today?" Josh panted hard and spat.

"Couple hundred, nothing special." Kenny lightly punched his shoulder. "Kinda outta shape there, dude. What are you up to—still doing guidance counseling?"

"Yeah, too bad we can't all be buff like you. But, nah, doing a little corporate work. Gotta make some money before I go out west."

"Good for you. You're gonna live the dream."

CHAPTER 43

IAN'S RECRUITING EFFORTS STARTED CLUMSILY. No one wanted to talk to him, and one woman threatened to call the police. But the next week, he started to get some nibbles. Using a roomy tea shop in Stonefort as his meeting place, his sessions, featuring the first cup free, brought more customers than the staff could ever remember.

Ian retrieved his mail every other day; he disliked the tyranny of the post office delivery schedule. But when he saw the thick cream-colored envelope, so obviously an invitation to something swank, he thought it was another in a series of careless sorting errors.

"Typical," he snorted. But it said *Ian Edwards* in fancy calligraphy and had his correct address. Ian felt it in his hand, enjoying its tidy weight. He didn't open it. When he brandished the invitation proudly after getting to the gym, Andre grunted his acknowledgement.

Ian opened it carefully with the blade of a scissor. "Wow, thank you Lori and Marti. I rate a plus-one. This might be the one wedding worth going to."

"You want me to fix you up?" Andre looked up from his phone.

"No, not at all."

"Something you want to tell me? Only Peter's allowed to bring a four-legged creature."

"Actually, I have several candidates in mind."

"OK, right. Describe one of them. And I'll be able to tell if you're lying."

"You're on. Dark hair, dark eyes, mocha skin, funny, and smart."

"In your dreams, dude."

Ian shrugged his shoulders and gnawed on a corner of the invitation.

Ian's outreach efforts hadn't yielded any new converts, but he met more and more people searching for meaning in their lives. All of the searchers who wanted to talk seriously were female, and aside from a few terrifying maniacs, Ian's chats brought him face to face with women who skewed towards being damaged, depressed, or disgusted.

"The world is full of possibilities. America certainly isn't perfect, but it is a country that promises second chances," he said earnestly, picking up on their angst. "Look at me, that's why I'm here. I'm a seeker. Whoever you were yesterday or the day before, you're not that same person right here, right now. The journey is everything. Take a chance on a change. What do you have to lose?"

Recruiting for PARSLEY involved a multi-step process.

Soul-searching, a critical step in bridging the divide between conversation and commitment, took a long time. Ian hadn't gotten any of his potential converts past extended introspection, but he had a strategy.

"I'm using a soft sell approach," he explained to Andre. "No hard marketing."

"I wouldn't buy water from you in the Sahara even if I was dying of thirst."

"Well, there's you dead."

"So, let me get this straight. You ask total strangers if they are happy with their lives. And then, when they say 'no,' you say, what?"

"What?"

"So hilarious. Really, I'm curious—like what the hell do you say?"

"I might tell them to buy a Powerball ticket and, when the astronomical odds indeed fail and all their dreams of material wealth crumble, to come see me for a cup of green tea and an interesting conversation."

"And they come back. Unfuckingbelievable."

Ian contemplated his invitation options. After a few minutes, he nodded. "The universe will tell me."

He drove to the retreat to work on the fire pit he'd started building near the outdoor patio. As he rummaged in the woods for more fieldstones, he heard someone calling his name. He turned in the direction of the voice and saw the woman he'd been describing to Andre.

"Ian, hi. Jade—remember me?" She brushed aside some branches and planted herself in front of him. Dark hair spilling out from beneath a baseball cap, she wore cargo shorts and a tank top that revealed a striking tattoo of a thorned rose on her left shoulder.

"Well, hello. Fancy meeting you here," Ian said. "Watch out for that poison ivy." He pointed to a patch near her feet.

"Hey," she said, moving towards him, "I wanted to continue our conversation, so I took a chance you'd be here."

"Great. I just need to get these rocks moved. Care to help?" He gestured to the wheelbarrow he'd loaded with stones of every hue and size. Jade bent down to grab a few remaining rocks, and his eyes were drawn to the firm cleavage peeking out from beneath her sports bra.

"Steady, steady," Ian said to the wheelbarrow, teetering under the load's weight. Descending slowly down the rocky slope, his ropy muscles bulged with effort.

"You're strong." Jade stopped to retrieve little rocks along the path. "These are good for small crevices."

Grunting, he dumped out the load by the rectangle he'd marked in the dirt and flicked dripping sweat off his brow.

"So, you promised me some tea and a good conversation." She pointed to the cafeteria. "In there?"

"So I did. Just let me wash up first." In the bathroom, Ian looked at his dirt-streaked face in the mirror and raised an eyebrow at his reflection before splashing cool water on his head and neck.

"Over here," Jade called from a high window ledge when he emerged. She motioned to the two tall glasses she had filled with ice and green tea. "Have some."

Ian hoisted himself up easily and downed the tea in two gulps. "Aah. So, who are you, Jade? Tell me more. I remember you saying you had spent time at a monastery or hermitage."

"Yeah, this isn't my first rodeo," she sighed. "I'm definitely on a spiritual quest. I've been staying at the Journey ashram over in Stonebury."

"So, you're Jade on a journey."

"In the flesh."

"It's catchy, intriguing. Say, total change of subject, but how do you feel about sitting? I notice that we're not."

"No, we're dangling. Is this some kind of trick question?" Jade stirred the remnants of her iced tea with a straw.

"Not at all. I'm an open book." Ian did his best to look her in the eye without smiling.

"Right. Truth be told, I hate sitting. I need to move. You can't imagine the trouble I got into as a kid because I couldn't sit still in school. They wanted to drug me into submission."

"Classic unenlightened discipline. It's toxic, you know." Ian swung his legs above the floor and examined the scratches on his knees. "We're all scarred from one-size-fits-all thinking."

"You're a mess." She grinned, pointing to streams of blood that had congealed on the sides of his legs.

"You have no idea. So, and this is not a trick question, how do you feel about weddings?" Ian looked at her seriously.

"What? You better not be hitting on me. Is this a proposal?" Jade's voice rose as she looked at him coolly.

"Of course not. Relax. I'm not the marrying kind. But, I've got a wedding to go to. How about being my plus-one on September 23? They're good friends."

"Ian, time out. Let's take a walk." Jade jumped down and waited for him to follow. As they stepped outside, she grabbed his arm. "I'm not saying no, but why would you invite basically a total stranger? I could be an axe murderer for all you know."

Ian wanted to say her spirit sang to him, she intrigued him like he hadn't been intrigued in a very long time, but that would seriously overstep PARSLEY-sanctioned recruiting boundaries.

"Sorry to push one of your buttons, Jade on a journey," he said, betraying none of his thoughts. "How about the concept of fun?"

"So fun is allowed in PARSLEY?" Her eyes twinkled suddenly, and Ian noticed that one seemed green and the other blue.

"Unofficially. You're quite short, you know." Ian stood on his tiptoes to exaggerate his height.

"OK."

"OK, what? You'll join PARSLEY or you'll come to the wedding or you know you're short?"

"Two out of three. You guess." They locked eyes until Ian looked away and pretended to think.

"Well, I'm hoping it's yes to the wedding and the height issue. And you probably need more time to think about PARSLEY."

"Bravo, you win." Jade raised her hand for a high-five.

"Excellent." Ian tapped her hand gently. "This is good, very good, but I have yet to get anyone to join PARSLEY. I'm rubbish at recruiting."

CHAPTER 44

PACO MANNED THE WINDOW OF THE GREAT FULL Bread truck, taking orders and money at their choice location down by the Hatfield Courthouse where offices teemed with legal professionals. It wasn't his favorite venue by a long shot because of some of the customers' power trips.

"They push my buttons in all kinda evil ways," he said to Marco when they loaded up the most recent batch of Rachel's finest. "Damn, these fresh-baked cookies makin' me hungry."

"Word. But that's your shift, bro." Marco didn't have much sympathy. He had a slower burn than Paco but that didn't mean that he was OK with being patronized, either.

Paco paused his now well-choreographed customer routine after a white middle-aged woman gave him too much attitude, tossing her money down on the counter instead of placing it in his outstretched hand. "Ay, mamacita—I don't bite."

"What did you call me?" Her ID badge swinging wildly on the rope she wore around her neck, she reared back as if a zoo animal had gotten too close. "I am not your mother. Just give me my grilled cheese. And my change."

Paco saluted her. "Coming right up, madam. You want the over-sixty-five discount?"

Jeff, manning the grill, caught the interaction, including the woman's sniffy harrumph, and shook his head at Paco who ignored him and made a great show of retrieving seven of the grungiest pennies he could find in the cash drawer.

"Next," Paco called to the customer behind the woman. She left the pennies and stalked off, clutching her eight dollar brie on gluten-free toasted focaccia.

"Bitch much?" The young construction worker next in line addressed the woman's back. Turning to Paco he said, "Hey dude, when you gonna have the gluten-free pupusas with sweet corn and black beans again?"

"See," Paco called over to Jeff. "They love pupusas, which you now know is what?"

"Corn masa," Jeff played along. "Griddle-cooked with love." He winked at a pretty woman who had joined the line. "Hey, did you like the Latin cole slaw with it?"

"Yeah," the construction worker said. "What's it called again?"

"Curtido," one of their lunchtime regulars chimed in. "Like fermented cabbage with jalapenos. To die for," he added, patting his ample stomach.

Ever since Paco and Marco adamantly insisted that Great Full Bread needed to add Latin-themed menu items, about a month into the venture, business basically doubled.

"We gotta do this, Coach. It's a no-brainer," Marco said. "It'll be a slam dunk."

"Absofuckinglutely," Paco said. "Kaching, mo' money." He and Marco bumped fists and made exploding sounds.

"It's our rich heritage of maize," Marco said in a newscaster voice, prompting Paco to dissolve into giggles.

"Whoa," Peter said. "So we add some papooses—"

"Pupusas," Paco and Marco corrected simultaneously.

"We ain't serving no dead Indian babies," Paco said.

"Native American," Marco reminded him. "And arepas, too. Coach."

"A-what?"

"You so white." Paco went for simplicity as he explained. "Arepas are the same as pupusas and gorditas, but different."

"Yeah, that really explains everything." Jeff said. "Hey, if they're money-makers, we can do some breakfast and lunch versions if Rach agrees. How about a demo?"

"You got it. Too bad we can't do chicharron coz pork is the bomb. But we gotta keep kosher. Maybe cheese and pinto beans, cheese and spinach or what's that other green all them hipsters like?" Paco snapped his fingers in the air to get some responses.

"Kale?" Peter asked.

"That stuff is for cows, man." Marco shuddered dramatically. "What about double cheese?"

"Yeah, but you gotta watch the expenses, bro. You wait, kale and pinto beans will sell through the roof." Paco nodded sagely.

And they were right. Marco's mother taught Rachel how to bake all of it.

"So pupusas are from El Salvador," she said as Marco occasionally translated. "Arepas are from everywhere. Every country has something like this. I'm also gonna teach you how to make churros so you got something sweet to sell."

"Churros are like donuts, right?" Rachel had a smudge of flour on her nose that Marco's mother gently wiped away.

"Girl, you got a lot to learn," Marco laughed. "Dunkin Donuts got good coffee, that's a fact, but churros leave donuts in the dust. You don't know what you don't know. Mami will set you straight."

After two days of experimenting, Rachel had Mrs. Torres's blessing for the long, ridged fried dough rolled three times in cinnamon sugar. She tried them out on Peter, Jeff and Tomassi.

"I can die happy now." Jeff licked his fingers happily. sucked the crumbs off his mustache.

"Warm, sweet, soft on the inside and crunchy on the outside." Tomassi helped himself to a second one and gave Rachel a thumbs-up.

"My ideal woman," Peter said to groans. Rachel bopped him on the head with a plate.

"Inappropriate, Pete."

Jeff finally told Paco to work on his bedside manner. "Look, all I'm saying is don't overreact to stupid stuff. Some people act like assholes when they're hungry. Let it bounce off you. It's not personal."

"I don't take shit from no one. But trust me, this ain't my first go-round with anger management."

"I get it. Just remember—you're here for a reason. We need you, we depend on you."

"I know you wasn't all 'Yay Paco' at the beginning. But, you took a chance. I don't wanna fuck it up. Plus, me and my lady got a kid on the way. I gotta think smart."

"Hey, congratulations. And you're right. Kids are expensive."

"Teach me how to deal with them crazies, and Ima do it. Being all turn-the-other-cheek don't come natural to me, just so you know. Ima copy you. You *my* coach, aight?"

Jeff patted him on the back and held out his hand. "I'm honored. Now let's get to work, Papi."

Paco smiled big. "Nice Spanglish."

CHAPTER 45

JUST DAYS BEFORE PETER AND BRUTUS FOUND THE documents at the dam, Josh finished the home stretch of a long run down by the river. He liked to run now; it cleared his head. Darkness had fallen, and he could barely see by the time he made it back to the parking lot down by the ferry. He knew he had to have at least one water bottle in the trunk. All Consortium employees received a case of Eautopia, and he had stuffed the refrigerator at home full of them. He leaned against the side of his old Subaru, spat and reached for his keys.

Opening the trunk, he found a crumpled paper towel, his old leather jacket with the broken zipper that must have fallen out of a bag full of clothes he and Emmie donated to Goodwill and a half-filled water bottle. He gulped it down in three sips and mopped his sweaty head. When he checked his phone, he cursed with annoyance because the battery had almost zero charge.

Driving home in the twilight, salt-encrusted, thirsty, and clammy, he glanced away from the road when a huge moth beat its wings across his face. Suddenly, he felt the impact of something thudding off the front end. Twisting the steering wheel, he narrowly avoided crashing into a tree.

"Shit—what the fuck?' The car shuddered to a halt, and Josh stepped out shakily. His headlights revealed a dying fawn lying half-stuck on his front bumper, bleeding heavily and moaning in pain.

"Oh, God. Sorry little buddy, I'm so sorry." Josh peered through the darkness to see if the doe or any other deer were near. The sounds the fawn made as it died pierced the night air and torched Josh's soul. Helplessly, he brushed back sudden tears and made himself bear witness to the deer's dying breaths.

"Sorry," he kept whispering.

His phone and the fawn both dead, he went to the trunk and fished out his old leather jacket. The bloody corpse sagged in his arms as he wrapped the jacket around it. He tried to lug the body to the side of the road, but its shattered bones, crushed insides and syrupy fluids made it impossible.

He swaddled the baby deer as tight as he could, the leather jacket slathered in gore. His feet slipping on the slick roadway, Josh struggled for traction as he dragged the deer to the side of the road and tried to rest the body gently against some rocks. Josh said a short prayer and then grabbed his jacket off the road. Shoving it in the trunk, he wiped his hands off on his trembling legs, on his shirt, anywhere he could, before nosing the damaged car back onto the dark road.

The car made loud grinding noises and pulled to the right the entire trip home. He went straight to the garden hose out back in the shared yard. Stripping off his clothes off, he hosed down, the nozzle squeezed tight to full-on jet spray.

"Josh?" Emmie held a flashlight and a 3-iron for self-defense as she came towards him. "Josh, is that you?"

"Yeah, babe."

"What are you doing?"

"I hit a baby deer. It died right in front of me, and I'm all bloody."

"Oh, babe. So long as it's not your blood. I'm going to get you a towel. Just wait there."

Despite the humid night air, Josh shivered as he stood rooted to the spot. Emmie hurried back, minus the 3-iron, and draped a big beach towel over his shoulders.

"Let's ditch your clothes in the trash. They're all bloody and gross. You sure you're OK?"

Josh nodded and picked up the sodden pile.

"Here." Emmie gently wrapped a smaller towel around his waist. "Don't want the neighbors reporting a flasher." She put her arm around him and lead him inside. "Come on, lean on me."

CHAPTER 46

NANCY CHOSE TO GO TO HER SURGERY ALONE, CLIMBING into her Uber at 4:45 A.M. Exiting the car, she aimed herself at the Pre-Op reception area, gave them her completed forms and filled out yet more paperwork.

"You sure you don't want a ride?" Peter asked repeatedly.

"No, but you can pick me up. Bet you won't recognize me."

A pretty but tired-looking nurse with a long blonde ponytail and butterfly-printed scrubs called Nancy's name. She chatted with two techs in standard blue scrubs while waiting for Nancy to make her way over.

"Hi, Nancy. I'm Lily, but you can call me Lilz. So, I'm not your procedure nurse; I'm just bringing you in so you can change into the beautiful ball gown we ask all patients to wear, especially the men. Then you can meet the mod squad."

"Oh, goody," Nancy said. "I appreciate the comedy, I really do."

"Check out my YouTube channel. Just kidding. Hey, it sure beats whimpering in the corner, I can tell you that. Did you leave your tiara and jewelry at home?" Nancy nodded dutifully. "Great, so here we are. This part of the procedure is called hurry up and wait." Lily offered up a high-five. "Go get 'em, girl."

In the airless tiny room where Nancy sat after she changed into her hospital finery, she played with her wrist band, courtesy of her most recent nurse, stared at the IV started by yet another nurse and endured an endless wait. There were no magazines more recent than 2015, and she dearly wished she still had her phone. Finally, an intern who looked all of twelve years old came in to go over her chart.

"And to get the practice," he grinned and showed her his shaking hands. "I'm a little nervous with actual patients. This is my first week, and the senior guys are beating me up."

"Well, practice makes perfect. Just don't operate on me, OK?"

"Deal." He asked her questions she had already answered so many times that she wondered if the point-lessness was part of the process.

Then she waited again, this time for the attending anesthesiologist. Her boredom combined with thirst, hunger, and stale hospital air to make her really sleepy. Nancy missed the little boy intern; he reminded her of Alex and Justin when they briefly forgot they hated her.

She perked up when her surgeon strolled in to crack a few jokes right after the nerdy anesthesiologist exited the room. They went over everything about the surgery again. After he left, Nancy actually nodded off before being summoned by yet another nurse. Groggily, she followed her team into the next room where she climbed onto the moveable bed that would take her to the operating room.

"Go to your happy place," someone said. She visualized the cerulean waters and warm sun of a tropical paradise. The process took over, and she tried to rise above the beeping machines, gleaming instruments, bright lights, and loud conversations. The anesthesia resident had trouble converting her weight into kilograms. He seemed to lack a fundamental grasp of basic algebra, and the attending scolded him. The resident fumbled with the mask as he pressed it over her nose and mouth. She tried to alert him to her continuing consciousness. He ignored her and brusquely mashed the mask into her face.

The surgery took 2 ½ hours once she was asleep. She slept for another 2 ½ hours in the recovery room, about which she recalled nothing. Waking up, her abdomen hurt like hell.

"You are the master of your pain," the recovery nurse told her. "Push this button and it will release a dose of your pain meds. But you can't get more than the calibrated dose."

'Everything hurts," Nancy moaned.

"Of course it does, but you're going to get up later after dinner to take a little walk."

"No way."

"Yes way." The nurse gave her another dose of pain meds by pushing the button on the pump. "Just stay ahead of the pain."

Nancy hated her floor nurse and, worse yet, she had a roommate. The nurse made her get up and totter across the room, hooked up to pumps and IVs. Nancy tried not to scream.

"Don't be such a wimp."

"Don't be such a witch," Nancy hissed, doubled over in pain.

Her roommate, a ninety-year-old woman whose IV beeped constantly except when it went into full-on alarm mode, about every twenty minutes, refused to lower the TV volume which stayed tuned to shouting matches on Fox News. Nancy pressed her pain pump constantly.

The next day, Nancy had a CAT scan. "We're going to perform a leak test. We just want to make sure everything's OK," her surgeon said. "You'll be able to start clear liquids in the next few days."

When all the IV's, catheters, plastic tubes, and compressive devices were unhooked on her discharge day, Nancy cinched her abdominal binder tighter and counted the minutes until she could leave. Peter came to pick her up as promised.

"Hey, slim. Your chauffeur is here, and your chariot awaits."

"Ha, not rocking the bikini just yet." Nancy moved very gingerly to the wheelchair the hospital insisted she sit in until the front door.

"Your mom is at your house. God, she's meaner than ever. No mellowing in her old age. Are you sure you can last a week with her?" Peter knew Nancy's mother well enough. She exuded wavelengths of hatred no sentient creature could defend against.

"Nope. The bitch is back. I figure two to three days max. I'll be fine. Peapod delivers, I've got all my meds and I'm post-up, hallelujah."

Despite constant nagging and vitriolic criticism, Nancy's mother achieved a minor miracle during her three-day visit when she brokered a temporary peace between Nancy and Alex. Justin had moved to St. Louis for work, so their detente ended up being negotiated in a tense phone conversation and evaporated after they both hung up.

Neither Nancy nor her mother felt anything but relief when she left. Peter looked in every day, and she seemed to be making progress.

"I'm fine already."

"If you say so." Peter had his doubts. She seemed pale and very out of sorts.

Ian and Andre came to visit after her mother left.

Andre had met her mother before in his phlebotomy days. "Much as I feel for Nancy, if the witch is there, I'm not visiting. She's a horror movie nightmare."

"Nancy's not exactly a picnic."

"When I was doing blood at the hospital lab, mommy dearest needed a stick, a couple tubes. Kids try to be brave. But she carried on like I was torturing her, and she called me the-n-word one too many times."

"No. How many times?"

"Once." Andre spat on the ground.

But after ten days, Nancy started to go downhill. She ran a fever and felt short of breath. The pain intensified and turned into left upper quadrant anguish. She finally agreed to call the doctor who told her to go to the emergency room right away. She asked Alex for a ride after Peter didn't call her back, and he finally drove her to the hospital after whining for a full five minutes about the inconvenience and her shortcomings as a mother.

"Nancy, I'm afraid you might have a leak in your staple line and an infection. We're going to readmit you right away to repair the problem," her surgeon said when he saw her in the ER.

Nancy spent the next nine days in the hospital, including three days in the ICU after a second surgery that left her thinking she'd died.

"I remember all the bright lights and strange people coming in and out. I lay there and couldn't move. So much noise, too—like bad dream noise." She tried to tell Peter, but he could barely make out the mumbled words. She cried constantly, unable to summon the energy to wipe her tears.

"You could have died." Peter couldn't hide his horror at her condition when he finally saw her.

"You wish," Nancy whispered. She looked like someone else, someone who had survived a close call with death. Misery and pain caused by the emergency surgery to clean out the infection and close the hole in her stomach left her shriveled and extremely weak. Her belly oozed fluids through a drain that the surgical team inserted. Powerful IV antibiotics and pain medications pumped through her system to combat the infection. The lethargy and dizziness made opening her eyes a huge effort.

"Why did this happen? I didn't cheat," she cried. "I followed the protocol."

Her surgeon didn't sugarcoat the situation. "This is uncommon but certainly not unknown. Maybe 2 percent of patients get this complication; surgery always has risks. When you're well enough to go home, you'll need visiting nurse care. The wound has to be kept clean as it drains. No eating until it heals. You're on IV nutrition and IV antibiotics."

"But I have to get back to work. My short-term disability only pays 60 percent, and I used up all my sick and personal days already."

"No, not possible. Stress about work only hurts the healing process. I'll write any letters or appeals you need. I'm not making predictions, but I've seen cases like this take eight weeks."

"I've got six weeks of coverage."

When Peter came to take her home, his stomach did a nosedive. "Jesus, Nancy. You're a hurtin' pup. Don't even think about work."

He drove very slowly but, even so, she cried out in pain at each bump in the road.

"Sorry, sorry."

Getting her into the house took over an hour. Each step looked like Kilimanjaro and demanded more strength than she could muster. Peter couldn't figure out how to make it any easier.

"I'm afraid to try to carry you. Maybe hold onto me like a piggyback." Peter crouched and motioned for her to climb on his back.

"I can't do it." She begged for pain medicine. "Just give me a shot."

"I don't know how, Nance. Just hang on."

Peter waited until the first shift of visiting nurses came over and left once Nancy zoned out into la-la land. He needed two shots of bourbon to calm down.

The visiting nurses came three times per day for the first two weeks until Nancy went off antibiotics. Then they came twice daily for the next two weeks. Her four-week visit to the surgeon felt as hard-fought and pivotal as Antietam in the Civil War.

"Please give me good news. I'm begging you."

"Nancy, you're almost there—so close."

CHAPTER 47

"I'M ALL SHOOK UP." JOHN TOMASSI SHOWED PETER his trembling hands as they stood in Peter's kitchen after Tomassi dropped by unexpectedly.

"Jesus, JT. Have a beer." Peter pulled two cold bottles of India Pale Ale out of his refrigerator and offered one to Tomassi who took an enormous swig.

Tomassi walked onto the deck and heaved himself into the Adirondack chair next to the glider. "Petey, I gotta tell you something. Sit down."

"What happened? Is Donna OK, the kids?"

"Not about them. You know a jogger found a body in the reservoir this morning."

"Yeah, it's all over town."

"It was Sherry Nicholas."

"What? No, that can't be right. No." Peter put down the pretzel he was about to pop in his mouth and practically choked on his own saliva.

"It's true." Tomassi held his head in his hands. "Believe it."

"John, I just saw her a few days ago when Ian and I were hiking. She was all rattled and saying people were spying on her, but she said shit like that a lot. She took us over to her tent and shopping cart full of stuff that would break your heart. I kind of blew her off."

"Yeah, everyone blew her off sooner or later. Her brain was so goddamned fried, and she didn't make sense half the time."

"I should have listened better, spent more time; maybe she really saw something. Shit, how could Sherry drown? I mean, she was a helluva swimmer. Like she was part dolphin or something."

"I know." Tomassi emphasized both words and gave him a meaningful look. "Sherry wasn't some random homeless woman, she's one of us. Why the fuck she came back, I never understood. She couldn't get out of here fast enough, and then she joins some kind of crazy cult out West. You know the chief had it in for her; Captain Fantastic, too. Bastard made me tell her if she camped out anywhere in town, she'd be busted. What am I explaining this for—like you're not the trespassing expert?"

"Come on, John. Lay off. You ever tell Donna about your hot and heavy month as Sherry's boy toy back in junior year?" Peter grinned at the memory of a youthful Tomassi excitedly begging him to ask Jeff for condoms.

"Long ago and far away. And no, so don't you mention it." Tomassi fell silent.

"This is so messed up. Ian even gave her his precious metal water bottle because she was thirsty. Of course, she wanted booze, but whatever." Peter blew his nose loudly into a paper towel.

"My patrol guys knew the drill, never busted her—just moved her over to Herb Baker's land. He didn't give a shit if she stayed on the back end of his property. He even put a picnic table out there for her. A goddam tire swing, too, like she was a kid."

"Mentally, she was."

"Yeah." Tomassi sighed.

"Did she definitely drown? I mean, no foul play?"

"Good question." The cop in Tomassi took over. "Got an autopsy lined up at the Medical Examiner's office. We knew it was her because of her tattoos, and she hadn't been in the water too long. The jogger who found her called it in right away."

"Shit."

"Listen." Tomassi lowered his meaty hand onto Peter's forearm. "I got a bad feeling about this. Something doesn't smell right."

"It stinks to high heaven. Eautopia's gonna try to make this go away but stay on it. Their precious water deal matters more than a human being."

"Yup," Tomassi said, getting up. He looked haggard, and Peter enfolded him into a less complicated version of the man-hug Paco and Marco had taught him. Tomassi bumped his chest hard. "Listen, you find her tent or anything up there you know belonged to her, call me right away—don't touch anything. This has gotta be more than a quick, open-shut, tie-it-with-a-bow case of some old crazy homeless broad drowning." His voice trailed off. After tapping on Peter's door with his fist, Tomassi trudged back to his car, muttering and shaking his head.

Peter called Ian, who insisted they had to rush back up to where they last saw Sherry. When they approached the formerly rocky and hole-ridden parking lot, they saw fresh paving, yellow caution tape and a newly installed chain link fence that closed off any entry. Peter backed up until he could park inconspicuously. When they got out, they spotted a rising mound of stuffed animals and cut flowers next to some balloons.

"A shrine? Jesus, word travels fast," Peter said. "How did people find out already?"

Ian nudged him. "Is that a TV crew over there?" He pointed to a cameraman filming close to the water.

"Let's go talk to them and see what they know."

"Not a good idea, mate. Let's go in the opposite direction. You'd make a lousy PI."

Peter and Ian walked quickly through the ravaged site. The yellow earth-moving equipment that Sherry tried to describe had destroyed a huge stretch of pine trees, leaving only piles of dried-up needles and tree roots torn asunder. The footings for a very large foundation were in place, too. Peter spat on the ground.

Ian took off his sunglasses and closed his eyes, sniffing the air like a bloodhound. "I feel like her tent was just over that hill. It smells right."

"I don't see anything. But I know she moved her stuff around all the time, so she wouldn't get busted. No harm in looking."

Ian led the way. Suddenly, he bent down by a small ditch, picked up a stick and poked deliberately. "I see something red and orange here. Isn't that one of her dream catchers?"

Peter quickly came over to check it out. "Yeah, I think so. Leave it. I need to tell Tomassi."

"Wait. What's over there?" Ian marched over to a big rock and whistled. "Now you really have to call him."

"What?"

"Her tent, I think. And look, it's been burned. Sherry,"

Ian said softly, sitting down on the ground. "Tell me what happened."

CHAPTER 48

EAUTOPIA AND THE CONSORTIUM SEALED THE DEAL with splendid opulence. The lavish private cocktail party, celebrated with flowing bottles of Taittinger Comtes de Champagne Blanc de Blancs, produced only in years when the vintage is exceptional, had its own confidential expense column privy to a select few.

"Only the best for the best," Brock toasted. "Hear, hear," everyone responded. They lifted their fluted glasses and purred with contentment at the aromatic notes of ripe hay, chalky caves and briny seas.

The guests included all the bigwigs from the Consortium and Eautopia. Since the site work would proceed quickly and without any fanfare until the official public announcement, a blackout on publicity kept a lid on the news.

Marti handled the Consortium's specialty champagne order for two cases at $3,500 each.

"I love taking their money," she said to Lori. "And I have to admit they have great taste, damn them."

"That's some pretty swanky booze. What exactly are they celebrating?"

"I don't know. Maybe they made another deal with Lucifer."

The gourmet appetizers, served in the executive penthouse suite on the fiftieth floor overlooking Hatfield and the river valley, featured beluga caviar, pate de foie gras, ripe wheels of brie, prosciutto di Parma wrapped around melon, and mini brioche lobster rolls garnished with chives.

Josh helped himself to leftovers the next day, along with the other staffers who'd worked on the deal but hadn't rated being invited. They'd also been required to sign a non-disclosure agreement. He slathered some Dijon mustard on crusty sourdough bread, lopped off a chunk of pate, cut a wedge of brie, grabbed a bottle of Eautopia water, and headed back to his office to work on the formal report. He almost sat on the white chocolate petit fours topped with a passionfruit ganache he'd stuffed into his pocket but remembered them at the last minute.

Josh burped contentedly, a very satisfying foie gras essence, but he barely looked up for hours as he made colorful pie charts and bar graphs that a third-grader might understand.

Yet he couldn't shake the mental image of a nuclear mushroom cloud, the kind he'd seen in history books and movies. The dense atmospheric poison obliterated the sheer natural beauty of the reservoir, tricking unsuspecting Mother Nature out of her glory. Frowning, he took his hand off the computer mouse and got up to stretch.

"I don't know about this. Forget two years," he whispered to himself. "Not sure I can last two months."

Meanwhile, Nancy tried to communicate with her boss at Alcon to make sure he understood her situation, but she left message after message without hearing back. Once she got his assistant, who promised to give him the message. Getting through to HR, never easy in the best of times, proved even more frustrating.

"Voicemail hell," Nancy muttered. "I don't get it."

Finally, she could see the goalposts. Maybe just three more weeks of IV nutrition through her pump, a process which Nancy, now practically a pro, still endured with difficulty. Nancy used the pump only at night for twelve full hours. She never slept soundly any way, but somehow, she catnapped through the dark hours, a trade-off for the freedom she got during the day.

"Of course, freedom means inching from the couch to the table to the TV. For a treat, I even go into the kitchen. Not that I can eat anything. I don't even remember what eating's like."

Nancy insisted on Peter eating a chocolate chip cookie from Great Full Bread in front of her and observed him like a tourist at the Eiffel Tower.

Healthy snacks were on Kenny and Marco's minds as they poured over the spreadsheet Kenny had created to evaluate team performance.

"Look, on Saturday and Sunday afternoons we don't win. Every kid's down at least one hit, and the fielding errors suck. It's gotta be what they're eating for breakfast and before the game." Kenny gestured with a pencil covered with bite marks.

"Hey man, don't chew pencils. You stupid? Lead poisoning, dude."

"Bad habit." Kenny didn't bother to look at the indentations from his teeth as he tapped the picnic table rapidly with the stubby pencil. "Our plan to get them here two hours before game time, hydrate and ditch the junk food has gotta help."

"Yo, KJ, you got your own place, right?" Marco spoked as he counted out the snacks they'd bought for the team. Kenny got the Bridgeville PD to buy two cases of Gatorade; Great Full Bread ponied up for oranges and protein bars.

"Yeah, kind of. I live with a bunch of guys. It's like a freaking frat house sometimes. Not great, but the way my shifts change, I can't see getting my own place."

"I'm still with my moms, but time to get my own crib." Marco moved a grape Gatorade towards the side. "Ima save it for me. Let's give this kid a yellow one."

"Sure. I never asked you this, but with Paco and his girlfriend expecting, it just popped into my head. You have any kids?"

"Hell no. Makes me like the only one. Truth—I'm a mama's boy. Ain't no one like Mami." Marco flashed a big grin before shading his eyes with his hand. He craned his neck left and right, looking for some early arriving players. "My sister already gave her three grandbabies, anyway."

"Yeah, that's funny—my sister's got two. Cute kids, but the little one whines all the time. Keeps my parents out of my hair, though."

"One day, you gonna wake up and find like baby triplets hanging all over you. Half a basketball team before you even know it. KJ all bald, fat and mega-whipped, that'll be you."

Kenny laughed and shook his head. "No fucking way. I want a dog really bad, though. Hey, you still seeing Luz?"

"Keep up, man. Old news. Why, you into her?"

"Nope. Just asking." Kenny stood up and whistled through his teeth at the kids congregating by the backstop. "Over here, guys."

CHAPTER 49

THE MEDICAL EXAMINER'S SUMMARY AUTOPSY REPORT for Sherry changed everything. It labelled her death a homicide due to the fracture of the hyoid bone, larynx and thyroid cartilage.

"That's throttling, strangling. This is a homicide, all right," Ian said to Andre and Peter after Vic tipped him off. "She had to be dead before being thrown in the reservoir. Or at least well on her way and then her lungs filled up with water. The report will show the time sequence."

"Are you fucking kidding me?" Peter almost vomited. Tomassi's bad feeling notwithstanding, he hadn't thought it would be a murder.

"Vic's got his claws into everything, damn. How the hell did he get the confidential information?" Andre put his hand on Peter's shoulder to comfort him. "And then he goes and leaks it to you of all people."

"Vic lives for moments like these. He probably wet himself." Ian had actually begun to like Vic and loved being in on the dirt. "In the UK, this used to be called 'the hangman's fracture.' Criminals were sentenced to hanging quite frequently, back in the day. People queued up to watch, big crowds—entertainment for the whole family. The technique was brutal before the mid-19th century."

"What are you, the History Channel?" Andre gave Ian a hard look to get him to shut up.

Ian ignored him. "They just hung off the rope's end 'til their necks broke. But if the hangman didn't jerk it hard enough or tie the knot tight enough, well—death through slow choking."

Peter gagged and spat into a paper towel.

"Why the fuck are you still talking?" Andre demanded.

"It was something we learned at the academy. Part of the History of Homicide sequence."

"What is a hyoid bone?" Peter finally spoke.

"It's in the neck, it's like the letter 'U' and if it's broken, you've got a guaranteed strangling." Ian pointed to his own neck to show the location.

"I'm gonna go home," Peter said quietly.

"You don't look too good. Are you sure you're OK to drive?" Andre consulted the schedule. "I'm booked until 5:00, and Ian's back-to-back until 6. You want me to call Jeff to pick you up?"

"No." Peter, moving slowly, reached for his keys and trudged out the door.

When Peter got in his truck, he started driving aimlessly. He didn't want to talk to anybody. He didn't want to see anybody. By the time he found himself up at the dam, he had been pulled over by the cops.

The siren shrieked behind him, and he saw the flashing lights of the Bridgeville patrol motorcycle. Peter eased his truck onto the far-right side of the road and wondered what was up. He definitely hadn't been speeding.

The approaching cop flipped up the helmet's visor.

"Kenny?"

"Tomassi wants to see you." Kenny Johnson cut an imposing figure in his leathers, but his sparse light brown facial hair suggested a teenager.

"He could've picked up the phone like a normal person. And that peach-fuzz on your lip is a pathetic excuse for a mustache."

"Hey, it's a process." Kenny leaned against Peter's truck. "This is a whole new level of fucked up. Tomassi wants you to meet him at the ferry path at 6:00. Very hush-hush."

"What is he, Mata Hari? Fucked up doesn't begin to describe this stuff with Sherry. You know, Tomassi never misses dinner, and Donna's gonna be pissed."

"I'm sure the two Big Macs he demolished for lunch will keep him going. And Donna will just have to deal like always." Kenny glanced around and saw some cars slowing down for a look. "Peter, I don't know what the hell is going on, but you're one of the good guys so don't step in more shit."

"Got it. You can tell John I'll be there." A couple of young kids on bicycles stopped to check out the motorcycle and take in the scene. Peter took notice. "Can I go now, Officer? You should give these yo-yo's a talking to about not wearing helmets." The kids pedaled off in a hurry, yelling about police harassment.

"Use your blinker next time, would you?" Kenny winked and patted the side of Peter's truck.

By the time Peter stepped into his house, his voicemail was full and he had twenty-five new text messages. He didn't bother with any of them.

Peter sat for a long time. Brutus jumped up on the couch and stuck his snout in Peter's face. He panted open-mouthed and cocked his head to the side.

"C'mon, B. You've got salmon breath. Take a hike." When Peter didn't pet him, Brutus nosed himself under Peter's slack arm and demanded satisfaction.

Peter checked his watch. Four thirty. Not enough time to do anything except take a nap. Closing his eyes, Peter saw visions of Sherry's fate. Shadowy figures snuck up on her as she sat cross-legged on the ground making more dreamcatchers. Sinister men in black cornered her at water's edge. In each instance, Sherry's neck was snapped by a pair of giant hands that squeezed her eyeballs out of her sockets.

When his alarm sounded at 5:45, Peter surfaced with difficulty. He felt terrible—groggy and disoriented, dizzy and nauseated. Brutus practically put on his own leash and dragged him to the ferry landing. Aside from a couple of birdwatchers and people sitting in their cars, he didn't see anyone. Then a pine cone hit him in the head.

"Over here." Tomassi stepped out from the trees onto a narrow stone path overrun by skunk cabbage.

"Just text me, dipshit."

"Walk with me, halfwit." Tomassi reached down to pat Brutus. "I wish I could have a stud like you."

"Man up and tell Donna no more yapping poodles. May they rest in peace." Peter remembered Pierre and Francie the most. They were fast as race cars but went into a tizzy about everything.

"Listen, between you, me and the mosquitos, there's no fingerprints. Do you understand what I'm saying?" Tomassi stared at him without blinking, his unibrow holding a steady line.

Peter thought for a moment and reached down to snare a discarded candy wrapper. "I'm thinking you mean there's no smoking gun."

"Bingo." Tomassi pointed to an empty vodka bottle. Peter shook his head after probing it with his shoe. "Yeah, no—leave it. Broken glass like that's a hazard. Gotta get the litter guys down here. Tomassi looked around and lowered his voice. "Based on the ME report, the perp wore gloves. We got jack for evidence and no witnesses. It's a clusterfuck."

"Jesus. What about forensics from the burned tent?"

"An accelerant. Nothing useful."

"So that's it?" Peter grabbed Tomassi's arm. "We gotta get justice for Sherry."

"It's an open case; I'll never let it go cold." Tomassi disengaged and put an empty potato chip bag in Peter's hand. "Do something useful for a change. Look, her picture, description, location, and, you know, the usual 'if you have information about this case, please contact the Bridgeville Police Department at blah blah blah,' is gonna be on the website front and center. Maybe we'll catch a break."

"Fuckers who did this."

"Never say never. We only need someone who saw something to come forward. But don't kid yourself, this isn't someone stupid like Skippy Lafford. This feels professional."

"It's all tied up in the Consortium and Eautopia. It's about the damn water." Peter put himself nose to nose with Tomassi. "You know deep in your gut, you felt it, John."

"Stay out of it." Tomassi stepped backward into some mud and very deliberately wiped his shoes off on a rocky outcropping. "You called in the tent, you done good. It's strictly by the book going forward. Goddam Vic's really got his head up someone's ass to get intel like that, never mind share it with Ian."

"They're buds now. The dynamic duo. But what's with the cloak and dagger bullshit. You can't call me or be seen with me?" They had resumed strolling along the leafy path.

"It's not all public yet. And yeah, I got a reputation to protect. Plus, phone records and text messages can be subpoenaed. And don't you go posting any trash talk on social media."

"Wow. I'm speechless."

"That's a first." Tomassi looked at his watch. "Geez, Donna's gonna think I got something on the side." Peter had to crack a smile. Tomassi loved being a married family man more than anything in the world. "What? I'm never late for dinner."

• • •

CHAPTER 50

"HISTORY IS WRITTEN BY THE WINNERS, NANCY."

"We need team players. Trust is easy to lose, Nancy."

Right on cue, each corporate hologram addressed Nancy as though she had the mental capacity of a snail. Nancy looked dully from man to man. They sat in a basement office in the Alcon Building. As she stared at them loopily through her painkillers that she'd injected through the PICC line in her arm, she saw they were clones, possibly even robots. Mid-forties, minimally moussed brown hair parted on the left, navy blue suits, crisp white shirts, majestically red ties, and gleaming black loafers.

Nancy had broken just about every kind of important rule laid down by the visiting nurses by leaving her house and driving to this meeting. Even the stairs were off-limits right after pain meds. Somehow, she drove to the office, but only after being told that her job depended on this meeting.

"We'd like to hear your version of events, Nancy. We come from a place of concern. You can tell us," said the first man whose name sounded like Biff Glasscock. Nancy decided that she would identify Biff by his meaty earlobes.

The other man, Woody Buffington, had very short fingers. Or maybe the first man was Woody Glasscock and the second one was Biff Buffington. Nancy truly couldn't puzzle it out, but she didn't really care. Although, she reminded herself, their names sounded oddly close to a drinking game she had played in college where a person created a porn star name by answering three questions: your first pet's name, the name of the street you lived on as a child, and she forgot the third one.

"Nancy? Have you forgotten why you're here?"

Nancy roused herself. Her still-open wound leaked through the gauze pad she'd taped over the drain in her abdomen and seeped unpleasantly down her underpants. She could smell her body rotting.

"You said this is an urgent meeting because you want to discuss my performance. But I don't understand how I work for you. I work for Joe Evans. At Alcon. Like I explained over the phone, HR knows all about my situation and why I'm on short-term disability."

Just then, Brock Saunders flung open the door and loomed over her. "Not any more. And your division reports to us."

Nancy flinched at the sight of him, her stomach, or what remained of it, spasming. Her vaginal muscles tensed wretchedly into a knot.

"Nancy Yates. You have been spun off," Brock boomed. His cologne filled the room. Biff and Woody pulled up a chair for him. "I'll stand. This," he said, gesturing at Nancy as though she were an inanimate object, "shouldn't take too long."

"What is happening here?" Nancy croaked. Before any of the men could speak, she cut them off, her strength rallying. "I've had serious complications from my surgery. I don't know what you're talking about."

"Your department at the Alcon Group was spun off to the Consortium's Financial Services Division. We have important issues to discuss." Biff took the reins and steered the conversation to somewhere Nancy hadn't anticipated.

Woody spoke up as Brock's eyes bored holes in Nancy's body. "Nancy, your performance review which, importantly, your previous managers filed prior to your surgery is a disaster. Work flow stagnation, deficiencies, errors, lack of timely communication, inappropriate communication, ethical lapses; all are duly noted with dates." He circled something on his legal pad.

"Now then," Biff continued, sounding very rehearsed. "Unless we can come to some kind of understanding, your place in the new paradigm is at risk. Is this the outcome you want?"

Nancy looked from Biff to Woody, deliberately ignoring Brock's presence. "I don't understand this negative performance review. There were no problems at all."

"Not according to this document. What happens today is crucial for your future at the Consortium." Both men stared at her without blinking. Brock cracked his knuckles loudly, over and over. "Nothing less than full cooperation is acceptable."

"OK, sure." Nancy's dripping armpits drenched her shirt. She shifted uncomfortably, wiping her palms on her loose pants.

"Good. Let's start with your explanation of how you came to view documents stolen from our new corporate partner, Eautopia."

"What? What do you mean?" Nancy sputtered in shock, her heart plummeting. "I was in the hospital, the ICU. I've had serious complications."

Glasscock cleared a phlegmy blockage in his throat. Brock filled the temporary void. "You committed big violations of corporate security laws."

"You should know," Nancy shot back.

"Touché. I faced my consequences. Are you ready for yours?"

Brock motioned for Biff to show Nancy some papers.

"Think hard. These should help." Biff slowly and deliberately arranged some photographs on the table.

Nancy gasped at the pictures of Peter holding the envelope containing the documents and flash drive. He was photographed entering and leaving her house. The two of them were silhouetted at her kitchen table looking over the papers. In a sequence of time- and date-stamped photos, Nancy held the flash drive and inserted it into her laptop.

A very powerful zoom lens showed the 9 x 12 envelope and the documents on her table. Clearly visible were the words: *Property of the New England Consortium Council.*

Tears, make-up and sweat ran down Nancy's face. "Do I need a lawyer?" She tried to get up and leave but her legs buckled. She clutched the table tightly.

The men stared at her coldly, Brock's expression terrifying although Nancy tried to avoid looking at him.

"What were you doing?" Brock moved his chair closer to her, near enough so she could see the grey peeking through the apricot hue of his hair.

"How dare you spy on me. Wait," she said, her head spinning. "Have you been following Peter since the Zenergy thing?"

"Russo's history. We can put him away. Here's a short video you might enjoy."

Brock pushed a button and a screen descended from the ceiling. She watched, mesmerized. The video showed Peter leaving the dam and heading to her house. Peter rang her doorbell and held the envelope. The last few seconds showed him, envelope tucked under his arm, pulling the door shut and checking twice before he drove away.

"Oh my God, he did shut it. You bastards, how dare you?"

Brock smirked and pushed another button. The next short video showed Peter and Ian hiking at the reservoir. Nancy could dimly make out a woman talking to them.

"Is that—no it can't be. Is that Sherry Nicholas?"

"Here's what you're going to do, Nancy. Save your-self. Tell us where he hid our property. Tell us everything about Russo's activities." Woody or Biff spoke to her while Brock leaned back in his chair and watched her closely.

"This is blackmail. I want—"

Nancy suddenly started having powerful bowel contractions. An occasional side effect of her surgery, she'd never had them this urgently. She scurried out to the hallway, clutching her belly and farting. She almost made it to the door of the handicapped stall before she lost control. The stinking mess combined with her cell-level horror at Brock's evil intentions sent her off the deep end. Crying, huddled in the corner, she wadded toilet paper into a sponge and cleaned off as best she could. Haltingly, she rose to her feet and tried to text Peter but there was no reception.

Nancy knew she had to get out of there somehow, some way. Opening the restroom door cautiously, she stepped into the waiting coven of Brock and his henchmen.

"Here you are," Buffington purred.

"You made me shit myself, you fucking bastards. Let me go."

"We're not done, Nancy." Brock pressed a white hand-kerchief to his nose.

"I'll call the cops, I'll sue you for harassment."

"Actually, you're just about to be arrested for theft and espionage. Felonies."

Nancy stared at them weakly, unsteady on her feet. "What do you want from me?"

"We want Russo. We almost have him, but we need you to make it stick. You give us Russo, and nothing happens to you. It's simple. You get to keep your job and benefits. Health care, retirement." Biff looked at her expectantly.

"No."

"You for Russo."

"No. I need time. I'm sick."

"Well, if you didn't become such a fucking fat pig," Brock suddenly whispered in her ear, his breath horrifying. "Work on saying no like you mean it, bitch."

Straightening up, he gave an almost imperceptible nod to his cronies. "You have an hour. Plenty of time to clean the shit off."

"We have eyes on you. No contact with Russo or anybody else." Woody and Biff finished each other's words.

"It's prison if you miss the deadline," Brock showed her his teeth and smiled as her face quivered. "Super max for Russo."

CHAPTER 51

THE CONSORTIUM AND EAUTOPIA CALLED A BIG NEWS conference to reveal their water bottling venture. The deal made headlines in the business world. Locally, the governor and state legislators practically pummeled each other like MMA fighters to get in front of the TV cameras. Brock Saunders gave interview after interview, pronouncing himself humbled at the chance to do some good. The giant facility neared completion as crews worked 24/7.

"I asked the good Lord for forgiveness and guidance. Things happen for a reason. I'm so grateful that our great metropolitan region can be an engine for growth." Brock had toned back the spray-tan and hair spray. "I want to thank all the people who made this possible."

"Brock brought home the bacon for whoever put him on the Water Board. They're laughing all the way to the bank." Lori said when she called Peter to give him her take on what just went down.

"I'm so mad I can't even see straight," Peter fumed. "I can't tell you how upset Jeff is. He's talking to some other people who got burned by Pioneer to see if they can take down Brock."

"Yeah, good luck with that. Are you OK? I feel awful that I didn't help you more when you came to me asking about the Consortium. I'm really sorry, Peter."

"I can't talk about it, Lor. Too upset."

But out of the spotlight, fault lines fissured. Stone-faced Town Council members up for re-election kept their profiles low. The citizens of Bridgeville burned with fury and outrage. Taking the pulse of public opinion, the Consortium all but disappeared from view, letting emissaries from Eautopia make the rounds to donate cases of water, tout the new job opportunities and promise peaceful co-existence. Brock Saunders limited his appearances to radio.

The college kids back home in Bridgeville for the summer weren't having it.

"Bridgeville is ours," they chanted in front of the reinforced chain link fence denying access to the site. "B-I-O; Bridgeville is ours."

While their elders railed against the lack of transparency in meetings conducted according to Robert's Rules of Order, the millennials named names and created a social action hashtag: #myBIO. Tweeting and retweeting, posting and reposting, podcasting and streaming, they created a firestorm. They even held a widely covered funeral for the reservoir, complete with remembrances and eulogies. Still, the Eautopia water plant neared completion.

Job applicants interviewed off-site undeterred by the controversy.

Peter blasted Nancy, Ian, and Andre. "Who knew? We did. And we fucking blew it."

Nancy knew Brock had eyes on her; she felt them. She tried to be invisible, saying nothing to Peter and shunning contact with him. The luxury of his outrage about the Consortium and Eautopia drove her to fury. In their only phone conversation after Brock's ambush, she let him have it. "Leave me alone. I don't need your melodrama; I'm done with all the bullshit."

"With pleasure," Peter said angrily. He didn't call again.

Nancy didn't dare allow Peter to see her. In one look, he'd know she'd somehow sold her soul to the devil. But he wouldn't guess that he was her free pass, her get-out-of-jail ticket. Nancy needed to play both Brock and Peter. One, a cruel and powerful sadist, had her trapped in a vise; the other, a selfish jerk, had brought ruin to her doorstep. After taking the last klonopin she'd hoarded for a really bad day, she dreamed she was a highly poisonous coral snake, lithe, pert and sexy like an old-time Hollywood ingenue, talking to Peter as she lay on his deck.

PETER: *You're so beautiful, but what's up with the big hat and sunglasses? It's almost night, Nancy Snake, no one will see you.*

NANCY: *I'm being blackmailed, terrible people want to destroy me.*

PETER: *I'm picking up very weird vibes. You're probably hungry. I might have some frozen mice in the freezer; I know how much you love a yummy snack.*

NANCY (*slithering closer*): *I'm so scared, but I'm not going down in flames. I can't save both of us.*

PETER: *I'm gonna chalk it up to your complications, but, wow—you are not yourself.*

NANCY: *I've never been more myself. If it's you or me, I choose me. You have only yourself to blame for what's coming from Brock and the Consortium. I fucking hate you. And, I'm sorry.*

CHAPTER 52

IAN LEFT FOR AN EXTENDED WEEKEND AT THE RETREAT, "I need to atone. We had some clues—we are complicit." He fasted for days and toiled until his fingers bled.

"This is some fucking dystopian shit," Andre said, working out with Peter. They put on the heavy boxing gloves and pounded the heavy bag, switching to the speedbag and back again.

"But it's real," Peter panted. "We, especially me, were such pussies. We had it in our hands. And now look."

Although Peter didn't include John Tomassi in his indictment, Tomassi shouldered some of the blame in a late-night conversation by the ferry. This time, Sean was the emissary. Jeff, working late with Rachel, let it be known that he felt guilty, too.

"Pete, sometimes, you're right," Tomassi said. "Actually, hardly ever – but this time you had the goods. It never even crossed my mind that the Consortium could pimp our water."

"We're guilty. At least I am. After Ian couldn't break the password and when Sherry got killed, I lost my focus."

"Nobody would've believed you. People would've looked at you like Chicken Little running around yelling the sky was falling."

"You really think?"

"Hell, yeah. You're a loudmouth loose cannon half the time." Tomassi tapped his knuckles gently on Peter's head before Peter shook him off.

"At least I give a damn."

Peter called Lori with an idea. "Maybe we've still got a shot at stopping production. I've still got the documents. Maybe we can get it shut down."

"No. Face facts, Peter. It sucks, but it is what it is."

"I'm not giving up."

Two days later, Peter had just about finished deadheading the marigolds lining his front steps when Tomassi showed up unannounced, looking for all the world like his head ached more than any amount of Tylenol could soothe.

"I don't know how to tell you this. It's bad. You're fucked." Tomassi spoke urgently as he exited his car.

"Don't be such a drama queen—what're you talking about?" Peter stood by his front steps and waited. "What now? I thought you couldn't be seen with me. Hey, you gotta taste one of these peaches I just picked, they're delicious."

"Too much is moving too fast. It got ahead of me." Tomassi suddenly spoke in jagged bursts. His shortness of breath scared Peter.

"What did? Jesus, just breathe—oh shit. You better not be having a heart attack." Peter pushed the pile of desiccated orange blossoms off the step and moved Tomassi like he weighed less than a kitten. "Sit."

Tomassi sank like a cement block. "Hyperventilating." He motioned with his fingers and croaked, "Paper bag."

Peter ran inside. "Here—you want me to hold the bag?
I'm calling 911."

He shook Peter off and held the bag over his own nose
and mouth. Tomassi took about ten breaths into the bag
and then took it away from his face.

Peter grabbed Tomassi's wrist and placed two fingers on his pulse. "I don't like it. Breathe, do the belly
breathing."

Tomassi nodded, his breathing growing less ragged.
"Nancy. Pushed you under the bus."

"John, should I call 911? How about Donna?"

Tomassi shook his head no. "Nancy folded." He paused,
winded completely. "Brock Saunders, the Consortium."
He put the bag over his mouth again and sagged against
the door frame.

"What?" Peter massaged Tomassi's slumped shoulders
and inspected him nervously. "Come on, Johnny. Breathe,
dammit."

Tomassi trembled visibly. "I can't fix this. Christ, I'm
dizzy." Tomassi motioned for Peter to help him up.

"Let's get some water." Peter put his shoulder under
Tomassi's sweat-soaked armpit and half-dragged him
into a chair near the window. He turned the box fan on
the highest setting and aimed it at Tomassi. "Damn it,
John—tell me you're OK." The cool breeze slowed the
torrents of sweat on Tomassi's face, but he glistened with
an unhealthy sheen.

"I have to talk to you." Tomassi's voice, slower than
usual gained some strength. "Fucking anxiety, I'm fine."

"OK, I'm listening. And you better get yourself checked
out. No dying in our fifties."

Tomassi, eyes closed, nodded. "A world of hurt coming your way."

"What the fuck are you talking about? Nancy wouldn't
sell me out. No way." Peter watched his old friend's

shaking hands. "Since when you been getting panic attacks?"

"Forget it. Consortium's got you." Tomassi leaned back, clearly exhausted. "Violating probation, the papers."

"That's bullshit. So I found their damn documents. So what?"

"Douchebag. Theft, trade secrets, that's what."

Peter relaxed for a nanosecond, insults were good. "Lies—all lies. They're full of shit. Wait, she actually ratted me out? What the hell is happening here?"

"You gotta get in front of this. Hear me? Call Lori or Vic. Do what you need to do." Tomassi emphasized each word slowly. He rose unsteadily but sank back down. "Get me outta here. I'll be fucked if they find out I warned you."

"You're a good man, John. The best. And you've got real stones." Peter chattered anxiously and helped him up. "Jeff's by the barn. Let him give you a ride home. Sean can drive your car since it's not the cruiser." Before Tomassi could protest, Peter texted Jeff who drove the tractor over as fast as it would go.

"Let's get you home, John-o," Jeff said, using a long-retired nickname for Tomassi. He mouthed the word, "Hospital?" and waited for Peter to nod yes or no. Peter gave an almost imperceptible no. Jeff arched an eyebrow but said nothing.

After Jeff bundled Tomassi into the car and took off, Peter hesitated. He didn't know whether to call Nancy and give her hell or to listen to Tomassi and call Lori. Pacing back and forth, he opted for Lori. When he went straight to voicemail, he called Vic.

"Hey, Vic. You still my defense attorney?"

"Maybe. Gimme a dollar and we'll see. What's up?"

"You still in the office?"

"Yeah, why? You want to drop by?"

"On my way."

Vic didn't take his eyes off Peter. The story stunned him into silence.

"Unfucking real. I get to play me in the movie. This is crazy shit."

"Yeah, well, John said it was beyond real, as in 100 percent true."

"Alright. Here's what we do. First off, you and Tomassi never spoke. Got it? Second, do not—and I mean absolutely do not—contact Nancy. You can't tip your hand. She's talking to the Consortium willingly or not, but either way, you know nothing. Third, I'm gonna call Ian and get him moving. Fourth is big. How are you gonna pay for this?"

"Vic, I don't know." Peter lowered his head into his hands. "And please don't ask Carmen. I'm begging you."

"Look, whatever. I gotta make some calls. In the meantime, you lock your trap and throw away the key. Capisce?"

CHAPTER 53

HERB BAKER, NOW SEVENTY AND FEELING POORLY, insisted on holding Sherry's memorial service behind the gnarled fruit trees where he let her camp out. The weather forecast called for a scorcher of a day in the mid-nineties, so the gathering started at ten in the morning.

Herb had served in Vietnam with Sherry's second oldest brother, Billy. Walking shakily on two canes, Herb stopped every few feet to acknowledge well-wishers and mourners. The long procession through the crowd took forever, but it gave him wings. By the time his daughter led him up to a wooden armchair placed on a makeshift stage, Herb looked like a younger man. He began to speak into a microphone, part of a system set up by his grandson who encouraged him to hold it further away from his mouth after some painful squawking static.

Peter stood next to Ian. Jeff and Annie were sitting with Donna Tomassi, and Jeff kept casting a watchful eye in Peter's direction. Jeff went ballistic when Peter told him about Nancy, who didn't show up, provoking more than a few whispers.

"She wouldn't dare," Peter said. "She couldn't look me in the eye for a second."

"That Judas bitch?" Jeff seethed. "Never. And Saunders is mine."

The organized police presence set a tone of respect, and Tomassi had his guys doing crowd control, parking and traffic. Tomassi, himself, wearing full uniform, stood by the stage, scanning the crowd.

Peter didn't see Carmen at first, but he felt her in the air. When he turned to slap a mosquito off Jeff's shoulder, he saw her. Carmen, in a crisp linen dress, looked sad, and leaned into a tall mountain of a man who had his arm around her. Peter nodded in her direction and then glanced away.

"Settle in, people. I've got some stuff to say, and I'm not getting down until I say it." The noise of the crowd hushed until the only the birds and the bugs were audible. Herb made eye contact with a few audience members who encouraged him to get going.

"Sometimes, I wonder who was luckier—me for coming back home to Bridgeville all scarred up in mind and body or Billy Nicholas for dying on Hamburger Hill. Yeah, I don't think you'd understand. We had a saying; every unit had a saying: The unwilling led by the incompetent to do the unnecessary. Remember that because I'm going to ask you to repeat it soon. But, let me tell you Hamburger Hill wasn't nothin to die for. Pain and fear and sacrifice. Men who weren't more than boys, screaming. And blood, so much blood." Herb had to stop because he was winded and crying. He took out a worn handkerchief and wiped his eyes before blowing his nose loudly.

"Now, some of you don't know Sherry Nicholas had two brothers die in the war. Bobby died at Khe Sanh in '68. She was seven. The Nicholas family couldn't handle those boys dying, and sorry to say, it wasn't home sweet home that kept Billy and Bobby from enlisting. And Sherry ended up fending for herself except for the ghosts and monsters at home. This is not a fairy tale I'm telling. And I know many of us wish we'd done more for Sherry." He stopped, seeming to forget what he wanted to say. His daughter whispered in his ear, and Herb resumed speaking.

"Sherry was murdered, strangled to death and thrown into the reservoir like a handful of mud, in her own hometown of Bridgeville. That's not the Bridgeville I dreamed about in country. And it's not the one she somehow found her way back to. Now I'm mad as hell about why we're here today, and I know most of you feel the same way. Why'd I say most of you? Because we have to weed out the lying bastards who're stealing our water." Boos cascaded through the air. Herb raised a shaky hand to ask for quiet.

"If I was a betting man, I'd put money on them pulling the strings to break her neck. See, Sherry—she'd never drown. Girl swam like a mermaid. And those sons of bitches, they're not to set foot on my land, but I'm sure some of their lackeys snuck in. If you see them, let me know and I'll kick them out myself." He tilted danger-ously to the right as he tried to stand. His grandson hov-ered close by his side, hands outstretched to catch him. Cheers filled the air along with chants of, "Herb—Herb."

Herb asked for a moment of silence. Then he shouted into the microphone. "What'd I want you to remember? Say it loud."

It started as a low rumble and then coordinated into a roar. "The unwilling led by the incompetent to do the unnecessary!"

"Yes, sir," Herb said. "Let's start backwards. The unnecessary is stealing away our water, never mind during a drought. This is our water, so where the hell do they get off selling it to some blood-sucking company to bottle it and make millions?" He waited, hands trembling with Parkinson's. The crowd coaxed him to continue.

"The incompetent—well that's easy. The Consortium and the damn town officials who made this secret deal. It wasn't theirs to sell. Yep, not theirs. Now who's the unwilling? We are," he yelled hoarsely. "We are unwilling to let this go. Am I right?"

The crowd erupted. "Herb—Herb."

People milled around afterwards, lining up to shake Herb's hand. When it was Peter's turn, Herb, eyes glazed, put his hand out automatically.

"No way. Get in here, Herb," Peter said, opening his arms wide. Herb sagged against him, and Peter righted him by the elbows after hugging him tight.

"Petey, I'm so tired. You need to make sure the bas-tards pay."

"I'm trying, I'm trying." Peter tried to get Herb to balance on his own two feet, but he swayed alarmingly. "Hey, can we get Herb into the shade and give him some water?"

Ian helped Peter guide Herb to the golf cart that his grandson drove over, and they lifted him into the seat. He clutched Peter's sleeve, his tremors heightened by fatigue.

"Don't be a stranger." Herb's voice, barely above a slow whisper, chilled Peter's heart. "I don't have much time."

Peter squeezed both of Herb's liver-spotted and gnarled hands. "You'll outlive us all, Herb."

The golf cart lurched off, sending clouds of dust into the air. After saying some more goodbyes, Jeff reminded Peter that they needed to drop by the commissary.

"We gotta check on the bake and take inventory. Rach's expecting us."

Rachel, taking a short break, saw them pulling into the parking lot and jogged over to offer hugs.

"Pete, you look so down. It's gonna be OK. Just be safe."

Jeff, surprised by the sudden burst of affection, held onto his daughter for an extra beat.

When Peter met up with Marco for the morning shift the next day, Marco patted him on the back.

"Memorials always sad, Coach. I been to too many."

"Yeah."

"But you been kinda down for a while now—not like you. What's happening?"

"If I told you, you wouldn't believe me. But I can't."

"What—you don't trust me? Coach, I'd put it on the line for you any day, any time. Take a bullet like the Secret Service. You gotta trust me."

Peter flinched. "Marco, Marco. Don't. I trust you completely, and I swear I'd tell you if I could, but this is some very evil shit. A betrayal by someone really close. And the consequences are really bad. You're like a son to me, but for your own good, your own protection, I can't tell you."

"You in trouble again, that's my problem, too. I know a guy who knows a guy. You read me? Maybe, we make this go away."

"No, the last thing I want is for you to get sucked in. You got your own stuff, and I don't know how this bullshit plays out. Come on." Peter checked his watch. "Enough true confessions. We need to haul ass. Let's get the show on the road."

When the breakfast run started, Marco reminded Peter to smile. "No long face, aight?"

Peter rallied, buoyed by Marco's contagious energy and Great Full Bread's appreciative customers. He bantered, he charmed, but his battery drained completely by the end of lunch. Once they sold out of almost everything and were cleaning the truck, Marco asked, "Does KJ know about this?"

"Absolutely do not tell him. This is my mess. I'll handle it." Peter shut the conversation down with uncharacteristic vehemence.

"OK, listen. Time out. I got some ideas about fancy paletas. We do some for the hipster vegans, some others covered in chocolate and coconut. Maybe chili powder. We got like ten kinds, but we could do twenty real easy."

"You've got bona fide business smarts. I'm in."

"I got a good head for this. Damn, how come I never knew before? Everybody always sayin' I'm never gonna amount to nothin'. Just a punk."

"What bullshit. People got a lot to answer for."

"Damn straight. So what kinda fruit base you want? I'm thinking we go heavy on the fresh watermelon, peach and strawberry. Gotta support and represent. No farms, no food, baby."

• • •

CHAPTER 54

THE DAY OF THE WEDDING, PETER TRIED FASHIONING a boutonniere to Brutus's plain brown leather collar, but Brutus pawed it off.

"Fine. Message received."

Peter followed Ian's advice to put Nancy's negative energy in a thick steel vault, locked up tight and buried deep underground.

"At least for the wedding and festivities," Peter said. "I can't let her spoil their happiness."

"Or yours," Ian said.

"If I'm happy, it's news to me."

"You're happy. Trust me."

After consulting with Lori and Marti, Peter wore a navy blazer, blue button down Oxford shirt, and tan khakis.

"No tie, hallelujah." But, he told Jeff and Tomassi they had to wear one. "Only the holy get excused."

Peter had slimmed down considerably from the last time he wore his good clothes, a pleasant surprise. "I look good, admit it, Brutus. It's all that hard work and clean living."

After one last check of his buttons, he and Brutus drove up to the orchard with time to spare. Peter parked his truck in a corner of the lot and stuck his head in the kitchen by the pavilion to see if Paco and Marco had delivered the special order. Carmen saw him as she rushed around and gave him a quick thumbs-up.

"It's all here," she yelled over the din.

"Great. Need any help?"

"No. Good luck—now out of my way," she said, rushing past him in a Hot Stuff apron shaped like a chili pepper.

"You, too." He watched her with a smile until he almost got slammed in the face by a tray full of steaming dishes. He inspected the Great Full Bread items that Paco and Marco had arranged on platters. Everything looked good to go.

The 6 pm ceremony started late, getting underway around 6:30. By then, the softer light of evening gave off a beautiful glow. The September sun had been strong enough to merit a 7 on the UV index, but the evening air felt comfortably cool.

Fiori Orchards never looked better. Carmen had her people working up until the last minute. Using a vintage-inspired floral theme perfectly matched to the rustic chic vibe, Carmen had arranged dense clusters of flawless white flowers on every table.

Ian and Jade arrived very promptly.

"I can't believe we're the first ones here aside from the brides and family." Ian looked around in amazement.

"No one shows up on the dot. It's more of a suggestion." Jade wore a fashionable pink strapless dress that emphasized her curves and the twisting rose tattoo that transfixed Ian.

Ian, in a white linen untucked shirt, exuded a tropical vibe. Looking around, he breathed in deeply and exhaled loudly. "No worries. It gives us more time to explore. Maybe we can meditate by the oak tree."

"What the fuck are you wearing?" Andre laughed as he and his date strolled over. "You look like a dental hygienist. Are you sure you want to be seen with this guy?" Andre asked Jade. "Meet Tiffany." The attractive young woman by his side smiled and gave a small wave.

"It's a guayabera, you toff. A fancy one, I'll have you know."

"Hi, I'm Jade. From the Journey ashram." Jade extended her hand, and Andre shook it heartily.

"Jade on a journey, it's nice to meet you finally. You can do better."

"Andre's my biggest fan—can't you tell?" Ian threw a mock punch into Andre's mid-section. "Tiffany, I offer you my condolences on having to spend time with this bloke."

"You got to be channeling some Cuban dominoes old dude in Miami." Andre returned the favor. "Where's your cafe Cubano and cigar?"

"So nice to meet you. Ian has only mentioned you about 200 times." Jade put her hand lightly on Ian's shoulder and smiled.

"Only to complain. Andre, somehow, Jade has agreed to suffer your company tonight. And, did AJ lend you last season's prom outfit?" Ian grinned with pleasure as he saw Andre squirm. His teen-age son was quite the fashionista.

"Prom outfit, my ass. Have you ever even been to a prom?" Andre plucked at his perfectly tailored tan summer-weight suit. "You couldn't catch me dead in some plaque-picking, x-ray taking scrub top, oh wait, I mean guayabera."

Rachel and her boyfriend strolled over, arm in arm. Rachel's hair, a delicate shade of pink, matched Jade's dress perfectly, and they bonded over the color. Rachel showed off her new tattoos after exclaiming over Jade's thorned rose.

"Look, one is a little food truck that says Great Full Bread." Rachel stuck out an ankle from her long halter dress. "And here's the one just for me." Rachel showed them the blue cursive R etched on the inside of her forearm.

"You afraid you're going to forget your name?" Jeff's voice boomed as he joined the group. Jeff had already ditched his sports jacket and loosened his tie.

"Dad—cut it out. Where's Mom?" She straightened his tie. "This is too short."

Annie and Donna Tomassi, each in floral summer dresses, stood over to the side of the tent, gossiping animatedly.

"Pete, you look so handsome," Donna called out. John Tomassi, unmistakable in a loud plaid sportscoat, caught up with Peter a few minutes later.

"Don't embarrass yourself, Reverend." Tomassi didn't take up space like his normal robust self to Peter's eyes, but he looked a hell of a lot better than the last time he'd seen him.

"What is that, a Scottish horse blanket? And thanks for your confidence."

"De nada. You good?" Tomassi looked at him closely. "I mean except for the obvious wardrobe malfunction."

Peter quickly checked his fly. "Asshole."

"Doofus."

Kenny Johnson strolled over, a walkie talkie in his hand. "No wedding crashers allowed." He pointed to his Fiori Orchards shirt. "Security."

"Oh, yeah. I feel safer now," Tomassi said. "Hey, you got some dirt on your lip." He and Peter cracked up.

"Jealousy is such an ugly emotion." Kenny affectionately stroked his sparse mustache. "Hey, do me a favor. This is a sketchy crowd. If you see something, say something."

• • •

CHAPTER 55

JOSH HESITATED TO CALL MIKE TOMASSI MUCH AFTER he started working at the Consortium. Mike, inundated with his course load, didn't have the time or inclination to hear Josh's misgivings about the water bottling project.

"Dude, it's a job. A well-paying job. The corporate world doesn't give a shit if you're unhappy. Just suck it up. Hey, I gotta go—study group in five minutes. Be safe."

But when John Tomassi asked Mike how Josh was doing, Mike told him he didn't like his new job at all.

"What's he doing?"

"Some analyst position at the Consortium. Would you believe his mother sent his resume in without Josh knowing about it? And then he gets the job."

"What? Why didn't you tell me he was working there?" Tomassi senior stopped drinking the beer he had just opened and waited, suddenly riveted to Mike's words.

Mike stared at him in disbelief. "Dad, what's the big deal? He's working on some big production facility. He hates it."

"You heard from him lately?" Tomassi's hand remained frozen in place, the beer bottle a perfect right angle away from his lips.

"No. What—you gonna nail him for littering?" Mike shook his head at his father.

"Nah, come on. Just asking. Josh is a good kid."

"No shit. He's probably buried under all those numbers like I'm buried under all this reading." Mike slammed shut the case book on tort law. "God, talk about boring."

When he didn't hear back after texting Josh for two days straight, Mike got worried. Josh always replied with funny emojis, if nothing else. So, Mike reluctantly contacted Mrs. Richardson to make sure everything was all right.

"Mike, it's so nice to hear from you,'" she said. "Josh and Emmie went on a vacation to Canada. They're not using their phones because it costs too much for international."

"OK, that makes sense. I just didn't know. Thanks, Mrs. Richardson."

The next day, Mike got a call from his dad.

"Mikey, you heard from Josh?"

"Again with this? How 'bout asking how I am?"

"Michael—this is your father calling to inquire about your health. There, that better?"

"No. So, I asked his mother. Josh and Emmie went to Canada, some kind of vacation. Too expensive to keep their phones on."

After a long pause, Tomassi said, "Hey, speaking of phones, call your grandmother. She's on my case something awful."

Josh and Emmie were long gone by then. They left Bridgeville quickly in the dark of night, driving cross-country to California in Emmie's Ford Focus. Josh donated his Subaru, damage and all, to the ASPCA. No questions asked—he filled out a few forms, mailed them the title and they sent a tow truck to pick it up. Emmie let her sister stay in their apartment, with the rent paid through the end of the month. Josh and Emmie each took out $5,000 from their bank accounts and rolled the twenty-dollar bills into rubber-banded packages of $200. Josh also bought a bunch of pre-paid Visa cards and some cheap burner cellphones.

"This is so sexy, Josh. We're like under the radar, like good outlaws."

Planning the trip had been great for their sex life, Josh had to admit. The tricky part had been Josh's mom.

"Going on vacation, Mom. We're gonna explore, most likely Canada." Josh gave her a bigger hug than usual.

"You already get a vacation? They must really appreciate all the work you do. Be careful, drive safe." Just as he backed the Focus out the driveway, she came running. "Wait," she yelled, waving something in her hand.

"What is it, Mom?"

"Here, take a little extra cash. Buy me some souvenirs; I've never been to Canada."

Car packed to the brim, Emmie and Josh stopped only for gas and bathrooms on their drive to Roanoke, Virginia. After a surprise delicious meal of Vietnamese pho from a tiny strip mall and a lackluster night of sleep in a cheap motel, they picked up Interstate 40 and blasted off to Tennessee. Memphis provided great barbeque that Josh ate on a park bench while Emmie picked at a salad. She wouldn't kiss him until he brushed his teeth.

"You've got meat breath."

From Memphis, they drove to Austin, Texas—a killer drive. More terrific barbeque eaten on a bench. They decided to chill in Austin for a few days, loving the music scene and spending next to nothing at a unisex barber shop to radically redo their hair. But, Emmie wanted to get to California as soon as they could.

"C'mon, Josh. I want to see the Pacific. I want to walk on the beach."

She now had an auburn asymmetrical bob, cut very short on the left side. Josh had grown a stubble beard to go along with his bleached taper fade. They drove close to Mexico on I-10, marveling at the scrubby landscape.

Tucson offered phenomenal tamales, including Emmie's beloved vegan options like black bean and blue corn. Finally, Emmie drove the last leg of the journey along

I-8 from Tucson to San Diego. Josh kept his baseball cap pulled low, reliving the events that sent them fleeing from Bridgeville. He kept peering out the window, amazed as the landscape changed from desert to scrub to massive sand hills to traffic jams to the glistening horizon of the Pacific Ocean.

CHAPTER 56

JOHN TOMASSI COULDN'T SHAKE THE FEELING — AN anxious feeling about Josh. And Tomassi's instincts rarely led him astray. At the station the next day, he dropped by Kenny Johnson's desk.

"This is a pig sty, Kenny. Too much crap here." Tomassi gestured with irritation.

"Sorry, Sarge." Kenny read Tomassi's mood loud and clear, and immediately made two stacks of files into one big one.

"You seen Josh Richardson lately?" Tomassi leaned his rump into the side of Kenny's desk that had been tidied up just for him.

Kenny brushed a pile of crumbs into his hand as he continued the housekeeping. "Yeah, I saw Josh running a couple weeks ago. He was sucking wind, let me tell you. I think he said something about doing some steady corporate work and making bank."

"Mike says he's on vacation in Canada with his girl. Lemme know if you see him. I gotta ask him something."

Kenny mumbled, his attention focused on an ant crawling along his desk.

Tomassi swatted the ant dead and flicked the corpse onto the floor. "You still coaching baseball in Hatfield?"

"Yeah. Team's getting better, actually." Kenny cautiously lifted some papers, half-expecting to discover a thriving ant colony.

"Doing good, Kenny. Department likes to see community outreach. Don't forget to put it on the review form for your file." Tomassi rose with difficulty. "And clean this shithouse up."

What no one knew is that Josh couldn't take it anymore. He couldn't unwind after hitting the deer. He chugged the first beer Emmie gave him before she could sit down. He couldn't eat the chips she put in front of him, he couldn't watch TV, he knew he'd be shit in bed, and he sure as hell couldn't sleep despite Emmie falling asleep in the middle of their conversation. Dread pumped through his veins, and his heart raced. He finally spooned her as she slept, smelling her fragrant hair and trying to match his breathing to her slow rhythm. He needed her skin-to-skin, nothing sexual about it, just to feel her aliveness. Stripping off his boxers, he pushed the big tank top she wore all the way up to her shoulders and held on for dear life. Slowly, he came back to himself.

"It's a sign, I know it's a sign. I'm on the wrong side of right." A kaleidoscope of images exploded in his brain— the deer, the reservoir, the Consortium, his mother, huge dollar signs the size of mountains, California, billions of water bottles.

"What?" Emmie roused herself with difficulty. "What did you say?" She wriggled against him and sighed happily.

"Just go back to sleep, babe."

"C'mere, you." Emmie grabbed his arm and pulled it across her breasts and under her chin. "Just close your eyes. You're OK—we're OK."

The sound of steady rain on the roof comforted Josh, and he hoped the downpour would wash the deer's blood off the car.

When the alarm blared at 6 A.M., Josh felt like he had been run over by a truck.

"I think I'm gonna call in sick."

"Yeah," she said, bustling around the room. "Just take the day."

Emmie left at 7:15, and by 7:45 Josh had enough of tossing and turning. He didn't have the stomach to eat breakfast.

The car looked like it had hit an elephant not a fawn.

"Piece of shit." Josh kicked the front driver's side tire, being careful not to make contact with the ruined front end. At least the rain had washed the exterior clean.

He walked slowly but purposefully back inside and sent his boss an email detailing the symptoms of his sudden stomach flu. Josh gulped a cup of coffee and decided to take a ride up to the reservoir. He grabbed his messenger bag and took out the folder with the projections and spreadsheets. He didn't bother to open it. Instead, he stuck it in the big envelope he'd received from HR. Shaking out all the glossy brochures and manuals, he jammed the folder inside. As he walked out the door, he doubled back to his bag and removed the flash drive, safe in its Consortium pouch, and chucked it into the envelope. Almost in the car, he cursed and pivoted back inside to the kitchen. He rummaged for a plastic garbage bag, a big towel, a roll of paper towels, and some tape.

"Just in case it's a hurricane in there with all the blood and whatever. I can tape the bag to the seat."

Striding purposefully back out to the car, he spread the towel over the gross front seat, climbed in and cautiously accelerated. It wasn't as messy as he had remembered.

Maybe Emmie had tried to clean it up while he was having his nervous breakdown under the hose.

"Go, come on." Josh didn't care about the clunking sounds his shuddering Subaru made. He just wanted to get to the reservoir, fast.

He was afraid the cops would stop him for driving an unroadworthy car, but if Kenny pulled him over, it would be OK. He and Kenny were cool. Tomassi, probably, not so much.

Josh looked down at this buzzing phone. His boss hoped he felt better soon.

"Thanks," Josh snorted.

He coaxed the car up the final hill and parked. He wanted to walk around the reservoir so badly that he started to run towards it. He left the envelope and everything else in the car. The morning air still felt refreshing, especially under the canopy of trees. When he could just glimpse the reservoir gleaming in the sunlight as he crested the steep bank, he noticed a hunk of rope hanging off a tree.

"What the hell is that for?" It almost looked like someone had fashioned it into a small noose. Josh untied the rope and stuffed in in his cargo shorts. At the water's edge, he took off his socks and put them in his other pocket. He tied his shoelaces together and draped his sneakers over his shoulder.

The rocks were too sharp and slippery. He waded back to shore like he was walking on hot coals. On his way back to the car, he stumbled and then tripped into a huge hole in the ground. It looked like space junk had tumbled down from the heavens.

"Son of a bitch," he yelled as he felt the stinging scrapes on his legs and hands. His ankle killed, too. "Terrific." But sitting there on the ground, rubbing his sore ankle and wiping the dirt and blood off with his sock, he saw the possibilities.

"Hmm. What about, wait—no. Fuck, it's the answer."

He got up and limped back towards the car, stopping to pick up a branch that looked like a decent walking stick. Right near it, he saw several cinder blocks that must have fallen out of the back of someone's truck. He could still see the tire tracks. When Josh got to the car, he used the paper towels to dab his scrapes. Opening the garbage bag, he slipped the envelope inside. After propping himself up against the doorframe, he tore strips of tape with his teeth and fastened the bag into a neat tight rectangle.

As he limped back towards the crevasse, Josh stopped short. He stood frozen as if struck by a thunderbolt, only his eyes darting back and forth. Gnawing on his lower lip until it bled, he headed back to the car. From the trunk, he gingerly removed the leather jacket he'd used to move the deer. It reeked so badly that he vomited, all coffee and stomach acid.

"Shit." He wiped his mouth and looked around. Furtively, he wrapped the oozing jacket around the neat package encasing the envelope and tied it with the rope he'd found. Crutch-walking with the branch, he retraced his steps to the hole, and tentatively lowered the jacket. It fit with room to spare.

"I want someone to find this. I can't do it—I'll go to jail. Someone will find this and do the right thing." He covered up the hole with sticks and leaves and hobbled ten yards before turning around to study the site.

"No, it's not good enough. Some animal will smell the blood and dig it up and rip everything to shreds." Josh thought for a minute. "It needs better protection, maybe deeper and heavier."

He tried to remember exactly where he'd seen the cinder blocks. He limped back and forth, using the stick for balance and tapping the ground near trees like a blind man. When he finally struck gold, one last hurdle remained. The heavy block, too awkwardly shaped to hold in one hand while crutching with the other, made him move like a mutant jackalope.

Josh threw the stick towards the hole and jump-hopped until he got there.

Crouching didn't give him the angle he needed, so he lay on his belly like a reptile and tied the rope encircling the jacket to the cinderblock. Grabbing handfuls of dirt, rocks, leaves, and sticks, he buried the smoking gun. Staggering to his feet, he paused for a minute and pissed on it.

Josh played his stomach flu like a fiddle for two days. His boss thought he had eaten at Chipotle or some other food emporium afflicted with mass e-coli breakouts.

"Is it still puking and the runs? I don't want you coming in when you're sick. Those damn employees don't wash their hands. You did a bang-up job on Eautopia, Josh. Maybe you worked too hard."

"Yeah, I'm really sorry that I'm missing work. But I could try to come in, I don't know what might happen. I mean, I would wash my hands carefully. I could ask my doctor about maybe using adult diapers or something."

"Good God, no. Absolutely not."

Josh had to cover the phone to muffle his laughter. He mouthed, "He's buying it," to Emmie who was laughing so hard that she fell to the floor and lay there, clutching her stomach and moaning.

"Is that your girlfriend? Don't tell me she's got it now, too. That's terrible. Take as much time as you need. More."

CHAPTER 57

MARTI AND LORI GREETED ALL THEIR GUESTS LIKE everyone had come to a great party that just happened to be their wedding. Murphy stood by them, handsome in a stylized Schnauzer trim of a tufted fur skirt below his shaved torso and bushy eyebrows. Marti's white tuxedo flattered her tall frame and fit her like a dream. Lori rocked a sexy low-cut cream-colored gown with a fish-tail hem.

They had very little trouble agreeing on their matching platinum rings. But choosing between Virgil's *Love conquers all* and The Song of Solomon's *I am my beloved's and my beloved is mine* as the inscription proved more difficult.

The ceremony also required some negotiating. Marti had her heart set on a wedding arch,

"I love those, but it has to be made from apple branches and white silk. I'm not Jewish but, so what? They're beautiful."

"Cool. I want a red carpet down the center aisle. It will show off my fishtail and my kitten heels won't get stuck in the grass."

"Red? What is this, the Oscars?"

"It's perfect. Red is the color of happiness, and I'm so happy."

Peter kissed each woman on the cheek as they settled in front of him after walking together down the aisle, arms linked.

Their families were not surprised by their choice. "Down with the patriarchy," Mr. Welles and Mr. Dunn joked when told of their non-participation.

Peter motioned to the crowd to sit down. Jeff tried to corral Brutus and Murphy, but they brayed in the aisle at all the hub-bub until he finally herded them over to Annie.

Peter had written the sermon of his dreams. After everyone sat, Peter smiled delightedly at the audience, put on his bifocals and started to read and extemporize from some note cards.

"Welcome, everyone. We are blessed to be here to celebrate the marriage of Marti Dunn and Lori Welles. I was thrilled when Lori and Marti asked me to officiate. I am, just so you know, legally certified by the Universal Life Church now, and I'm loving being a holy man."

Tomassi's guffaw was audible. Peter glared at him sternly before grinning. "Beware my righteous wrath, infidel."

Jeff, sitting in the first row, aimed a not-so-gentle kick at him to get Peter back on task. When he connected, Jeff grinned happily

Peter resumed his remarks after rubbing his shin. "The earth nurtures us and gives unselfishly of her bounty; we are uplifted by her love. As we gather here above our beloved river in this beautiful orchard, surrounded by apple trees laden with fruit, it is no coincidence that apples are the theme of this occasion."

He looked down at his note cards and began to read in a stentorian tone.

"Gaia, the earth mother in Greek mythology, gave Hera, the queen of the gods, some precious apple trees which were tended by the Daughters of the Evening and guarded by a fierce dragon. The apples from these trees were golden and tasted like honey. They also had magical powers—they

could heal, they grew back as they were eaten and if someone threw one of these apples, it always hit the target like a
bull's-eye and then came, boom, right back into the throw-
er's hand. And, believe it or not, a golden apple stolen from
Hera's garden caused the Trojan War."

The sun started to set in the west as the moon became
visible in the east. Peter stopped to take it all in. "Hey, the
Harvest Moon, right on cue." People in the crowd stood
to see it, creating an audible roar of appreciation.

"Settle down, people. Now, in Norse mythology, apples
represent eternal youth, while in Celtic mythology, apples
can give immortality and are the fruit of the gods. I just
want to make a point that might exonerate the apple from
being blamed for tempting Eve. Turns out it may never
even have been an apple. Go back to the book of Genesis.
In the Bible, it is written that God commanded Adam and
Eve not to eat the fruit of *one* tree that grew in the Garden
of Eden. Well, get this: there were no apple trees in the
Near East. So, lay off the apple—it was innocent."

Marriage is considered one of life's sacred gifts,
although I have to say it didn't work out for quite a few
of us here today. But you, Lori and Marti, you are perfect
together. Let's cherish this moment as we celebrate our
brides on this glorious occasion of the Harvest Moon, the
Blood Moon and a lunar eclipse. If that isn't the universe
blessing us than I don't know what is. Here's a beautiful
poem by William Butler Yeats that's perfect for tonight.
It's called *Song of the Wandering Aengus.*

> I will find out where she has gone
> And kiss her lips and take her hands;
> And walk among the dappled grass,
> And pluck till time and times are done
> The silver apples of the moon,
> The golden apples of the sun.

Peter looked around the crowd, some wiping tears, and smiled proudly.

"If there is anyone who dares, anyone who could possibly object to this wonderful union, speak now or forever hold your peace."

Brutus barked loudly, sparking a huge roar of laughter. Peter put his finger up to his lips.

"Lori and Marti, you're on."

Lori took Marti's hand and kissed it. "I am so in love with you. Although I draw the line at camping, I promise to go to Fenway to watch the Red Sox without complaining even though I'd much rather be playing eighteen. I love your adventurous spirit and your unbelievable good nature. You are my everything." Marti held Lori's hand over her head like a prize fighter.

"Lori," she said. "I'm going to keep this short and sassy, just like you. Here we are, in front of our friends and families—finally it's our time. You are my dream woman. I never thought I would find you, but I'm the luckiest woman in the world. I love you with all of my heart."

Peter had to quiet the shouts of approval from the crowd. "Do you take each other in this union of marriage? To continue being best friends and partners for life, for richer and poorer, in health and in sickness? To honor, cherish and love for the rest of your days?"

Marti and Lori kissed each other and yelled, "We do."

"I thought so. Now we come to the rings. The wedding ring's shape is round, just like an apple. There is no beginning or end, just like the earth and just like your love. Our brides' rings are engraved with a beautiful line from The Song of Solomon: *I am my beloved's and my beloved is mine.*"

Lori barely waited for Peter to cue her before saying, "Marti, I give you this ring as a symbol of my enduring love. With this ring, I give you all that I am and cherish all that you are."

Marti whisked away tears before speaking. "Lori, I give you this ring as a symbol of my enduring love. With this ring, I give you all that I am and cherish all that you are."

Peter threw his arms wide open before bellowing, "Friends, by the power invested in me by the Universal Church, my cup runneth over to pronounce Lori and Marti, wife and wife."

Everyone rose to their feet, cheering loudly as the brides kissed. And kissed. The festivities began promptly, with champagne toasts and fireworks. After feasting on Carmen's delicious menu, the band cranked up the volume. Somehow, the first dance included Peter, who energetically clapped and two-stepped. The dancing continued non-stop until the band put down their instruments and asked everyone to step out for the Blood-Red Moon and eclipse.

Peter took a breather outside the tent and happily grabbed the ice-cold Sam Adams that a smiling John Tomassi tossed him. Tomassi looked ten years younger and pleasantly buzzed as he cha-chaed in place.

"Reverend Twinkletoes, the one and only."

Just then Carmen, walked up to Peter and handed him a Fiori Orchards t-shirt. Tomassi did his best Groucho Marx eyebrow wiggle and poked Peter in the ribs.

"Later," he growled to Peter before stopping for a second. "Carmen."

"John." She took in his undulating eyebrow and shook her head, somehow managing to make her own sweatiness look dewily chic.

"On the house, Pete," Carmen said, stepping back from the soggy embrace Peter offered.

"Carm," he yelled, stripping his shirt off and shimmy-ing. "Can you dig it?'

Carmen covered her face and screamed. "My eyes."

"You know you got to have this." He pulled the T-shirt on over his head. "Better? Dance with me, Hot Stuff." Peter grabbed her hand and maneuvered over to the dance floor.

"Wait, I gotta make sure the clean-up's OK." But she swayed to a Motown medley, keeping an amused dis-tance from Peter's gyrations.

When *Superfreak* came on, Jade pulled Ian onto the dance floor and engaged him a in a barely disguised grind. At first, he resisted but then threw out all the stops, hips swiveling to the beat.

Andre yelled approvingly. "Way to get your Brahmin on."

Ian gave him his special prayer and grinned ear to ear.

CHAPTER 58

AFTER THE EVENING'S THEATRICS, PETER FOUND Carmen, utterly exhausted, leaning against the bar. He offered her his hand, and, after a brief hesitation, she let him lead her towards the bonfire. They sat down on a log in front of the flickering flames near the s'mores station. Peter grabbed a stick and expertly toasted a s'more.

"For you, Carm. You pulled off a helluva night."

"You, too." She slowly pulled off the most charred bits

of marshmallow and savored them. "Mmm. you burned these just right."

"I aim to please. I know how you like 'em." Peter helped himself to some of the gooey chocolate she was ignoring. "Good stuff. These never get old."

"No, but we did." She watched the fire, sinking into a melancholy silence, her-half-eaten s'more drooping off the long stick.

"Yeah, we did. So what? Tell me what's on your mind. I can take it. Is it my stench?" He took the stick from her and rested in on the ground.

"No, you smell like you. Just let me sit and you be quiet." To his surprise, Carmen leaned against him and sighed. "I'm so tired."

"Lean on me. Hey, can I sing you the song?"

"No."

Peter didn't move even though his right arm was trapped in an awkward position. "Carm?"

"I wanna say something. I'm angry at you for spoiling other men for me. I'm done. They're just not you. There, I said it, for all the good it does."

Peter cautiously put his arms around her. "Carm, my young friends tell me you have to ask permission now to touch a woman."

Carmen sat us straight and looked at him. "You asking?"

"Yeah, I'm asking."

Carmen chuckled and arranged his right arm so her head fit into the space between his shoulder and elbow. "Don't get too cocky."

"The new me would never brag about my amazing anatomy." She snorted, and Peter felt carried away by waves of tenderness and nostalgia. He inhaled her aroma and rested his head on top of hers. "Not like the old me."

"Shhh."

"Right, I promise not to speak." Every ember in the fire glowed brighter as he held her.

"Thank God."

Peter couldn't resist kissing her neck softly. "I'm a dumb guy—you know it's true. But I'm here for you. Just tell me what's going on."

"You're not ready for this." She disengaged and looked carefully at his face.

"Try me."

"OK. I think we missed it. We missed our shot. And it sucks." She shifted uncomfortably. "God, I'm too old to sit on this log. My ass is killing me."

Peter patted his lap. "I'm pretty comfortable."

Carmen exaggerated her double-take. "We haven't been this close in years. Now you want me to sit on you?"

"Well, for starters. Why not?"

"Uh, because everything."

"Look — here we are four years later, and I'm still me, and you're still you. I'm going grey and you're just getting more beautiful. How is that fair?"

Carmen shook her head. "Pete—"

"We got caught up in a tragedy. Life gave us a sucker punch, and you broke my heart. You know it. But you did what you felt was right under terrible circumstances. You made it very clear you were better off without me."

Carmen's shoulders heaved suddenly as she buried her face in her hands. Peter hesitated. "Are you saying I was wrong not to push harder? You threatened to get a restraining order when all I wanted to do was see you, talk to you."

Carmen wiped away mascara-tinged tears with the bottom of her lace blouse. "Do you have a tissue?"

Peter shook his head no. Using the sides of his hands, he gently whisked away some tears rolling down her cheeks. "My fingers are too rough for your pretty face."

"You never recover from losing a child. Children shouldn't die before their parents. She was old enough to know better; we raised her to know better but look what happened. It still makes me sick to my stomach. I'll never know if she slipped, or someone pushed her, or she jumped."

Peter kissed her forehead. "Don't do this to yourself. Some stuff is just unknowable. But you found a way to carry on. You built the orchard up into the most successful operation in the area. You're raising your grandson, you're there for everyone."

"Yeah, but not for you or me. I blamed you for making me so happy that I took my eye off the ball. So stupid, when I look back. Did you hear me? I *blamed* you." Her eyes blazed angrily.

"I know, believe me—I know."

"The orchard was running on all cylinders. And when my mother died, you were my rock. We were great together. But, I got selfish, and everything centered on you and me. I saw the warning signs, you saw them, too. Becky couldn't handle herself. But I thought, "Oh, she's making her choices, and I may not like them, but they're hers to make. She'll straighten out.' Thing is, she didn't have enough time left, and I didn't know." Carmen choked back a sob.

"No one could know. Stop beating yourself up." He reached for her, but she shook him off.

"Wait, let me finish. And when you got stuck in all the freaking Zenergy trouble—I wanted to kill you. You drive me crazy."

"Just a minute. Give me a chance to say something."

"No, you don't get a minute, and you don't get a chance. Listen to me. What happened with Sherry and the water just destroys me. And out of respect for this beautiful wedding, I'm not even mentioning the bitch I'd like to slaughter." Carmen grabbed his hands and looked at them like she had never seen hands before.

"That goes double for me." He stopped and watched her, surprised. "I guess you heard from Vic. But don't tell Tomassi what I said."

"As if. But you, Vic said you're in jeopardy. You get caught up in things that are too big, fights you can't possibly win because they don't fight fair. Why do you do this?"

"I—"

"As for you and me," Carmen interrupted, squeezing his hands, "we started to talk a little after seeing each other in Vic's office, yeah, but about nothing important."

"Hey, those were your rules."

"Murder and evil don't get to win, you hear me? I've got enough guilt to last till the end of time. I am so sorry, Pete." Shaking with emotion, she collapsed into his embrace.

"Carm, you were wrong to put all this on yourself." He spoke softly and tried to soothe her like the trembling puppies he rescued. "Why couldn't you let me carry some of the load, us together? I'm an ox, give me the burden. I'm a beast."

"You certainly are." She poked a finger into his belly and sniffed. "Or at least you used to be. You're too skinny—I've never seen you like this."

"That's a new one. Maybe you can fatten me up." He puffed up his cheeks, and Carmen chuckled huskily.

"Maybe."

"What? Well at least this beast isn't a total caveman." He traced her rosebud mouth with his calloused index finger. "May I?"

"No – me first, and I don't have to ask." She kissed him hungrily until he broke away.

"Are you putting the moves on me, Carmen Fiori?"

"If you don't know, things are worse than I thought."

"Hey, ladies should always come first and often. Even cavemen know that." He held her close, their deep kisses dissolving the years.

"Are you thinking what I'm thinking?" Carmen asked. She tilted her head in the direction of her house, not too far from where they sat.

"That I should have brought Viagra with me? Yup."

"We'll make do," she said, her hand lightly acknowledging the bulge of his hard-on. Starting to get up, she clutched suddenly at her back. "Oh, my God. Ouch, ouch."

Peter struggled to rise from the log to come to her aid and yelped in pain. "I can't move. Goddammit, I'm stuck." Bent over at a forty-five-degree angle, he had to support himself by putting his hands on his thighs. He look at her ruefully, and they both burst into gales of laughter that escalated to shrieks and shouts.

"I just peed myself." Carmen clamped her legs together but couldn't stop giggling.

Peter, still bent at the waist, held out his hand. "I have that effect on women. Come on, Hot Stuff. Help me."

"You big idiot, help *me*. And forget the Viagra. We need a bucket of Advil."

He grimaced as he shuffled towards her. "Maybe a wheelchair."

• • •

CHAPTER 59

PETER AND CARMEN LEANED ON EACH OTHER AS THEY made slow progress back to Carmen's place. Carmen, her spasms almost gone, ran a hot shower for Peter in the guest room bathroom. When he got out, he saw she had laid out an old pair of faded Patriots sweatpants he recognized as his own.

"No shirt for you, handsome," Carmen said, waiting for his entrance as she reclined on the bed in pair of cotton pajamas. Gesturing to her attire, she smiled. "Very sexy, I know."

He lay down gingerly and reached for her. Carmen ran her fingers through his chest hairs as she slowly melted into him, kissing his shoulder.

"You always are." Peter held her on his bare chest. "Can't wait for tomorrow," he said, dozing off in seconds.

"It's already tomorrow," she whispered.

Peter woke up first and made a bee line for the bathroom. He brewed a pot of coffee and munched on a crisp apple. With Jimmy still at Aldo's, they had the house to themselves. He brought Carmen a steaming mug of coffee but couldn't bring himself to wake her. He watched her breathe, grateful beyond belief to have this moment.

"Pete? Is that you or am I dreaming?"

"The one and only. Here." He handed her the mug, grinning broadly. He sat quietly as she blew ripples onto the hot brew and took small sips.

"Don't go anywhere." Carmen turned on a light jazz station before making her way to the bathroom.

Peter wandered around her bedroom, noting the changes from four years ago. He looked at a framed picture of Aldo, Carmen, Becky, and Jimmy. It seemed like ancient history. Suddenly, Carmen's arms encircled his waist.

"Hey, I know you." Peter scooped her up carefully and placed her gently on the bed. "Nice outfit." Carmen had ditched the sleepwear and slipped into a silky short negligee. Their mouths met, and his hands caressed her breasts and buttocks. "Not asking, OK?"

"Me neither."

They took their time at first, but Carmen made him jump when she ducked down and licked his shaft.

He groaned and drew her back up to his mouth. "Rain check. It's all you, baby."

Kissing his way down her body, Peter teased her nipples before settling in between her thighs. She held onto his shoulders and came hard as he tongued her.

Peter rolled over and pulled Carmen on top of him. "You sexy beautiful woman, get over here." As he filled her completely, their bodies knew what to do, the terrain already mapped.

"Oh, Pete." Carmen arched her back and threw back her head.

Her breasts bounced as she rode him, coming over and over. Finally, Peter couldn't hold back, gripping her hips and exalting until he slackened.

They tumbled onto their sides, all tangled legs and arms, neither one able to summon a coherent word.

"Wow." Peter hugged her close. "Where you been?"

"Mmmm." Carmen curled into him and kissed his chest. "Missing you."

CHAPTER 60

PETER LAY BACK ON THE COUCH, TRYING TO FIND A late ballgame to watch on TV. When the doorbell rang, he looked around in annoyance. At 11 P.M., no one should be on his doorstep. Jeff had just left after going over the menu for the week. Carmen had gone to Bermuda for a short trip she'd booked months ago with friends. The bell rang again and again. Brutus barked and charged at the door. Peter put down his beer and got up slowly, looking cautiously through the side glass panels.

Nancy stood on his door stoop. Peter flung the door open and stared at her in disbelief.

"What the hell do you want?"

"We need to talk." Nancy looked shrunken, and her skin hung weirdly like ill-fitting clothing. She didn't pet Brutus, who waited expectantly.

"Are you wearing a wire?" Peter practically spat at her. "You have some nerve coming here. Get the fuck off my property."

Nancy positioned herself closer to the wood siding like she was waiting out a sudden downpour. "I'm coming in." She stalked past him and turned off the TV.

"I asked you to leave not come in. Get out."

Nancy sat down. "I shouldn't be here, I know." Her voice sounded breathy and weak.

"Well since you barged into my house, how about telling me how you live with yourself. How could you betray me to Brock Saunders of all people and the Consortium?"

Peter picked up his phone and shot off a text to Jeff. *Nancy here.*

"You stupid bastard. You have no idea what you playing detective did to *my* life. Don't even mention that asshole's name. Believe it or not, I protected you."

"Uh-hunh." Peter didn't even bother to look at her. He checked his phone for a reply. "Smells like bullshit to me."

"I'm not leaving. You need to hear me out before you judge me. I want you to know exactly what happened. You owe me."

"I owe you nothing. Save the big reveal for someone who gives a shit. I'm not gonna ask you again—get out."

"No. Shut your trap and listen. I don't have money or a farm or a family to fall back on. I've got me—that's it." Nancy looked at him defiantly. "So is the cavalry coming to save you? Anyone coming to your rescue? Stop checking your phone. No one gives a shit about you either."

"Wait just a fucking minute. Sherry is murdered by cold-blooded killers, the Consortium sells our water to the highest bidder, and you're having a pity party? Boo-hoo, poor me."

"You're the drama queen. Gotta be the big hero and center of attention. Everything's all Peter, all the time, never mind the hell you bring down on everyone else. Well guess what—I'm not your collateral damage. Do you even *know* what happened to me?"

"Cry me a river, Nancy. You have exactly two minutes before I call the cops. You're trespassing." Peter folded his arms across his chest and glared at her.

"Oh, that's rich. Me, trespassing. Your forte not mine." She shifted uncomfortably. "They threatened me. That piece of shit said he owned me. They said I would go to prison, they'd take my job, my pension, everything. All because of you. And you'd rot in a super max somewhere."

"Prove it. Prove they threatened you."

"This is how you thank me? I took their best punches to protect you. They've got you in photos and videos."

"Show me the proof. There's no way in hell you can justify throwing me under the bus. They threatened you? Please—they threaten everyone. Since when are you Brock's bitch?" He stared at her defiantly, keenly aware that he might have crossed a line.

Nancy recoiled as if she'd been struck. "What the fuck don't you see? I saved your ass. They already had you, and I didn't give them anything they didn't have. You motherfucker. I'm not Brock's bitch."

"Nancy—"

Nancy started crying. "They've been spying on you since Zenergy. Where's your gratitude?"

"Gratitude, what a joke. Look, maybe you were deprived of oxygen during your surgery and are too brain-damaged to understand the consequences here." Peter drummed the cocktail table impatiently, still stalling for time.

"Fuck you. I did what I had to do." Nancy reached slowly into her purse and wrapped her hand around something. "I've got the power now."

"What, you have a gun? Go ahead, shoot me." He put his hands up in the air.

"You'd love that, wouldn't you?" Nancy left her hand where it was, and Peter couldn't see what it held. But out of the corner of his eye, he saw flashing lights from an approaching cop car.

"If you came here for forgiveness, you're crazy." Peter put his hands down and looked at his phone. He saw a text from Jeff that said *BPD coming.* His heart fluttered. Were they coming to save him or arrest him?

"You're fucking Carmen again."

"What?"

"Do you remember when we fucked?"

"Shit sex a hundred years ago isn't worth remembering."

Nancy surprised him by standing up quickly, her fists clenched in fury. "I remember!"

She grabbed the beer bottle and hurled it at his face. He ducked instinctively, and it shattered loudly, gashing a football-sized hole in the wall behind his head. As she screamed curses, Officer Bill O'Leary flung open the door.

"Stand still, and let me see your hands," O'Leary yelled.

Peter, speechless, did as told. But Nancy picked up anything she could find and threw it at Peter. A framed glass picture smashed hard into his head, staggering him. As the blood poured from Peter's temple, O'Leary subdued Nancy but not before he threatened to use his taser.

Peter numbly surveyed the broken glass and ruined photo at his feet. He was dimly aware of more police arriving. Hesitantly, looking through a red curtain of blood at O'Leary, he stooped to pick the frame off the floor, one Carmen had chosen, running his hand over the cracked glass. His great-grandfather and assorted relatives, fresh off the boat in uncomfortable formal wool suits, stared back solemnly in grainy black-and-white. Blood dripped and puddled over their faces as he stared at them mutely before losing consciousness.

CHAPTER 61

RACHEL GOT THE PANICKED CALL FROM JEFF WHEN she and her boyfriend were leaving the movies. He had also sent five texts.

"Dad?"

"Pete's in the hospital. It's bad. Nancy attacked him."

"What? No, no way. Is he gonna be OK?" Tears ran down Rachel's face, and she clutched her boyfriend's arm.

"Get Marco to handle tomorrow with Paco. I can't do it." Jeff barked instructions as his phone buzzed with a text from Lori. Still on her honeymoon in Hawaii, she'd tapped Vic to get over to the hospital. They already had worked out a strategy.

"I'm calling him right now. I'll be there as soon as I can."

"No, it's a zoo here. Focus on the truck. So many cops. I don't know if Pete's under arrest or what. Nobody'll tell me."

Hours passed on the eighth floor of the Hatfield Medical Center, Peter, tossed and turned, chained to his bed. The handcuffs dug into his wrist. He pulled against them and his IV tape ripped.

"Don't do that." He could hear a man's voice.

Peter fought against the fog of his brain. He battled to open his eyes, but their heavy weight defeated him. Somebody pushed him down, and he fell in deep water. He couldn't surface no matter how hard he labored. He struggled to escape certain drowning.

The police presence in and outside Peter's hospital room seemed to grow hourly. Jeff paced outside the room, and button-holed Tomassi the minute he saw him trudging down the hall.

"John, talk to me." Jeff, unshaven and bleary-eyed, looked beat.

"Just give me a minute with him, Jeff." He patted him gruffly on the shoulder and went in.

Once inside, Tomassi approached Peter's bed. "Hey," he said, pulling up a chair. He motioned for some space to the crowd in the room.

"Wake up, Pete. Come on."

Peter moaned and tried to free his hands. Tomassi sighed and looked up at everyone still in the room.

"Kenny, what are you doing here? You're off shift now."

"I wanted to be here for Peter, Sarge." Kenny stopped talking and pointed. "What's he doing?"

"Shit," Tomassi yelled. He pushed the call button for the nursing staff. "Nurse, nurse. Anybody there?"

A male nurse answered. "Yes?"

"He's pulling his IV out. There's blood everywhere."

Two nurses rushed in and shooed everyone out. Tomassi took a call and walked around the hallway, trying to find good reception. Jeff went down to the parking lot to see Marco and Paco in the truck. In the elevator on the way down, Jeff texted Ian.

Finally, Jade texted him back on Ian's phone. *Be there soon.*

Jade urged Ian to hurry up. "Don't you want to see Peter?" At 9 A.M., now a frequent visitor to BIG, she sat cross-legged on the gym floor and stared impatiently at Ian as he entered the seventh minute of his plank pose.

"I'm going for fifteen minutes," he said, sweat pouring off his head. "Nothing's going to change in that time."

"I think I'm more worried about him than you are." She got up and started throwing a medicine ball against the wall. "Don't you care?"

Ian did his best to ignore her. "Not going to work. I have intense powers of concentration. And I don't do manipulation."

"Ha." Jade walked back over to Ian and quickly straddled him.

He maintained his perfect form until she sat on him. Surprised and teetering on his arms, he yelled. "Get off me. What are you doing?"

She started tickling him, and he collapsed onto the floor. No longer in a peaceful frame of mind, he tried to flip over but she had much better leverage and resisted him for as long as she could. When he could finally pin her on her back, he was lying on top of her, and they were both laughing.

Suddenly shifting gears, Ian disengaged his limbs from hers, stood up and shook out his track pants. Chagrined at his obvious erection, he turned away. "This shouldn't happen. Sorry."

"Sorry for what? You're apologizing for biology, for being a healthy male. You're apologizing for finding me attractive. Now you've hurt my feelings." She reached her hand out for him to help her up. Her hard nipples pushed out from her shirt. Saying nothing, he pulled her up.

His face flushed scarlet and accentuated the bright blue of his eyes. "I just failed spectacularly—I'm supposed to be guiding you. Let's press restart."

"Let's not." She stepped in close, releasing his hand and slowly moved her face towards his. He reached out with both hands towards her waist to deflect her from getting any closer. She spoke softly as if to soothe a skittish colt. "I come in peace."

"I can't handle this," he said, riveted to the spot, lowering his hands.

"Yes, you can. No touching, Ian." She got so close she could count his eyelashes.

Staying within a nose of her face, he dropped his hands. "No touching?"

"No," she murmured. She paused and locked eyes with him.

He bent over, drawing impossibly closer, until their lips imperceptibly brushed against each other. A drop of sweat dripped from his forehead onto her lips. She tasted it with her tongue flicking over her lips and said nothing. She held his eyes.

Slowly, Ian found her open lips with his own. He kissed her again, the softness of her tongue and mouth astonishing him. Struggling not to touch any part of her body, he almost lost his balance. He half-expected her to slap him. Instead, she gently bit his lower lip and held it between her teeth, before releasing it slowly.

Ian placed his warm hand on her shoulder and traced her tattoo down to where her shirt began, breathing hard. She could feel the blood pulsing in his veins.

"I think it's time to go now." His voice sounded thicker, and his hard-on was unmistakable.

Jade moved her palms against his chest and felt his heart pounding. She tilted her head to the side as if assessing its rhythm. Dabbing a rivulet of sweat from his chin with her fingers, his stubble bristled against her touch. The scratchiness held her attention, and she smiled. "I'm more than ready." She took his hand and placed it on her left breast. "You feel my heart?"

Ian nodded. He swallowed hard and slowly removed his hand. Jade turned him around and guided him towards the door like he was a lost child.

"Peter needs us—let's go."

Ian, still not talking, followed Jade into the hospital. They found Jeff furiously shaking the vending machine as they exited the elevator.

"Jeff, what's happened?" Ian asked anxiously. "Is it Peter?"

"No, it's my Doritos, dammit."

"But what's going on with Peter?"

"Nobody's telling me. Tomassi's here. Carmen's on her way from the airport." Jeff gave up on the vending machine, but not before one last kick. "Jade, you still hanging out with this character?" He nodded his chin at Ian.

"Jeff, let me handle this." She took two singles out of her pocket and carefully smoothed them before inserting them into the vending machine. When she pressed the tab for Doritos, the new bag came out forcefully and pushed the stuck one to the bottom. Jade retrieved both of them and handed the bags to Jeff, who tore one open on the spot.

"I love her." Jeff addressed Ian, his mouth teeming with neon orange crumbs.

"Easy, Jeff. Chew." Ian took the second bag away from him for safe-keeping.

"If you two really want to help, can you smuggle Brutus in? Not kidding."

"Not a bad idea," Ian said. "Put a vest on him, and he's an emotional support dog, right?"

"OK. Wait, what's that smell?" Jade sniffed the air.

The elevator pinged its arrival. The doors had barely trundled open before Vic stepped off in a cloud of eye-watering cologne.

"Hey, what's with all the socializing?" Vic grabbed a Dorito out of the open bag that Jeff held loosely in his hand. "So, take me to my client already."

CHAPTER 62

"LET'S WALK AND TALK," JEFF SAID. HE, VIC, IAN, AND Jade moved down the hallway in a tight beehive cluster like scheming schoolchildren.

"Who's here?" Vic asked. "And I talked to Lori already. We're both on it."

"Like half the Bridgeville PD. It would be a great time to rob a bank," Jeff said.

"Tomassi?"

"Yeah, John's in with Pete."

"I don't like it. Get in there and yell 'Fire.' I want to see Tomassi, but not with a crowd."

"You should announce free donuts, instead. But if we were back in the UK, I'd advertise chips, aka French fries." Ian smiled knowingly. "They call it the blobby bobby."

Jeff laughed, the first lift in his mood since Peter's attack.

"Where's Carm—she here yet?" Vic checked his phone for any information about Carmen's expected arrival.

"No." Jeff shrugged his shoulders. "I haven't seen her."

"So, listen. Ian—this your girlfriend? Honey, he's all talk, no action. Don't say I didn't warn you. I gotta find Tomassi." Vic ducked into a nurse's station to grab a cookie from a plate.

"Hey," Tomassi marched towards them. "Didn't I just see the big V?"

Ian pointed to the nursing station. "Cookies."

"Come on. Vic, stop stuffing your face. We got business to discuss." Tomassi walked to one side of the station as Vic left out the other side.

"Give me a sec. Nature calls."

Jade walked over to Tomassi and stuck out her hand. "Hi, I'm Jade."

"Nice meeting you, and I hope to God you're Ian's girlfriend and not Vic's. Lie if necessary—I'm delicate." He winked at Jade and leaned against a pillar.

"Actually," Jade called out, "we met at the wedding."

"Right," Tomassi brightened, his worry lifting momentarily. "Jade on a journey. You're a helluva dancer. Now I remember."

"Stop with the flirting, John," Jeff said. "Your long-suffering wife will kick your ass. Plus, you suck at it."

Vic walked purposefully towards them. "Sergeant, I'm going to see my client now. Then we'll talk." Vic waved two fingers in the air as a salute.

"What's his problem? Like I don't know he and Lori got a back-channel going with the Consortium. Please. Hope Lori's not too pissed about her honeymoon getting interrupted."

"Back channel about what?" Jeff asked. "And Lori won't be pissed, she's family."

"Affirmative on the back channel," Ian said to Tomassi, who nodded appreciatively.

Tomassi cheered when he saw Carmen walking down the hallway.

"The cavalry is here."

"Where is he, John?" Carmen grabbed Tomassi's hand. "Take me to him." She hugged Jeff and whispered something to him.

Ian and Jade said brief hellos and trailed after them towards Peter's room. As she entered, Carmen did a double-take at the sight of Peter.

"Oh, my God. No. Can I talk to him, John?" The horrified look on her face mirrored Jeff's.

Tomassi glowered. "You can try. Jesus, it's a tight fit in here. C'mere." He tried to go in at the same time as Jeff and managed to slide past the bed but crashed into the sink with his lower back. "Fuck," he yelled. "Watch it, Jeff. Sorry, Carm."

"I've heard the word before. You OK?" Carmen sat at the edge of the chair next to Peter's bed and blinked back tears. Gauze bandages and twenty staples adorned his head, the handiwork of the ER doctor. Blood seeped through the gauze. Ugly bruises bloomed around his eye and cheek. "Why is he restrained?" She gently touched his non-IV arm. "Pete, it's me. Wake up, please wake up, baby."

Jade watched the proceedings solemnly. "Excuse me, I'm going to try to find a bathroom."

"I'll help you," Ian said.

"I don't think so." Jade walked away with Ian right behind her.

"Wait, Jade."

CHAPTER 63

TOMASSI AND VIC BOTH WAVED JEFF AWAY AS THEY finally shared air space.

"We need a minute. Just go see your brother," Tomassi said. "Maybe he's conscious."

"I'll be back to find out what the hell you're doing. And for the record, you're both killing me."

Tomassi gave his head an almost imperceptible shake. In a split second, Kenny popped up in on Vic's left in a pincer move General Patton would have admired.

"Boo, enough already." Tomassi got in Vic's face. "No more cookies, no more little boy's room. We're going for an involuntary commitment for Nancy Yates. You got a problem with the blue paper, Vic?"

"You're doing a blue paper? Alright for now, Sergeant."

"What the hell does that mean? Speak English for the love of God," Jeff said angrily after quickly joining the group.

Vic took a second to explain. "It's the form for involuntary commitment. It's on blue paper. Don't worry about it. We're actually all color-blind, so it might even be purple."

"Vic, John, you suck. Kenny, you not so much. She should be in jail. She's already arrested, so what's happening now?" He looked at Tomassi who signaled him to hold on.

"Jeff, yeah—she's in custody. If Vic could just get his inner asshole to shut up." Tomassi stopped talking and glared at Vic. "Have some compassion for the family."

Kenny jumped into the conversation. "She's been assessed as a clear threat to others, possibly to herself. And under the law, we can get a temporary psych hold."

"She's fucking nuts, and she assaulted my client. The blue paper only lasts three days. We're going for the white paper next."

"Let me guess," Jeff said. "The paper is white. And she's gonna vacation in the psych ward." Jeff's frustration was barely contained.

"Bingo. Genius brother here. I mean, sort of right." Vic took a moment to think of better phrasing as Tomassi's body language went from annoyed to angry. "They evaluate and find her incompetent. The hospital files for a court order to authorize psych hospitalization and treatment. Could be three months, could be much more."

Jeff exploded. "She could've killed him. Pete looks like he went ten rounds blindfolded with Mike Tyson in his prime. Where's his justice?"

"Look, just like Officer Johnson said. She's on a blue paper because the police think she went off the deep end and could be a danger to others and herself, not just Peter. The medico-legal process takes over. And you need to let me do my thing." Vic's attempt at patience didn't go unnoticed by Tomassi or Kenny, who looked at him like they had just discovered that dogs could play the piano.

"Where's Carmen?" Vic asked.

"I don't know. Ladies room? I gotta get to the truck right now."

Paco and Marco had been texting Jeff non-stop for updates.

Carmen stroked an unbruised section of Peter's face, gently running her fingers over his stubbly jawline. "I want to fucking kill her," she said to Tomassi when he came into the room.

"I get it, believe me. But, right now, the law views her as in acute mental distress. Like a really high risk because she's not in her right mind. She's being held in a psych unit."

"Don't be such a fool. She served him up on a plate. What makes you think she didn't want to finish the job?"

He patted her on the shoulder and sighed. They watched Peter until the orderlies came in to take him for more tests.

"C'mon, Carm. Let me treat you to something good from Great Full Bread. I know the owners."

Vic dispatched Ian to do some legwork. He particularly wanted Ian to get pictures of the Consortium's parking lot and all the vehicles that exited entered for the next few days.

"Hit the DMV database, cross-reference plates, get into the nitty-gritty. Let's get profiles on who comes in and out."

"Good idea," Ian said, taking notes on his phone.

"Yeah, no kidding. Hop to it."

Jade insisted on tagging along even though Ian wouldn't tell her what Vic wanted him to do.

"So what's our next move?" she asked. The strained silence between them had faded but not vanished.

"Ours? Between you and Andre.' He shook his head. "Well, I hope he's having fun at Disney World with the kids."

"Come on, Ian. Let me help. And text Andre about Peter. He'll be mad you didn't tell him." She reached into his sweatshirt pocket and took out his phone. "Here."

Ian looked at her quizzically. "You have severe boundary issues. Hands out of my pockets, Miss."

Jade tapped him on the head with his phone. "What about Andre's clients? You're supposed to be covering them. You won't even be able to train your own regulars if you're off investigating. Put me to work. Think of it as part of my journey's healing process." She flashed a winning smile at him.

"I dunno. Jade, you are complicating my very simple life. I don't like complications." Ian stood up very straight as he faced her.

"But?" Her voice betrayed a touch of uncertainty.

"No but." Ian reached for her hand and contemplated her palm.

"You should be looking at your own if you want to read your life."

"I'm reading yours. Does this crease right here mean you drive a very handsome Brit crazy?" He ran his finger over the spot to see if he could smooth it out, but the skin held its pucker.

"Exactly." She closed her fingers over his and they held each other's smiles until Ian brought her hand up to his lips.

Rachel walked in on them. "How is he?" she asked shakily. "I'm so scared for him."

"Go see your dad, he's over there. Vic's got some tasks for us." Ian pointed down the hallway. Jade gave Rachel a hug and murmured encouragement.

Rachel barely held it together as she flung herself into Jeff's arms.

"Rach, he's gonna be OK. Good doctors, good lawyers, good friends. Right now, we need to focus on Great Full

Bread because he can't. Hey, good family, too." Jeff massaged her slim shoulders. "Rach, it would kill him if the business fell apart because of Nancy."

Rachel nodded. "I have to see him. I'm staying put." She waited in his room, tidying up all the empty coffee cups and smoothing the sheets.

"I'm really worried about her. It's too much stress. I knew it," Jeff said to Carmen out in the hallway.

"They've always had a tight bond. Annie's got to call around to get more help, especially now that her wrist is a mess again."

"Sean's really busy. Rachel goes ballistic when I hover. Too bad Mike Tomassi and his buddy, Josh, aren't around. They were good. Who else?"

"Marco?"

"Yeah, I gotta ask Marco to be a superhero. And maybe his mother will help."

Jeff texted Marco to meet him at the commissary. Marco was sorting ingredients when Jeff made his pitch.

"You got it. I'm here for Coach, you, the business, Rachel. Just so long as you keep doing the numbers. Hey, maybe you teach me some day."

"Absolutely. I'll show you when everything's back to normal. Plus, you're getting extra in your paycheck."

Marco found Rachel crying later that day right by the door to the commissary. "It's gonna be OK. You gotta have faith. Ima get Mami to help. Today you got me." He held up his hand for a high-five, but she cried even harder.

"You already do so much. I just don't want anyone to think I can't do it, like the pressure's making me crack. I really need Pete to be OK. He's my rock."

"Mine, too." Marco found a shredded napkin in his back pocket and smoothed it before offering it to her. He patted her awkwardly on the arm although he really wanted to give her a hug. Jeff would probably appear the minute he touched her, and Marco knew how Jeff felt about him getting too close to Rachel.

"We need your mom." Rachel wiped her face and blew her nose carefully on the driest part of the napkin.

"She's in. Come on, don't cry." He held the door for her as they went inside and grabbed aprons.

"My dad's always watching me like a hawk to see if I relapse. He's gonna make me if he keeps up like this." Rachel threw him a hairnet and put one on herself.

"It ain't happening, girl. I got you. No relapses. Coach being out of action is tough, but we gonna get through this. He's strong, he's gonna be fine." Marco held out his fist for her to bump. "Gimme some gloves, jefe. Safety first."

Rachel finally smiled. She made a delicate fist and tapped his waiting knuckles.

CHAPTER 64

WHEN PETER CAME HOME FROM THE HOSPITAL, he still had terrible bruising on his face plus the twenty staples sealing the deep gash from mid-ear to his scalp. Rachel brought Marco and Paco over for their first real face-to-face since the attack.

"You gonna get a mad scar, Coach."

"I guess my leading man days are over. Hollywood will never call." Peter winced as he smiled. "Christ, that hurts. Don't make me laugh."

"Yo, Coach," Paco said. "They say laughing's dope

medicine. Here, have a paleta—mixed berries." He inspected Peter's face closely and whistled. "Damn."

"You could always play what's-his-name. Frankenstein." Marco sat next to Peter on the couch and gave a blissed-out Brutus an extended belly rub. "Twins, man."

"Get the hell out of here and make us some money, guys. You too, Rach. This monster needs a nap."

Lori, deeply tanned, and Marti, painfully sunburned, arrived at Peter's house immediately after their flight landed. Their delayed honeymoon had been worth the wait, but they cut out a couple of days' plans to get back to Bridgeville.

"Hawaii truly is paradise," Marti said. "New England looks like another planet."

"With alien life forms," Lori added.

"It is." Peter tried to focus on them, but he felt exhausted from all the visitors.

"We sent you happy positive energy every day. Could you feel it?" Lori patted him on the arm.

"I thought it was just gas"

"Very funny."

Marti showed him the T-shirt they'd bought him. And the picture frame made out of koa wood. "In questionable taste maybe, but we understood you needed a new one."

"Ha. Very true. Say, Lor, I know you were pulling the strings behind the scene. What's going on. Vic wouldn't say much."

"That's out of character," Marti observed.

"Well, obviously the good news is that you're not in jail." Lori took a bulging folder from her bag and started sorting through papers.

"Yet," Marti said. "No, seriously—I'm kidding."

"Could still happen, right? Nancy's in a locked psych unit. But, I gotta say, she seemed sane to me." Peter sunk back wearily onto a pillow propped up on the couch.

"What exactly is the status of the documents and flash drive?" Lori asked.

"I burned the documents and smashed the flash drive to smithereens with a hammer."

"Good. Then what?"

"Then nothing. I did absolutely nothing. And there's a stinking humongous water bottling plant up at the reservoir."

"Yeah, but you're OK. No evidence to discover."

"Except for what the Consortium's got and Nancy's testimony." Marti picked at her peeling sunburned arms as she thought.

"Can you believe they tailed me everywhere after Zenergy? I'm too stupid to even see someone spying on me for two years."

"Yeah, but who would ever suspect big-league intrigue in boring old Bridgeville?" Lori asked. "Cat and mouse stuff."

"No shit. I'm a regular dumbass mouse, looking for cheese and living a little mouse life." Peter sighed. "The cat won, and Eautopia's pumping our water into millions of plastic bottles."

"No." Marti stopped picking at herself for a minute. "The cat won the war, but they didn't get the mouse. Tell him, Lor."

"Harassment, Peter. They spied on you illegally for two years. They violated your civil rights, your constitutional rights and thought they could get away with it. We threatened to file charges, bad publicity, the works."

"Tables turned, baby." Marti high-fived Lori. Peter sat there, stunned into silence.

"Wow. Vic basically told me to back off and get well. That you guys had a playbook."

"Yeah, it's called grab them by the short hairs and stomp on their balls." Marti turned to Lori. "Although that probably isn't the legal term."

Lori leaned over to kiss her. "You got it right, babe. That's exactly the legal term."

"Your lips to God's ears." Peter surprised them by wobbling to his feet and holding his arms open wide. "Get in here, girls."

CHAPTER 65

NANCY LEARNED THE WAYS OF THE PSYCH UNIT without much trouble. After she got out of the padded rubber rooms, as the patients called them, roommates came and went, some screaming, some scarily frozen in silence. Daily activities were written on the chalkboard, and some of them had to be earned through good behavior. Air conditioning kept the floor cold, so much so that staff always wore jackets or sweatshirts. If Nancy had earned bonus points, they let her watch TV cuddled in a small fleece blanket in the common room. But that happened only when an aide sat next to her and she kept her hands on top of the blanket at all times. Once she tried to keep the soft blanket and take it back to her room, and she lost major points. Plus, she got called out in Group Meeting.

"Sorry," she mumbled.

"Now you'll remember," came the stern reply. "Rules have to be followed or own the consequences, Nancy."

She got surprising and immediate attention to her physical problems resulting from the surgical complications. Despite being medicated to the gills, Nancy quickly got schooled on her new superpowers as an inpatient in a major teaching hospital. No longer a lowly outpatient for her post-infection needs, she went from fumbling all alone to briskly efficient twenty-four-hour medical management. Hospital personnel poked and stuck her purposefully. They spoke to her. Nurses handled her IV nutrition and wound care. They put ointments on her itches and were kind when she wept.

As a psych admit on a white paper, Nancy's situation typically wouldn't have been noteworthy. But as an older female potentially facing an attempted murder rap, she aroused considerable curiosity and interest. She had frequent visits from hospital residents and fellows. Nancy still wailed and cried in her twice daily individual therapy sessions, but almost never in group meetings where she felt called to mother. Her sheer presence, pathetic as it seemed to her when she could form a thought, seemed to comfort many of the younger patients.

"Can we call you Mom?" asked several of them, some just out of high school, some as old as her own sons, who never visited. A few called her Mizz Nancy, showing respect for her age and status as the matriarch of the locked unit. Occasionally, she saw a detox inpatient, who acknowledged her with a sorrowful nod from the depths of abject misery and tremors.

Nancy's body shrank, but she didn't notice unless she saw her reflection in the silver-toned paneling of the elevator. She wore nothing but baggy sweats and slippers. Her hair had a huge white skunk stripe of undyed roots. Her flesh hung in folds, even on her face. When she changed her sweatshirt, ignoring her drain and pendulous loose rolls of drooping skin, she hurried. She hated seeing all the rashes and hives everywhere on her body. Mushrooming itches and erupting welts demanded that she scratch at herself with long jagged nails. A sympathetic nurse on her team tried to stop Nancy as she raked her body.

"It's a side effect of the meds. You have to stop." The nurse gave her an oatmeal bath, slathered her body with super-strong hydrocortisone and cut her nails. Nancy cried with gratefulness.

But still, Nancy scratched.

"You're going to give yourself more infections. Then, you'll never get out of here. Come on, focus on how much weight you've lost since your surgery." Her primary medical nurse tried to get Nancy to smile. "Let's check today's number."

Nancy dutifully got on the scale. "What does it say?"

"185. Wow, that's forty pounds in like two months. You're doing so great."

Nancy clapped her hands, and then started to cry. "What about my itches? I'm so itchy again, I want to scratch all my skin off. Help me, please."

"Honey, I'll talk to your doctor, but you need to tell him, too. You're having some kind of extreme reaction. But you can't scratch so much, or you'll end up here forever."

"Forever like never leaving?" Nancy took a while to compute that amount of time.

At night, Nancy tried to remember to rub and irritate the skin underneath her folds, especially around her breasts and thighs. Soon she had a fungal infection. Then she worked on her underarms. One roommate suggested rubbing feces on the festering sores.

Nancy shrugged. The roommate had been there before.

"I'm playing the long game," she said to herself over and over, not sure if she was speaking out loud or whispering in her head.

In therapy, she swore she didn't remember attacking Peter. They pressed her on why she would attack a lifelong friend. She told them she didn't do it. Someone else did, if it happened at all.

"No, they're lying, everyone's lying."

Her other stock phrase worked well, too.

"No, I don't remember." She wailed almost at will.

"We'll work slowly, Nancy. We'll get there," the residents and fellows said. They prescribed more drugs, more cognitive and dialectical behavior therapy, more itch cream.

But she recalled almost every detail of her confrontation with Peter. Her arrest was the blank area.

Every now and again, she told her roommate. "Oh, I remember. He bled like a pig."

"Haha, a dead pig."

"I remember."

If her roommate blabbed, Nancy bet no one would believe her.

"She's nuts. I barely believe her if she says it's morning." Nancy said this to herself or so she thought. The psych meds had powerful side effects. Some were good, like deep sleep. Others not so good, like the nightmares she couldn't shake and the sepia tones that now were the only colors she saw. People's faces all looked the same, too, kind of blurry and blubbery. She tried to remember to keep scratching. She played the long game.

Nancy wished she could tell Peter about her Oscar-worthy abilities, but he wasn't on her visitor's list.

"For obvious reasons," she whispered to no one.

CHAPTER 66

THE NEW ROTATION OF RESIDENTS BOTHERED NANCY. They kept pressing her, asking all kinds of questions about what made her attack Peter, whether he had ever hurt her physically and sexually.

"You were friends for over forty years. Why now?" An earnest young woman with big black glasses put the focus on her in group therapy.

"I told you. I don't remember."

"Did he sexually harass you? Did he cross the line when you might have said no? Did he make you do things you didn't want to do?"

Her questions hit Nancy like bricks. She started shaking and crying.

"Wow, bullseye," muttered another resident.

"No," Nancy couldn't speak over her sobs. "No."

"You're safe here now, Nancy. You can still report him," said the group leader.

The other patients became unnerved and upset by Nancy's distress. Some got up and left the room. Others started to rock back and forth.

"It's important for you to work through this. You don't have to keep this secret. He can be held responsible for his sexual aggressions."

Nancy's gut-wrenching wails resulted in her being taken back to her room. She lay on her bed and pulled the pillow to her belly. Her guttural cries didn't diminish until they gave her a sedative.

275

Later that day, the psychiatrist on call wanted to see her. A friendly young orderly named Gerald guided her with a steadying hand on her back.

"Nancy," the bearded male psychiatrist said. "This is a big breakthrough for you. And we all know it's hard. Sexual misdeeds of all kinds damage us as people. You are not the only one. Victims of abuse, even decades ago, are speaking up and calling out their aggressors publicly. Tell me about what happened. What did Peter Russo do— did he force himself on you?"

"No, no. Not Peter." Nancy, her emotions tamped down by the sedative, spoke slowly and softly. "We only had sex once. We wanted to."

"So, you are saying it was consensual?"

"Yes."

"I see."

"But, but someone else raped me. He hurt me so much. And he's back." Nancy broke down again.

"He's hurting you again? Raping you?" The psychiatrist couldn't proceed. Nancy fell to the floor and lay there shaking and moaning.

In subsequent days, Nancy refused to speak to anyone. She wouldn't eat or bathe. The staff fussed over her, but she didn't relent until they discussed feeding tubes.

"Can I see a chaplain?" She surprised everyone when she spoke.

"Jewish, Christian, Muslim—which faith? Does it matter?"

"No."

"I want to believe," she said to the grandmotherly woman whose name tag said Chaplain Sue Shaffer.

"In what, Nancy? I see your intake form has nothing indicated for religion. What do you want to believe in, a Judeo-Christian God?"

"In anything."

The chaplain waited for more, but Nancy sat deject-edly, dabbing at her eyes and nose.

"Nancy, I know this is a very difficult time for you"

"I'm afraid."

"But you're in a safe space here. Your abuser, well—there are measures that can be taken. In the meantime, we can meet regularly. Do you pray?"

"For what? I'm nothing, I'm alone. No money, no friends. I want Brock Saunders to die a million painful deaths, slow ones. Is that praying?"

"Brock Saunders—the one from Pioneer Premium Properties who ripped off so many people?"

Nancy nodded. "Yes."

"Is he the man who raped you and is back hurting you?"

"Yes."

The chaplain stiffened. She wrote some notes and placed the paper in Nancy's file. "I'm sure you've heard the phrase an eye for an eye. We can talk about the Old Testament and how to get reciprocal justice."

"A tooth for a tooth." Suddenly, Nancy burst into tears. "I can't pay. They'll kick me out, and Brock will find me. Will God pay?" She sobbed loudly.

"Nancy, paying isn't a problem."

"What—who is paying?"

"Honey," the chaplain said. "You've got better benefits than God."

The answer made her cry even harder. She saw Brock in her dreams that night, skinned alive and dipped in bleach, his cock stuffed in his mouth. He screamed over and over as God smiled. Nancy folded her hands gently across her healing belly. She got up and went to the nursing station where she found Gerald.

"Mizz Nancy?"

"I'm so hungry. Could I have something to eat?"

CHAPTER 67

JOHN TOMASSI, HOLDING DONNA'S SKY-BLUE CLUTCH purse, stood alongside the old Weber grill on Peter's deck and watched his wife dead-head the huge marigolds that grew wildly every which way.

"What, did you give them steroids?" he called out to Peter.

"That's survival of the fittest, baby." Peter walked over with two cold beers and gave one to Tomassi. "The blue is very you."

Tomassi laughed. "Maybe Carmen will let you hold hers one fine day, Frankenstein. You should be so lucky."

"Maybe." Peter eyed the sky-blue clutch Tomassi held in his meaty paw and shook his head. "Beyond whipped, Johnny boy."

"I heard that, Pete," Donna said. "And should you be drinking beer?"

"Cut him a break, Donna. He's damaged goods. Amazing hearing on that woman," he whispered before switching back to his normal bombastic volume. "Wow, Lori and Vic came through like champs. They scared the shit out of the Consortium."

"That's why I pay them the big bucks."

"Speaking of big bucks, what're you doing with the settlement money?"

"I vote for buying a nice diamond ring for Carmen," Donna said. "She's the one, Pete. You can't let her get away again."

"Geez, honey. Why don't you just buy him a net?"

"No squabbling, children. You'll make my head hurt. Anyway, she has like three already."

"Women have ten fingers," Donna said. "Are you listening, Johnny?"

"What?" Tomassi mugged at Peter. "Doofus, for a so-called ladies man, you know nothing." Tomassi adjusted the clutch under his other elbow. "Why doesn't this come with handles?"

"Listen, I want to add some money to the reward the Bridgeville PD has for info on Sherry's murder. And, Marco's cousin's team lost their sponsorship, so I'm gonna do that."

"As what, Great Full Bread or Reverend Russo's Holy Rollers?"

"Ha ha. Plus, get a load of this. Marco texted me this morning he and Kenny just discovered that all the team's equipment got stolen. Everything, even the damn bases."

"Goddamn drugs, again. Junkies'll stop at nothing. You'll cover that?"

"Yeah, of course. Kenny said he might stop by later with a list of what they need."

"Kenny and Marco. The world works in strange ways. So, it'll probably be bats, baseballs, batting helmets, maybe some mitts."

"The bases," Donna reminded her husband.

"Hey, that's not Kenny." Tomassi craned his neck at the sound of a car pulling into the driveway. "It's Ian."

"Where's your better half?" Peter yelled.

"Hello to you, too. And if you mean Jade, she's on a silent retreat. Can't see either of you blokes doing even an hour of silence let alone a week."

"They don't speak for a week? You couldn't pay me to do that," Tomassi said.

"Now that's what I'll do with some of the money. I'll pay you to go on a silent retreat."

"With Jade? Not exactly a sacrifice."

"I heard you, Johnny." Donna stepped out of the house with a bowl of snacks. "Ian, he's quite taken with your girlfriend."

"Great dancer," Tomassi said, putting his arm around his wife, kissing her cheek, winking at Peter and opening his mouth wide like a baby bird for the pretzel Donna offered.

"She's not my girlfriend. She is Jade, her own self, possessed by no one." Ian reached for a pretzel, grinning at the collective hoots and guffaws. "Now, if you're talking about Andre, he's on a training course in surveillance and evidence collection."

"So, he's taking the big plunge?" Tomassi nodded approvingly. "Good for him. The PI exam for getting licensed is tough."

"He's gonna ace it," Peter said.

"Andre's gung-ho. Oh, and here's a free tip, Sergeant. Sky-blue in a man-purse is so last year. Navy is more your color, anyway."

"Watch it, yoga man. I'll give you the special prayer that you save for Vic."

"You're on to me. Say, Peter—really good karma to give the money for Sherry and the baseball kids."

"What about Carmen's ring?" Donna asked, wiping her hands off on a paper towel and reclaiming her clutch from her husband.

"You can't expect miracles, Donna. This guy," Tomassi jerked his chin towards Peter, "isn't that smart. Hey, I hear the Consortium's in negotiations for a chunk of a mondo desalination project up the coast." Tomassi shared some of the latest dirt after his third beer loosened his tongue.

"What?" Peter stopped in his tracks like he had turned to stone.

Tomassi hesitated as Ian and Donna vigorously shook their heads side-to-side. "No," Donna mouthed.

"Nothing. Just nothing." Tomassi stuffed an astonishing quantity of chips into his mouth, pulverizing every last crumb.

"Sergeant, did you sign up for the yoga clinic I'm doing on Saturday morning? Your posture is appalling." Ian stood ramrod straight next to Tomassi.

Tomassi snorted. "Don't even."

"Yeah, John. You get those expensive leggings you ordered from Lulu-whatever?" Peter got right into Tomassi's line of vision, elbowing Ian aside.

"I'll lu-lu you in a minute."

"You probably got two pairs so when you split one trying to pull 'em up over your manhood, you got a spare. Hey, now—so tell me how the Consortium's gonna drain the ocean and kill all the marine life. This I gotta hear. Don't be shy."

Tomassi groaned. "You're like a dog with a bone. Just leave it. I got mixed up with something else."

"Pre-Alzheimer's?" Ian ventured with a sly grin.

"That's you."

Peter had already googled it. "What the fuck?"

"Here we go," Tomassi sighed. "Me and my big mouth."

"Listen to this: Brockie-fucking-Saunders is the liaison between the Consortium and a foreign group collaborating to build a massive desalination plant right by the Rhode Island border."

"Johnny, how could you?" Donna rubbed Peter's back sympathetically and stared hard at her husband. "Don't read any more, Pete. It'll just upset you."

"Well, it should upset everyone." Ian's voice became dead-serious. "The toxic brine these massive plants produce is barely diluted poison before it gets dumped back into the water. And Brock is the pointy end of the spear."

"C'mon, Pete. There's nothing you can do." Tomassi instantly regretted his words. Peter's eyes lit up like a bull fixating on a matador's gleaming red sash.

"Oh, yeah? It says here this reverse osmosis technique for getting the salt out doesn't work in icy weather. Great—we only get ice like half the year. This fucking desalination plant gets built, it'll destroy everything—the ocean, the rivers, the air, the land. It won't work, either, and the fish and birds will all die."

"Don't get so carried away." Tomassi punted Peter's dire prediction.

"No, we gotta get in front of this while we still got time. Motherfucking Brock doesn't get to be a one-man wrecking ball for the planet, not again. Time to bring the piece of shit down once and for all." Peter appealed to Tomassi, Ian and Donna, his arms half-raised.

"I'm in," Ian said. He toed the space between two deck boards. "Here's my line in the sand. Anything beyond means all the rules get thrown out." Donna nodded her assent and looked at her husband.

"That's the line gets you out of downward pissing pussycat? Then what the hell; I'm in, too. But don't tell anyone."

CHAPTER 68

Jeff drove Peter over to Fiori Orchards for dinner that night. Peter didn't feel too confident driving in the dark yet because of the dizzy spells that still seemed to come out of nowhere. When Jeff heard about them, he didn't want Peter driving at all.

"I can drive by feel; I know these roads by heart." Peter's protests fell flat.

"Can you see a kid on a bike by feel? A loose dog? I'm protecting the public from you, idiot."

Carmen came out when she heard the tires crunch on the gravel and gave Peter a big kiss and a mug of ice water.

"You need to drink more."

"More vodka?"

"Go hang out with my dad. Jeff and I want to talk about you."

"Yeah," Jeff said. "Beat it."

Aldo greeted him warmly. He made Peter sit next to him and listen to the Red Sox game on his boombox. Carmen and Jeff finished conferring, and Jeff bopped the horn before slowly pulling away to avoid stirring up a cloud of dust.

"Old school, Aldo. I like it."

"The TV guys are a bunch of pansies. They wear make-up, for Chrissake."

Jimmy came running out of the house when he heard Peter's loud laugh. He hugged him and gently touched the staples still in Peter's head.

"Those hands better be clean, young man," Carmen said.

Jimmy nodded and proposed a re-match of Scrabble.

"You're on," Peter said. "Rack 'em up."

Carmen looked at Peter and Jimmy playing Scrabble with Aldo. The noise from the ballgame mixed with their joyful chatter as they sat at the picnic table under the kaleidoscope of red, yellow and orange leaves. The wave of emotion hit her without warning. Almost in tears, she thought of her confrontation over four years ago with the grief therapist. Maybe being happy wasn't bullshit; it just snuck up, mixed in the moment with gratefulness, awe and heart-wrenching sadness for what might have been. She missed Becky. She wanted to tell her, *Hey, I figured it out. This is happy.*

Peter watched the following afternoon as Carmen expertly polished her nails. He smiled as she blew on her fingers and inspected them from different angles.

"Nice color."

"Thanks. The smell doesn't bother you?" Peter shook his head. "Yeah, reds work on me."

"Whatever that means, yes." He closed his eyes, trying to rid himself of his almost constant headache. The cool breeze fluttering the leaves helped up to a point.

"Why don't you lie back. Come here." She patted the chaise lounge and settled herself on it. "Just lean back on me."

"I might squish you."

"I can think of worse ways to go."

"Jeff told you about the damn dizzy spells, didn't he?"

"Yeah. It'll take time, baby." She put her arms around him and kissed the top of his head. "Watch my nails."

"I hate being like this." He shifted carefully, popping one eye open to avoid smudging her manicure.

"Shhh. To quote the great Ian, just be present in this moment. It's a beautiful fall day. We're together, and Rachel and Jeff have the business under control with Marco."

"Ian's a legend in his own mind."

"Sometimes, and I can't believe I'm gonna say this, he actually gets it right."

Rachel loved working with Marco's mother. Mrs. Torres at first refused to be paid for her work. They clicked as a team, even when Marco wasn't around. Rachel somehow had trouble communicating just how much she wanted Mrs. Torres to collect a fair salary.

"You gonna learn Spanglish, chica." Marco came by to help with production when he could.

"Si. This is probably a stupid question, but your mom's from Puerto Rico. I mean she was born there."

"Yup. I know where you goin'. Puerto Ricans are US citizens, dummy. How come they don't teach you nothin' in them good Bridgeville schools?"

"Really." Rachel nodded emphatically. "Sorry, I didn't mean to be rude. I just didn't know if not getting paid was about taxes or something."

"Yeah, it's OK. We cool. She just wants to help Coach out. Mami, por favor." Marco implored his mother, who at this moment, stood on a stool in front of the long prep counter, almost shoulder-deep in bread dough.

"Please, Mrs. Torres. I mean, Tia." Mrs. Torres had made it clear to Rachel that she wanted her to be less formal.

"Aight. You remembered. Mami likes that." Marco gave Rachel a thumbs-up.

"OK." Mrs. Torres gave in and smiled.

Jeff cheerfully added Mrs. Torres to the payroll. "I'm really glad she's with us. I think we should talk about expanding. We could double our business if we had more product."

"But, Jeff," Marco said. "We need like another truck. We're maxed out."

Rachel agreed. "Yeah, Dad. Let's talk to Pete. He'll go for it. And it's exactly like Marco said, not just more product—another truck."

"Yeah, I'm almost in. But we have to get Pete better. Good point, though. We definitely can't expand with just one truck."

"How 'bout a trailer? We could sell out of both sides, I seen them at farmers markets. Got a bigger prep area in the middle and we won't sweat to death."

"I don't know."

Marco bounced on his toes with excitement. "Bigger freezer, too, for all the paletas. Need a truck to pull the trailer, right?"

"Whoa, Marco. Slow down." Jeff did some mental calculations. "If we use Annie's Jeep, it could work."

Rachel cocked her head at him. "You know that means Mom gets a new car, right?"

"Yeah. Whatever she wants. Well, maybe not new"

"Relax. Mom's not the Mercedes type. She'll just want another SUV."

Sean offered to help scout out a used trailer. "Don't buy a new one, Dad. I'll make some calls."

Rachel gave her brother a big smile. "Awesome. Hey, have you seen Mike or Josh lately? They did such an ass-kicking job when they helped get us up and running."

"Mike, yes. Josh, not recently."

"Do you know if he's still with his girlfriend? Josh, I mean."

"You got a boyfriend last time I looked." Sean stared at her pointedly.

"I still have eyes, Sean."

Peter broke into a grin when Jeff told him about the expansion idea. "Let's get two trailers. I mean it."

"Pete, you cannot be serious. Let's start with one."

"I'm dead serious. We could do it, people are being turned away all the time because we run out of product."

"No. We keep it manageable, that's always the goal. I'm happy with the way things are. We got great people working with us. You're mending, Annie and me are solid, Sean's good, and Rach, well, she's mostly OK."

"What do you mean, mostly? She's baking up a storm, she runs the business, she's clean, she's got a nice boy-friend—what else do you want from her?"

"Numbskull, I don't want anything from her. I want things *for* her. And her relationship isn't doing so hot—lots of tension there. But I really like Zack."

"So, you go out with him. You gotta trust her more."

CHAPTER 69

PETER AND MARCO PARKED THE GREAT FULL BREAD TRUCK down by the river after selling out of everything during the hectic breakfast and lunch hours. Exhausted but happy, they strolled to the water's edge. Peter clutched two bottles of seltzer in one hand and a big bag of pretzels in the other. Marco carried two fishing poles and a bucket while Brutus trotted purposefully alongside them. They settled down by the big rocks and laughed as a quacking flock of ducks dive-bombed them.

"Dinner," Peter shouted. He shielded his still-healing head wound protectively in case the ducks got too close for comfort. Marco tented his hands over Peter's face, too.

"Yeah, right. You gonna feed them not cook them."

"Only to fatten them up. Duck a l'orange could be tomorrow's special."

"Nah, Peking duck. I like them little pancakes and dipping sauce. Hey—don't pick your scab, Coach. Gonna get infected."

The fish weren't biting, so after relaxing in the verdant shade, they packed up. Right when they came through the last grove of trees, they saw an off-duty Kenny Johnson buffing a spot on the truck's Great Full Bread logo. He looked up when Brutus started barking.

"Peter, Marco," Kenny said, walking over and offering Brutus his hand to sniff. "I've got a big favor to ask. I've been wanting to for a long time, but I had to wait until Peter could get off the most wanted list and behave himself in public." Kenny winked and slapped hands with Marco. "Can I drive this baby?"

"Well, now. Do you have the right kind of license? Wouldn't want you to get in trouble." Peter gave Kenny a very stern look while Marco guffawed. "The police strictly enforce the laws around here, you know."

"Hey, KJ—you want some ice with that burn?"

Kenny smiled and looked down at Brutus humping his leg. "Hey, I have Brutus's seal of approval. That's gotta count for something."

"Yeah, maybe," Peter said. "Wait, do you have a dog?"

"Not yet; my folks used to. Sparky." Kenny scratched Brutus in exactly the right spot behind his ears. "I love dogs. Come on, Peter. Give me a chance to drive the truck. Marco, help me out here."

"Well, lemme try and think of something positive to

say. Sure as shit ain't gonna be the 'stache. Wait, I got it. He's a good customer who tips, and he's OK for a cop. We all got some history together, Coach."

Kenny nodded and pointed at Marco. "The man speaks the truth. Except about the 'stache. Besides, Brutus will guide me."

"How much time you have, Kenny? I've got a proposition for you. See," Peter said, clapping him on the shoulder, "you can drive the truck but there's just one tiny catch. The only place you can drive to with my permission is the animal shelter. Take Marco, too. There's a couple of dogs that need a home—I got the call the other day—and I think you're the answer to one of their prayers. What do you say?"

Kenny grinned and vaulted into the driver's seat. Marco handed him the keys and flopped down on the passenger seat. Brutus scrambled in to help Marco supervise as Kenny revved the engine.

"Hey, man—don't flood it."

"Kenny, you never answered my question." Peter spread his arms wide and waited expectantly.

"You'll see, have faith." Kenny eased the truck out of the parking lot in a cloud of exhaust.

"We gotta get a tune-up, Coach." Marco yelled through cupped hands as Kenny accelerated.

"You're speeding," Peter shouted back. He rummaged in his pockets for a treat to give Brutus later and settled onto a picnic table, taking care to avoid fresh splatters of bird poop. Scrolling through his phone, he saw Sean had texted about a good lead on a food trailer. Texting back and forth, they set up an appointment with the seller for later in the week.

Before long, Peter heard the truck wheezing back to the river. "Damn, that sounds bad."

Kenny swung in close to Peter. "Sweet ride. I kept expecting the engine to explode."

"Yeah, yeah." Brutus jumped out of the truck and raced after some squirrels. "Hey, where's Marco?" Peter heard the little woof before he saw the puppy cradled in Marco's arms. "Who's this?"

Kenny took the fluffball from Marco. "Hey, I think he pissed on you."

"That's on account of your driving. This ain't Nascar."

Kenny cooed to the pup and then offered him to Peter. "Meet Slugger."

"Slugger?" Peter stroked his fur and whispered. "Did you choose him or did he choose you?"

"You don't get to choose nothin' in life. Little Slugger had a rough start, Coach," Marco said. "But some TLC, and he'll be good."

Kenny shook his head sadly and reached over to Peter for the dog. "Amen. C'mere, little dude."

They all turned at the sound of the approaching ferry, watching as the water churned. Gulls cried, and the ducks waddled away. Peter, Kenny and Marco waved at the ferrymen, weathered and tanned in their bright orange vests. Assorted cars and bicyclists exited up the ramp. Savoring the cool damp smell of the river, Peter draped his arms across the younger men's shoulders. The waves, lapping against the shore, cast a spell as they stood comfortably quiet and still.

READER'S GUIDE FOR *RIVER RULES* BY STEVIE Z. FISCHER

1. Many communities grapple with nature preservation, particularly if the choice is between open space and economic growth. Does Bridgeville's experience ring true to you?

2. Peter and Jeff are two years apart and very close. Jeff seems to have more of a traditional lifestyle than Peter plus he carries the load of running the farm. Was it fair for their father, Artie, to cut Peter out?

3. Peter went his own way, dropping out of college and working in the aerospace industry on the assembly lines. He helped Jeff, but did Peter do enough? Did Jeff do enough to make the inheritance fairer?

4. Did Tomassi do enough for Peter after he got arrested?

5. Nancy's tough road is one shared by many women: health problems, career struggles, divorce, and date rape. It is realistic for her to have endured all of these?

6. Nancy doesn't seem to think that she betrayed Peter to the Consortium. How much did Brock's role affect her decision?

7. Brock's brutality towards Nancy doesn't seem to catch up to him. When Nancy tells the chaplain who raped her and who she is terrified of, can Brock be held accountable?

8. Who is your favorite character in the book? Your least favorite.

9. Following your conscience and extending a helping hand motivate Peter and several other characters. How important is doing the right thing in protecting nature, family and friendships?

10. What about Becky, Carmen's daughter? She wasn't as lucky as Rachel. She became a teen mother and died at 23. What does the book suggest about how difficult it is to be a young woman? A middle-aged woman?

11. How hard do you think it was for Josh to follow his conscience? What do you think of his actions?

ABOUT THE AUTHOR

STEVIE Z. FISCHER writes about the interplay of people, nature and power in small-town New England. Her first novel, *River Rules*, looks at how everyday heroes can be forged as lives are changed by forces seemingly beyond our control. Stevie's focus on the bonds of friendship, love of nature, and refusal to be marginalized shines through in *River Rules*. Although she has worked in jobs ranging from cheese slicing to strategic analysis, nothing has been so transformational as paying attention, walking her dog and never meeting a stranger. Stevie teaches writing and lives in Connecticut.